Goose bumps rose on her arms, a shiver ran down her spine . . .

Bethany was within four feet of the man when a warning bell sounded in her head. Surely her eyes were playing tricks on her! But as she squinted into the darkness, the erratic candlelight hissed and flared, illuminating the man's face.

The calm of the courtyard was shattered by Bethany's shrill scream. The silver tray crashed to the bricks. Teacups broke into shards, and a half-filled pot of tea exploded on impact.

Theodosia slammed open the door and rushed outside and through the tangle of empty tables. "Bethany!" she called, urgency in her voice . . .

She saw immediately that the man slumped in his chair, his chin heavy on his chest. One hand dangled at his knees, and the other rested on the table, still clutching a teacup . . .

"Theodosia, what are you . . ." From across the way, Samantha's voice rose sharply, then died.

Another strangled cry tore from Bethany's mouth. She pointed toward Samantha, who had crumpled in a dead faint . . .

Theodosia's brain shifted into overdrive. "Haley, call nine-one-one!"

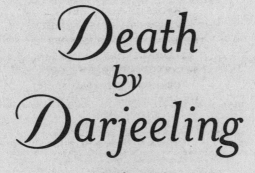

Death
by
Darjeeling

LAURA CHILDS

BERKLEY PRIME CRIME, NEW YORK

THE BERKLEY PUBLISHING GROUP
Published by the Penguin Group
Penguin Group (USA)
375 Hudson Street, New York, New York 10014, USA

USA I Canada I UK I Ireland I Australia I New Zealand I India I South Africa I China

Penguin Books Ltd., Registered Offices: 80 Strand, London WC2R 0RL, England
For more information about the Penguin Group, visit penguin.com.

DEATH BY DARJEELING

A Berkley Prime Crime Book / published by arrangement with the author

Berkley Prime Crime Books are published by The Berkley Publishing Group.
BERKLEY® PRIME CRIME and the PRIME CRIME logo are
trademarks of Penguin Group (USA).

For information, address: The Berkley Publishing Group,
a division of Penguin Group (USA),
375 Hudson Street, New York, New York 10014.

ISBN: 978-0-425-17945-1

PUBLISHING HISTORY
Berkley Prime Crime mass-market edition / May 2001

PRINTED IN THE UNITED STATES OF AMERICA

33 32 31 30 29 28 27 26

ALWAYS LEARNING   PEARSON

This book is dedicated to Peg Baskerville,
true friend and voracious reader.
May you rest in peace
and enjoy all the time heaven allows for reading.

ACKNOWLEDGMENTS

Thank you to Mary Higgins Clark for helping point the way; Grace Morgan, agent extraordinaire; Judith Palais, senior editor and tea shop visionary; fellow writer R. D. Zimmerman for his insider's view and wise words; Jim Smith for his friendship and encouragement; and my husband, Dr. Robert Poor, for all his love and support.

Visit our website at www.laurachilds.com.

CHAPTER I

THEODOSIA BROWNING LEANED back from the clutter of her antique wooden desk, balanced a bone china cup and saucer on one knee, and took a much-needed sip of Lung Ching tea. Savoring the emerald green color and delicate sweetness, she absently pushed back a meandering lock of the naturally curly auburn hair that swirled about her head, creating a haloed visage somewhere between a Rafael painting and a friendly Medusa.

Calmly, calmly, she told herself.

On this fine October afternoon with the temperature in Charleston hovering in the midseventies and the back door propped open to catch the languid breezes wafting off the nearby Cooper River, the Indigo Tea Shop seemed to be the epicenter of several minicrises, with all the fallout landing squarely in Theodosia's lap.

Her customs broker, usually so masterful at snipping red tape and shepherding shipments from far-flung continents, had just called with disastrous news. Three cases of silver tips from the Makaibari Tea Estate in India had been unceremoniously dumped on a dock in New Jersey and left to sit in pouring rain.

Then there was the issue of the Web site.

Theodosia directed her gaze to the colorful concept boards that lay scattered at her feet. Even with marketing and design expertise from Todd & Lambeau Design Group, one of Charleston's topflight Web design firms, launching a virtual tea shop on the Internet was proving to be a major undertaking. Selling bags, boxes, and tins of exotic teas as well as tea accoutrement required more than just being cyber savvy; it was a long-term commitment in terms of time and money.

And wouldn't you know it, Drayton Conneley, her assistant and right-hand man, had gotten a last-minute call to host a group tea tasting. Drayton was out front right now, charming and chatting up a half dozen ladies. That meant final preparations for tonight's Lamplighter Tour still weren't wrapped up.

Ordinarily, Theodosia reveled in the oasis of calm her little tea shop afforded. Tucked between Robillard Booksellers and the Antiquarian Map Store in the historic district of Charleston, South Carolina, the Indigo Tea Shop was one stitch in a romantic, pastel tapestry of Georgian, Federal, and Victorian homes, courtyard gardens, and quaint shops.

Inside this former carriage house and tiny treasure, copper teapots hissed and bubbled, fresh-baked pastries cooled on wooden racks, and patrons scrambled for a coveted seat at one of the creaking hickory tables. Leaded glass windows, a wavering scrim to temper the intense South Carolina sun, cast filtered light on pegged wooden floors, exposed beams, and brick walls.

Floor to ceiling, a warren of cubbyholes held jars brimming with black powders, crumpled leaves of nut brown and ochre, and shiny whole leaves that shimmered like Chinese celadon. And what a tantalizing spectrum of aromas! Piquant gunpowder green tea from south China, lightly fermented Ceylonese garden tea, delicate fruited Nilgiri tea from the Blue Mountains of India.

The ringing phone nudged Theodosia from her reflections.

"Delaine's on two," called Haley, popping around the corner from the kitchen to hover at Theodosia's elbow.

Haley Parker, Theodosia's young shop clerk and baker extraordinaire, worked days in the tea shop and attended college classes a few evenings a week. Although Haley currently listed her major as communications, she had, over the past three years, alternated between sociology, philosophy, and women's studies.

Theodosia looked up hopefully. "Could you help her?"

"Delaine specifically asked for you," said Haley, her brown eyes dancing with amusement.

"Lord, love us," murmured Theodosia as she reached for the phone.

"Mercury's in retrograde," Haley added in a conspiratorial stage whisper. "Going to shake things up the next couple days."

Theodosia exhaled a long breath. "Delaine, lovely you should call."

Delaine Dish owned Cotton Duck, a women's clothing boutique that featured casual yet elegant cottons, silks, and linens. Delaine was also the neighborhood gossip.

"Tell me you're not unaware of this man, Hughes Barron," came Delaine's somewhat strident voice.

"I'm unaware, Delaine." Theodosia stood and stretched a kink from her neck, preparing for a siege.

"Well, he's made an offer on the Peregrine Building."

The Peregrine Building was three buildings down from the Indigo Tea Shop on Church Street. It was an ornate, limestone edifice that had been an opera house at the turn of the century and now housed a handful of professional offices and shops on its lower two floors.

"My dear," continued Delaine, "you are an astute businesswoman. You understand complex issues such as zoning and commercial use."

"What are you really worked up about, Delaine?" asked Theodosia, unswayed by Delaine's flattery.

"Architectural integrity, of course. God knows what sins a developer with Barron's reputation might wreak on a building such as that."

The word *developer* rolled off Delaine's tongue with obvious distaste, as though she were discussing manure.

"Tell you what, Delaine . . ." Theodosia stifled a giggle. "I'll speak to Drayton. He's—"

"A muckity-muck with the Heritage Society!" interrupted Delaine. "Of course, dear Drayton. Who better to have a pipeline to all this!"

"I couldn't have said it better."

"Theo, you're a gem."

"Bye, Delaine." Theodosia hung up the phone, and carried her cup and saucer into the small kitchen. The air was delightfully fragrant from baking, the room dominated by an oversized commercial stove.

"You wouldn't have to be on the Internet if you just hired Delaine," said Haley. She yanked open the oven door, took a quick peek, and closed it again.

"Delaine's a character," admitted Theodosia, "but she does add a certain delirious passion to the neighborhood." Theodosia lifted the plastic cover on a tray of cranberry scones. "These look heavenly."

"Thanks. Hope this'll be enough for tonight. Oh . . . one more minute and you can take a fresh batch of butter cookies out to our guests."

"How's it going?" Theodosia nodded toward the front of the tea shop.

"Drayton is being his erudite self."

"Your vocabulary continues to expand at a rapid pace, Haley."

"Thank you, I'm taking a class called verbal integrity."

"Outstanding," said Theodosia. "And the credits hopefully lead one step closer to a degree?"

Haley slid the oven mitt onto her hand, and shifted her thin, lithe body from one ballet slipper to the other. "Actually, I'm thinking of taking a sabbatical from school so I can focus on more *practical* things."

"Mm-hm." Theodosia peered through a doorway hung with dark green velvet curtains that separated the front of the tea shop from the kitchen and her small office.

Six tasters were gathered around one of the large tables, listening eagerly as Drayton Conneley, professional tea blender and one of only ten master tea tasters in the United States, delivered a lively lesson in tea connoiseurship.

Formal as always in tweed jacket, starched white shirt, and bow tie, Drayton ladled four heaping teaspoons of jasmine pearl into a carefully warmed white ceramic teapot. This was followed by a gush of hot water heated to precisely 150 degrees Fahrenheit. As steaming water infused tea particles, a rich ginger color developed, followed by a sweet scent reminiscent of almonds.

"How do you know how long to allow tea to steep?" asked a white-haired woman who wrinkled her nose appreciatively.

"Green and white teas are best at between one and two minutes," said Drayton. "A Darjeeling, which we all know is delicate and fruity, shouldn't be infused longer than three minutes. And that *is* a hard and fast rule." Drayton Conneley peered over tortoiseshell half glasses that were perpetually sliding down his long, aquiline nose, giving him a slightly owlish appearance.

"Even fifteen seconds too long, and a Darjeeling will go bitter. But a Formosan oolong, especially if the leaves are tightly rolled, is an entirely different matter. Have no fear in boldly pushing the steeping time to seven minutes," advised Drayton in the carefully modulated tones his friends described as his *basso contante* voice.

Sixty-two years of age, the only child of missionary parents who originally hailed from Sullivan's Island, across the Intracoastal Waterway from Charleston, Drayton had spent the first twenty years of his life in Canton, China. It was in south China that Drayton developed his taste for tea and his passion for it, spending weeks at a time on the Panyang Tea Plantation in the high steppes of the Hangzhou region while his parents ministered to Christian

Chinese in far-flung provinces. Upon returning to Charleston, Drayton attended Johnson & Wales University, the area's prestigious culinary institute, then spent several years in London working at Croft & Squire Tea Ltd. and commuting to Amsterdam where the major wholesale tea auctions of the world are conducted.

Today Drayton had arranged six different teapots on the lazy Susan that occupied center stage of the table. Each teapot was crafted in a unique motif, ranging from a colorful ceramic cabbage to a Chinese Yi-shing teapot of molded purple clay. Steeping inside each teapot was a different type of tea, and fanned out in front of each taster were six small cups for sampling. An ornate silver tray with a rapidly dwindling assortment of cookies seemed to be in constant rotation around the table.

"I'm never quite sure when the water is ready," a woman in a yellow twin set drawled in the slow tones of a Savannah, Georgia, native as she eagerly reached for what proved to be the last butter cookie.

"Then, dear lady, I shall teach you a famous Japanese adage that is both edifying and rippingly depictive," said Drayton. "Carp eyes coming, fish eyes going . . ."

"Soon will be the wind in the pines," finished Theodosia as she bustled out from the back room.

"The fish eyes are the first tiny bubbles," Theodosia explained as she set a fresh plate of butter cookies on the table. "The carp eyes are the large bubbles that herald a good, rolling boil. And the wind in the pines is, of course, the beginning rush of the teapot's whistle."

These charming metaphors drew a quick spatter of applause from her delighted guests as Drayton looked on, pleased by the dramatic entrance of his beloved employer.

But then, most people were charmed by Theodosia Browning the moment they met her. She was all sparkling blue eyes and barely contained energy, with a broad, intelligent face, high cheekbones, and full, perfectly formed mouth that could pull into a pucker when she was feeling perplexed.

Theodosia retrieved an apron from behind the counter, and tied it around the waist of her Laura Ashley dress. Although not overweight, neither was Theodosia thin. She was solid, had been all her life. A size ten that occasionally veered toward a twelve, especially around Christmas and New Year's when the tea shop overflowed with scones, benne wafers, cream breads, and sweet butter biscuits. And holiday parties up and down Church Street featured buffet tables groaning with she-crab soup, roast duckling, and spicy shrimp with tasso gravy.

Theodosia's mother, a confirmed romantic and history buff, had named her only daughter after Theodosia Alston, wife of former South Carolina governor Joseph Alston and daughter of former vice president Aaron Burr.

In the early 1800s, when Theodosia Alston reigned as First Lady of the state, she had cut a colorful figure. But her notoriety was short-lived. In 1812 she was a passenger on a sailing ship that sank off the coast of North Carolina. When the bodies of the unfortunate souls washed up on shore, only the remains of Theodosia Alston were missing.

As a young child, Theodosia had sat with her mother in the garden swing and speculated on what had really become of the historical Theodosia. As they whiled away afternoons, listening to the gentle drone of bees, it was exciting to imagine any number of chilling scenarios.

Had she been kidnapped by her father's enemies? Did the pirates who plied their sinister trade off the coastal waters capture poor Theodosia Alston and sell her into slavery? And years later, when the estate of an old North Carolina woman was sold, why did a portrait of the old woman, painted when she was young, look startlingly similar to the missing Theodosia?

But in Charleston, that fine city that began as Charles Town, when rice, indigo, and tobacco from the plantations were in demand throughout the world, legend and history blended into a rich patois.

And Theodosia Browning found running a tea shop to be a civilized melding of merchant and Southern hostess.

Rather like throwing open one's parlor and awaiting whatever surprise guests might drop in.

But Theodosia, now at the age of thirty-six, had not always been the owner of a tea shop.

Years ago (though she'd prefer not to count them) Theodosia had been a student at the prestigious University of Charleston. As an English literature major, she'd been swept up in the poetry and prose of Jane Austen, Mary Shelley, and Charlotte Brontë. Determined to compose her own romantic, lyrical poetry, Theodosia had adapted the bohemian style of wearing a flowing purple velvet cape, walked the grounds of the old Magnolia Cemetery for inspiration, and taken a part-time job at the Charleston Rare Book Company.

But a month before graduation, Theodosia's father passed away and, with her mother long dead since she was eight, she had only a small inheritance on which to live. Knowing the life of a poet can be one precarious step down from that of starving artist, Theodosia took a job in an advertising agency.

Because she was blessed with a knack for creativity as well as a genius for business and marketing, she rose through the ranks swiftly. She began her career as a lowly media estimator, graduating to account coordinator, eventually becoming vice president of client services.

But fourteen years in a cutthroat, results-driven arena took its toll. Long hours, tight deadlines, nervous clients, and high-stakes creative decisions led to her gradual disenchantment. Theodosia searched for a way to step off the merry-go-round.

While serving on a pro bono marketing committee for Spoleto, Charleston's annual arts festival, Theodosia stumbled upon a quirky opportunity. The artistic director for a participating theater organization was trying to unload a little tea shop on Church Street that his mother had run years ago. Intrigued, Theodosia took a hard look at the dusty, unoccupied little tea shop that was up for sale and thought, *What if?*

Mulling her decision for one long, sleepless night, Theodosia made the ultimate executive decision and used her small savings to put a down payment on the property.

Convinced that the congenial atmosphere of a tea shop would be far more satisfying for the soul than helping to market credit cards, computer peripherals, and pharmaceuticals, Theodosia threw herself wholeheartedly into her new venture.

She learned how to evaluate the twist, tip, and aroma of tea leaves and acquired a spectacular shop inventory of loose and boxed teas from notable wholesalers such as Freed, Teller, and Freed's in San Francisco and Kent & Dinmore in England.

Serendipitously, America's sole surviving tea plantation, the Charleston Tea Plantation, was located just twenty-five miles south of Charleston on the subtropical island of Wadmalaw. So Theodosia was able to acquaint herself with owners Mack Fleming and Bill Hall and their 127-acre plantation that grew nearly 300 varieties of tea.

From Fleming and Hall Theodosia was able to learn about the harvest process. How to select the newest, most tender leaves. The use of withering troughs to circulate air through the leaves. Techniques on macerating leaves to break down cell walls.

She went so far as to glean special tea recipes. A wonderful orange pekoe dessert soufflé from a chef at the Four Seasons in San Francisco, a recipe for tea-smoked chicken from the Peninsula Hotel in Hong Kong.

And Theodosia hired Drayton Conneley away from his role as hospitality director at Charleston's famed Vendue Inn.

It wasn't long before the newly energized Indigo Tea Shop, as tea salon, retail tea shop, and gift shop, became a profitable enterprise and a popular stop on Charleston's many walking and carriage tours. Much to Theodosia's delight, her tea shop also came to be regarded by her neighbors as the social and spiritual hub of the historic district.

The clip-clop of hooves on the pavement outside the Indigo Tea Shop signaled that the horse-drawn coach had arrived to carry their tea-tasting visitors back to their respective inns and hotels.

"I hope you have tickets for one of tonight's Lamplighter Tours," said Theodosia as final sips were taken, mouths carefully daubed, and linen napkins refolded. "Many of the historic homes on the tour are private residences that graciously open their doors only for this one special event. It's really quite remarkable."

Sponsored by the Heritage Society, the Lamplighter Tour was an annual tradition in Charleston, held during the last two weeks of October when the long-anticipated cooler nights had returned. These evening walking tours of notable avenues such as Montagu, Queen, and Church Streets afforded visitors a leisurely stroll down cobblestone lanes and a golden opportunity to step inside many of Charleston's elegant, lofty-ceilinged grande dame homes and cloistered courtyard gardens.

"If I may impart my own personal recommendation," said Drayton, pulling back chairs and offering his arm to the ladies, "I would heartily suggest our own Church Street walk. It begins at the Ravenel Home, a stunning example of Victorian excess, and concludes in the formal garden of the elegant Avis Melbourne Home where our gracious hostess and proprietor, Miss Theodosia Browning, has been engaged to serve a repertoire of fine teas, including a special Lamplighter Blend created just for this event."

"Oh, my," said one of the ladies. "How intriguing."

"You have characterized it aptly," said Drayton. "Our Lamplighter Blend is a lovely marriage of two traditional black teas with a hint of jasmine added for high notes."

Theodosia glanced toward the counter and grinned at Haley, who had just emerged from the back room, her arms filled with gift baskets. Haley was always accusing Drayton that his role as Parliamentarian in the Charleston Heritage Society led to oratorical extravagance.

"Of course," added Theodosia in a droll voice meant to

be a casual counterpoint to Drayton's, "we'll also be serving blackberry scones with clotted cream."

Pleasured groans emanated from around the table.

Catching the subtle exchange between Theodosia and Haley, Drayton snatched one of the baskets filled with small tins of tea and tied with white ribbon and held it up for all to see. "Be sure to take a quick perusal of our gift baskets before you leave. Miss Parker here has recently taken up the art of weaving traditional South Carolina sweetgrass baskets and has become quite an accomplished artisan."

Haley's face reddened at Drayton's announcement. "Thank you," she murmured.

And, of course, ladies being ladies, veteran shoppers, and enthusiastic tourists, at least three of the delightfully done gift baskets were carefully wrapped in Theodosia's signature indigo blue tissue paper and tucked safely in the carriage as they departed.

"Did you bring Earl Grey down?" asked Theodosia after the door had swung shut and the shadows lengthened enough so she knew there wouldn't be any more customers for afternoon tea.

Haley nodded.

"Earl, come on, fellow," called Theodosia as she clapped her hands together.

A furry muzzle poked through the draperies, then an angular canine emerged and padded softly across the wooden planks of the floor. When the dog reached Theodosia, he laid his head in her lap and sighed contentedly.

Earl Grey, Theodosia's adopted dog, looked a far sight better today than when she had first found him. Hungry and shivering, curled up in a cardboard box in the narrow cobblestone alley that ran behind the tea shop, Earl Grey had been an abandoned, unwanted mongrel that probably wandered the streets for weeks.

But Theodosia found his elegant head, soft, troubled eyes, and quiet temperament endearing and took to him immediately. She nursed him, groomed him, named him, and ultimately loved him.

When Drayton had objected to a stray dog being named after the popular nineteenth-century prime minister who first brought back the famed bergamot-flavored tea from China, Theodosia insisted the name was more an old English reference to the dog's mottled coloration.

"I can't see that he's particularly gray," Drayton had argued, his tone just this side of vexation.

Indeed, the dog was more salt and pepper.

"There. On the inside of his left hind leg," Theodosia had pointed out. "That area is distinctly gray."

Drayton was nonplused by the dog. "A mixed breed," he'd declared with arched eyebrows.

"Like blending a fine tea," Theodosia had said with artful cleverness. She'd placed her strong hands atop the animal's sleek head and gently massaged the dog's ears as he gazed up at her, limpid brown eyes filled with love. "Yes," she had exclaimed, "this fellow is a blend of Dalmatian and Labrador. A Dalbrador." And from that moment on, Earl Grey of the Dalbrador pedigree became the beloved, official greeter at the Indigo Tea Shop and a permanent resident of Theodosia's cozy upstairs apartment.

"How many more sweetgrass baskets can you manage?" Theodosia asked as Haley, standing on tiptoe, arranged a half dozen of the gift baskets on a shelf behind the cash register.

"How many do you need?"

"My guestimate is at least fifty between now and the holidays. If our Web site is up and running by then, double it."

"Bethany can help me finish maybe another dozen," said Haley, referring to her friend, Bethany Shepherd, who was temporarily living with her in the little garden apartment across the alley. "But we'll have to buy the majority."

"No problem," said Theodosia. "I was planning a drive out to the low country anyway. After I pop in on Aunt Libby, I'll round up some more baskets."

Sweetgrass baskets were a staple in the makeshift stalls along Highway 17 North. Handmade from bunches of sweetgrass, pine needles, and bulrush, then bound together by fiber strips from native palmetto trees, the baskets exuded both functionality and beauty, and the women of the low country took great pride in their handiwork.

"How is Bethany doing?" asked Theodosia, her face softening with concern for Haley's friend whose husband had died in a car accident just eight months earlier. In the past couple of months, the shy Bethany had helped out in the tea shop a few times, and Theodosia was hoping the young woman would soon find her rudder again.

"Good days, sad days," said Haley in measured tones. "It's not easy being a widow at twenty-seven. I think if Bethany didn't have the internship to sustain her, she'd really be at loose ends."

"So at least that part of her life is successful," said Theodosia.

"Yes, thanks to Drayton." Haley glanced gratefully toward Drayton Conneley, who was talking on the telephone, briskly finalizing details for that evening's tea service. "If he hadn't put in a good word for Bethany at the Heritage Society, I don't know what she would have done. Bethany slaved to get her master's degree in art history, but it's still impossible to land any type of museum curator job without internship credentials. Maybe now . . ." Haley's voice quavered and her large brown eyes filled with tears.

Theodosia reached over and gently patted Haley's hand. "Time heals," reassured Theodosia in a quiet voice. "And in Charleston, time is an old friend."

CHAPTER 2

*D*ARKNESS HAD SETTLED on Charleston like a soft, purple cloak. Palmettos swayed gently in the night breeze. Mourning doves that sheltered in spreading oak and pecan trees had long since tucked downy heads under fragile wings.

But up and down Church Street the atmosphere was alive and filled with magic. Candles in brass holders flickered enticingly from broad verandas. Clusters of Lamplighter Tour walkers thronged the sidewalks, gliding through dusky shadows only to emerge in pools of golden light that spilled from arched doorways of houses buzzing with activity, open this one special evening to all visitors who had a ticket in hand and a reverence for history in their hearts.

Fat, orange pumpkins squatted on the steps of the Avis Melbourne Home. On the sweeping porch where a half dozen white Ionic columns imperiously stood guard, young women in eighteenth-century garb greeted visitors with lanterns and shy smiles. Their hair was nipped into sleek topknots, their step dainty and mannered, unaccus-

tomed as they were to layers of petticoats and the discon-
certing rustle of silk.

Inside the Avis Melbourne Home, the room proportions
were enormous. This was a residence designed for living
on a grand scale, with gilt chandeliers dangling overhead,
rich oil paintings adorning walls, and Italianate marble
fireplaces in every room. The color palette was soft and
French: salmon pink, oyster white, pale blue.

More costumed guides, members of the Heritage Society, accompanied visitors through the parlor, dining room
and library. Their running patter enlightened on architecture, antiques, and beaux arts.

Down the long center hallway, footsteps barely registered on plush wool Aubusson carpets as guests found their
way outside to the courtyard garden.

It was here that many of the tour guests had now con-
gregated, sitting at tables that ringed a central three-tiered
fountain. Foliage abounded, the sound of pattering water
pleasantly relaxing.

Theodosia ducked out the side door from her command
post in the butler's pantry. For the last hour she and Drayton had been working nonstop. He oversaw the preparation
of five different teas, while she hustled silver teapots out to
Haley for serving, then ran back for refills. At one point
they'd been so harried she'd asked Haley to make a quick
phone call to Bethany and plead for reinforcement.

Now, as Theodosia surveyed the guests in the garden, it
looked as though she could finally stop to catch her breath.
Haley and Bethany were moving with practiced precision
among the twenty or so tables, pouring tea and offering
seconds on blackberry scones, looking like French waiters
with their long white aprons over black shirts and slacks.
The tables themselves had been elegantly draped in white
linen and held centerpieces of purple flowers nestled in
pockets of greenery.

"Theodosia, darling!"

Theodosia turned as Samantha Rabathan, this year's
chairperson for the Church Street walk, tottered across the

brick patio wearing three-inch heels and flashing a winning smile. Ever the social butterfly and fashion maven, Samantha was fetchingly attired in a flouncy cream-colored silk skirt and pale peach cashmere sweater, generously scooped in front to reveal her matching peach skin and ample endowments.

Theodosia tucked a wayward strand of auburn hair behind one ear, and rested the large teapot she'd been holding on one of the temporary serving stations. Even in her midnight blue velvet tailored slacks and white lace top, an outfit that had received admiring glances from several of the gentlemen in the crowd, she suddenly felt like a brown wren next to Samantha's plumage.

"We've got a packed house, Samantha." Theodosia swept a hand to indicate the contented crowd enjoying tea and treats on the patio. "Your walk is a huge success."

"It is, isn't it," Samantha agreed with a giggle. "I was just calling around on my cell phone and heard that the Tradd Street walk got *half* our turnout." She nudged Theodosia with an elbow and dropped her voice to a conspiratorial purr. "Did you know we sold ninety more tickets than last year? It's a new Church Street record!"

Last year Delaine Dish had been the Church Street chair. For some reason unknown to Theodosia, Samantha and Delaine had a weird, catty rivalry going on between them, one she had no desire to explore, much less get in the middle of.

"Oh, my," Samantha cooed as she fanned herself briskly with one of the tour's printed programs. "Such a warm evening."

And off she went across the patio, the heels of her perfect cream shoes dangerously close to catching between the stones, her cell phone shrilling once again.

"I can't imagine why she's warm," whispered Drayton in Theodosia's ear. "She not exactly bundled up."

"Be nice, Drayton," said Theodosia. "Samantha worked hard on ticket sales and lining up volunteers."

"You can afford to be charitable," he said with a sniff.

"Samantha's always been sweet to you. My guess is she's secretly in awe of your past life in advertising. She knows you've sold the proverbial ice to Eskimos. But in complete, unadulterated fairness, this *has* been a group effort. A lot of good people worked very hard to pull this off."

"Agreed," said Theodosia. "Now tell me what results you've gathered from our rather unscientific poll."

Drayton's face brightened. "Three to one on the Lamplighter Blend! I'd estimate we have less than half a pot left."

"Really?" said Theodosia, her cheeks flaring with color, and her usually calm, melodious voice cracking with excitement.

"The people have spoken, madam. The tea's a knockout."

"So we package more and include it on the Web site," she said.

"No, we *feature* it." Drayton favored Theodosia with an uncharacteristic grin as he picked up the silver teapot she'd set down earlier and started toward the house. "The pantry awaits. The end of the evening is blessedly in sight." He paused. "Coming?"

"Give me a minute, Drayton."

Theodosia stood half hidden under an elegant arch of vines, basking in the glow of success. It was the first tea she'd blended by herself. True, she'd started with two exquisitely mellow teas from the American Tea Plantation. And she'd had Drayton's excellent counsel. But still . . .

"Excuse me."

Theodosia whirled about and found herself staring down at two tiny women. Both were barely five feet in height, quite advanced in years, and wore identical green suits. *Twins,* she thought to herself, then peered closer. *No, just dressed alike. Probably sisters.*

"Mavis Beaumont." Birdlike, one of the ladies in green extended a gloved hand.

"Theodosia Browning," said Theodosia, taking the tiny

hand in hers. She blinked. Staring at these two was like seeing double.

"You're the woman with that marvelous dog, aren't you?" said Mavis.

Theodosia nodded. This happened frequently. "You mean Earl Grey."

"That's the one!" Mavis Beaumont turned to her sister and continued. "Miss Browning has this beautifully trained dog that visits sick people. I had occasion to meet him the time Missy broke her leg."

The sister smiled and nodded.

"Early Grey is a therapy dog," explained Theodosia just in case they hadn't realized he was part of a very real program.

On Monday evenings Theodosia and Earl Grey visited the O'Doud Senior Home and took part in pet therapy. Earl Grey would don his blue nylon vest with the embroidered patch that identified him as a certified therapy dog, and the two would roam the broad halls, stopping to interact with the aging but eager-to-talk residents, visiting the rooms of people who were bedridden.

Earl Grey had quickly become a favorite with the residents, many of whom enjoyed only occasional visits from their families. And just last month, Earl Grey had befriended a woman who'd suffered a terrible, debilitating stroke that left her entire right side paralyzed. In the woman's excitement to pet Earl Grey, she had tentatively extended her rigid right arm for the first time in months and managed a patting motion on the dog's back. That breakthrough had led to the woman going to physical therapy and finally regaining some real use of the arm.

Mavis Beaumont grasped Theodosia's arm. "Lovely party, dear."

The sister, the one who apparently didn't talk, at least not tonight, nodded and smiled.

"Good night," called Theodosia.

"What was that all about?" asked Haley as she shuffled past shouldering a huge tray.

"Fans of Earl Grey."

"That guy's got some PR agent, doesn't he?" she joked.

"Say, thanks for enlisting Bethany," said Theodosia. "I sure hope we didn't ruin her plans for tonight."

"Are you serious?" said Haley. "The poor girl was sitting home alone with her nose stuck in Gombrich's *Story of Art*. Not that there's anything wrong with curling up with an art history book, but between you and me, this was a great excuse to get her out and talking to real people. Believe me, this is the best thing for her."

From her post at the far end of the garden, Bethany glanced toward Theodosia and Haley and saw by the looks on their faces that they were talking about her. She gave a thin smile, knowing they had her best interests at heart, feeling thankful she had friends who cared so much.

With her elegant oval face, pale complexion, long dark hair, and intense brown eyes, Bethany was a true beauty. But her body language mirrored the sadness she carried inside. Where most young women her age moved with effortless grace, Bethany was sedate, contained. Where amusement and joy should have lit her face, there was melancholy.

Picking up a serving tray, Bethany walked to the nearest empty table. She cleared it, taking great pains with the bone china cups and saucers, then moved solemnly to the next table. Centerpiece candles that had glowed so brightly an hour earlier were beginning to sputter. The Lamplighter Tour visitors were taking final sips, slowly meandering back inside the house, saying their good-byes. The evening was drawing to a close.

Bethany glanced across the patio to where Theodosia and Haley had been standing just a few minutes earlier. Now they were nowhere to be seen. They must have ducked inside the butler's pantry to start their cleanup, she thought to herself.

Bethany crisscrossed the brick patio, picking up a cup here, a plate there. When she finally broke from her task and looked around, there were only two tables where people remained seated.

Correction, make that one, she told herself as the foursome sitting at the table nearest the central fountain stood up and began to amble off slowly, chatting, admiring the dark foliage, pointing up at overhanging Spanish moss.

Bethany glanced toward the far corner of the patio. Against the large, dense hedge that formed one border of the garden and ran around the perimeter of the property, she could just barely make out the figure of a man sitting quietly alone.

Bethany tucked the serving tray against one hip and started toward him, intent on asking if she could refill his teacup or perhaps clear his table.

But as she approached, goose bumps rose on her arms, and a shiver ran down her spine. The night had turned suddenly chill. A stiff breeze tumbled dry leaves underfoot, whipsawed a final brave stand of camellias, and sent petals fluttering. The candle on the table nearest her was instantly snuffed, and the candle sitting on the man's table began to sputter wildly.

Bethany was within four feet of the man when a warning bell sounded in her head. Surely her eyes were playing tricks on her! But as she squinted into the darkness, the erratic candlelight hissed and flared, illuminating the man's face.

The calm of the courtyard was shattered by Bethany's shrill scream. The silver tray crashed to the bricks. Teacups broke into shards, and a half-filled pot of tea exploded on impact.

Theodosia heard Bethany's cry from inside the butler's panty. She slammed open the door and rushed outside and through the tangle of empty tables. "Bethany!" she called, urgency in her voice, worry swelling in her breast.

Anguish written across her face, all Bethany could do was back away from the table and point to the man sitting there alone.

Heels clicking like rapid fire, Theodosia approached.

She saw immediately that the man slumped in his chair, his chin heavy on his chest. One hand dangled at his knees, and the other rested on the table, still clutching a teacup. As Theodosia quickly took in this strange scene, her fleeting impression was that the tiny teacup decorated in swirling gold vines seemed dwarfed by the man's enormous hand.

"Theodosia, what are you . . ." From across the way, Samantha's voice rose sharply, then died.

Another strangled cry tore from Bethany's mouth. She pointed toward Samantha, who had crumpled in a dead faint.

Haley and Drayton had followed close on Theodosia's heels. But now they quickly bent over Samantha and ministered to her.

Theodosia's brain shifted into overdrive. "Haley, call nine-one-one. Bethany, stop crying."

"She's all right, just fainted," called Drayton as he gently lifted Samantha to a sitting position.

"Bethany, get a glass of water for Samantha," Theodosia directed. "Do it *now*. And please try to stop crying."

Theodosia turned her attention back to the man's motionless body. Gently, she laid her index and forefinger against the man's neck. Nothing. No sign of a pulse. No breath signs, either.

Theodosia inhaled sharply. This wasn't good. It wasn't good at all.

During her college days, one of Theodosia's more unorthodox professors, Professor Hammish Poore, had taken his entire biology class on a field trip to the Charleston County Morgue. There they'd witnessed two autopsies first-hand. Although it had been more than a few years since that grisly experience, Theodosia was still reasonably familiar with the body's sad signs that indicated life had ceased.

This poor man could have had a sudden heart attack, she reasoned. Or experienced an explosive brain embolism. Death from asphyxiation was a possibility as well.

But if something had obstructed his airway, someone would have heard him choking.

Wouldn't they?

Theodosia was aware of hushed murmurs of concern in the background, of Drayton shaking his head slowly, speaking in solemn tones about Hughes Barron.

This was Hughes Barron?

Theodosia fixed her attention on the hand holding the teacup. In the flickering spasms of the candle she could see the man's fingernails had begun to turn blue, causing her to wonder: *What was in that cup besides tea?*

CHAPTER 3

❧❧❧

THE MAGIC OF the night was suddenly shattered by the harsh strobe of red and blue lights. Three police cruisers roared down the street and braked to a screeching halt. Front tires bounced roughly up over curbs, sending a gaggle of curious onlookers scattering. The *whoop-whoop* of a rapidly approaching ambulance shrilled.

Klang und licht, thought Theodosia. Sound and light. So much excitement, so much kinetic energy being exerted. But as she stood under the oak tree in the dark garden, surveying the slumped body of Hughes Barron, she knew no amount of hurry or flurry on the part of police or paramedics would make a whit of difference. Hughes Barron was beyond help. He was in the Lord's hands now.

But, of course, they all came blustering into the courtyard anyway: four police officers from the precinct headquarters on Broad Street, all with polished boots and buttons; a team of EMTs dispatched from Charleston Memorial Hospital, who jounced their clattering metal gurney across the brick patio; and six firemen, and who seemed to have shown up just to feed off the excitement.

The two EMTs immediately checked Hughes Barron's

pulse and respiration and hung an oxygen mask on him. One knelt down and put a stethoscope to Barron's chest. When he ascertained that the man no longer had a heartbeat, activity seemed to escalate.

Two officers immediately cornered Drayton, Haley, Bethany, and Samantha for interviews and statements. Another team of officers began the business of stringing yellow police tape throughout the garden.

A tall, muscular policeman, with an impressive display of stars and bars on his uniform and a name tag that read Grady, turned his attention to Theodosia.

"You found him?" Grady had a bulldog face and a heroic amount of gear attached to his belt: gun, flashlight, radio, handcuffs, billy club. Theodosia thought he looked like a human Swiss Army knife.

For some reason—the illogic of the situation or the shock at finding someone dead—this Swiss Army knife analogy tickled Theodosia, and she had to struggle to maintain an impassive expression.

"Actually, no," she said, finally answering Grady's question. "One of the young ladies who works for me, Bethany Shepherd, noticed something was wrong." She gestured toward Bethany, who was across the courtyard, talking to one of the other officers. "She was the one who alerted us. I just checked the man's pulse."

Grady had pulled out a spiral-bound notebook and was making rapid scratches in it. "How did she alert you?"

"She screamed," said Theodosia.

One side of Grady's mouth twitched downward, passing judgment on her answer. Obviously, he didn't consider it helpful.

"And was the man breathing?" pressed Grady.

"No, unfortunately. Which is why we called nine-one-one."

More scratches in Grady's notebook.

"And your name is . . . ?"

"Theodosia Browning. I own the Indigo Tea Shop on Church Street."

"So you don't know what happened, Theodosia?" said Grady.

"Just that he died," replied Theodosia. Her eyes went to the crisscross of black and yellow tape that was now strung through the garden like giant spiderwebs. Police Line the words blared, black on yellow. Do Not Cross. Vinyl tape had been wound haphazardly around bushes of crape myrtle and cherry laurel trees, through the splattering fountain and beds of flowers transported from Charleston greenhouses and dug in for this one special night. Now plants and blossoms lay crushed.

Grady cocked one droopy eye at her. "You don't know what happened, but you knew he was dead."

"My impression was that he was cyanotic. If you look at the tips of his fingernails, there's a curious blue tinge."

"Lady . . ." Grady began.

"You seem upset," said Theodosia. "Could I offer you a cup of tea?" She looked around. "Can we get anyone a cup of tea?"

That small gesture seemed to break the tension of the moment.

Grady suddenly remembered his manners and touched his cap with a finger. "Thank you, ma'am. Maybe later. Could you wait over there with the others, please?" Grady pointed across the courtyard. "I need to confer with the medical team."

Theodosia peered toward the far corner of the garden to a round, wrought iron table, still festooned with its purple floral centerpiece. In the darkness she could just barely make out Drayton and Haley sitting there, looking rather glum. Samantha was sprawled in a wicker chair, sipping from a glass of water, fanning herself with a program. Only Bethany was illuminated by the lights from the house. She stood near the door of the butler's pantry, deep in conversation with two officers.

"Certainly," said Theodosia. She took one step back, had every intention of joining the others, when one of the

EMTs, a young man with shaggy blond hair, picked up the teacup and sniffed suspiciously at the contents.

"Put that down." The voice echoed out of the darkness like the rough growl of a big cat.

Caught by surprise, the EMT sent the teacup clattering into its saucer. Luckily, it remained upright.

Grady spun on his heels. "Who are you?" he demanded.

The man with the big cat growl led with his stomach. It billowed out between the lapels of his tweed jacket like a weather balloon. Bushy brows topped slightly popped eyes, and a walrus mustache drooped around his mouth. Although his stance conveyed a certain poise and grace, his head stuck curiously forward from his shoulders.

"Tidwell," said the man.

"Show me your ID?" Grady wasn't budging an inch.

Tidwell pulled a battered leather card case out of his pocket, held it daintily between two fingers.

Grady flipped the leather case open and scanned the ID. *"Detective* Tidwell. Well, okay." Grady's voice was smooth and dripping with appeasement. "Looks like the boys downtown are already on top of this. What can I do to help, Detective?"

"Kindly stay out of my way."

"Sure," agreed Grady cheerfully. "No problem. But you need any help, just whistle."

"Count on it," said Tidwell. He swiped his stubbled chin with the back of his hand, a gesture he would repeat many times. When Grady was out of earshot, Tidwell mumbled "Asshole" under his breath. Then he focused his full attention on Hughes Barron, still sitting at the table as best he could, wearing the oxygen mask one of the EMTs had slapped on him.

"Excuse me," said Theodosia. In her crepe-soled shoes, Tidwell hadn't heard her approach.

He swung around, wary. "Who are you?"

"Theodosia Browning." She extended a hand to him.

"Browning, Browning . . ." Tidwell narrowed his eyes, ignoring her outstretched hand. "I knew a Macalester

Browning once. Lawyer fellow. Fairly decent as far as lawyers go. Lived in one of the plantations out on Rutledge Road."

"My father," said Theodosia.

"Mnh," grunted Tidwell, turning back toward Hughes Barron. He lifted the teacup, dropped his nose to it, and sniffed. He swirled the contents like a wine taster.

Or a tea taster, reflected Theodosia.

Tidwell reached into a bulging pocket and pulled out his cell phone. His sausage-sized fingers seemed to have trouble hitting numbers on the keypad. Finally, after several tries and more than a few expletives, his call went through.

"Pete, get me Brandon Hart." He paused. "Yeah." Tidwell sucked on his mustache impatiently. "Brandon?" he barked into the phone. "Me. Burt. I need your best crime-scene techs. That skinny one's good. And the bald guy with the tattoo. Yeah, tonight. Now. Pete'll fill you in." He clicked off his phone.

"You're Burt Tidwell," said Theodosia.

Tidwell swiveled his bullet-shaped head, surprised to find her still standing there. "You still here?" he frowned.

"You're the one who caught the Crow River Killer."

Something akin to pride crossed Tidwell's face, then he fought to regain his brusque manner. "And what might you know about that?" he demanded.

"Just what I read in the paper," said Theodosia.

CHAPTER 4

SUNLIGHT FILTERED THROUGH the windows of the Indigo Tea Shop. It was 8:30 A.M., and the daily bustle and chores that routinely went on had been largely forgotten or quickly dispatched. A few customers had come and gone, Church Street shopkeepers mostly, who'd come for takeout orders or to try to glean information about last evening's bizarre goings-on.

Now Theodosia, Drayton, and Haley sat together at one of the tables, a pot of tea before them, rehashing those unsettling events.

"I can't believe how long the police spent talking to Bethany," declared Haley. "The poor girl was almost in tears. And then that awful, rude man came along, and, of course, she *did* burst into tears."

"You're referring to Tidwell?" said Theodosia.

"Was that his name?" asked Haley. "He had no right to push everyone around the way he did. We couldn't help it if someone had the misfortune to drop dead. I mean, it's terribly sad when anyone dies suddenly, awful for their family. But for crying out loud, *we* didn't have anything to do with it!"

"If you ask me," said Drayton, "that fellow Tidwell was far too diligent for his own good. He not only pestered everyone, but he also kept a small contingent of visitors tied up for over forty minutes. And those were people who'd been talking on the front steps, nowhere near that man, Hughes Barron! He even interviewed Samantha, and she was shrieking around *inside* the house most of the evening."

"Maybe because she fainted," said Haley. "She really did seem upset."

"Momentarily upset," said Drayton, "because she feared that a tragedy might reflect badly on the Lamplighter Tour." His voice was tinged with disapproval.

"Oh, I can't believe Samantha is that callous," said Theodosia.

"But she *was* worried about it," interjected Haley. "Over and over she kept saying, 'Why did this have to happen during the Lamplighter Tour? Whatever will people think?' "

Theodosia gazed into her cup of Assam tea. The evening *had* been nothing short of bizarre. The only lucky break was the fact that Tidwell hadn't made public his suspicion about a foreign substance in Hughes Barron's tea. Police photographers had shown up, and the evening's participants questioned, but, as far as she knew, it hadn't escalated any further.

The fact that some type of foreign substance might have been introduced into Hughes Barron's tea, and the fact that Burt Tidwell has shown up, had piqued Theodosia's curiosity, however. And she'd made it a point to nose around last night's investigation. As the last so-called civilian to leave, she hadn't arrived home at her little apartment above the tea shop until around 11:00 P.M.

But even in the familiar serenity of her living room, with its velvet sofa, kilim rug, and cozy chintz and prints decor, she'd felt disquieted and filled with questions. That had prompted her to take Earl Grey out for a late walk.

Meandering the dark pathways of the historic district,

inexplicably drawn back to the Avis Melbourne House, Theodosia had seen a new arrival: a shiny black van with tinted windows. The forensic team. From her vantage point in the shadows, she had heard Tidwell's gruff voice chiding them, nagging at them.

A curious man, she had thought to herself. *Paradoxical. A genteel manner that could rapidly disintegrate into reproachful or shrewish.*

Back home again, Theodosia had fixed herself a cup of chamomile tea, ideal for jangled nerves or those times when sleep proves elusive. Then she sat down in front of her computer for a quick bit of Internet research.

On the site of the *Charleston Post and Courier,* she found what she was looking for. That venerable newspaper had loaded their archives (not all of them, just feature stories going back to 1996) on their Web site. Conveniently, they'd also added a search engine.

Within thirty seconds, Theodosia had pulled up three articles that mentioned Burt Tidwell. She learned that he had logged eleven years with the FBI and ten years as a homicide detective in Raleigh, North Carolina.

During his stint in Raleigh, Tidwell was one of the investigators responsible for apprehending the infamous Crow River Killer.

Theodosia had recalled the terrible events: four women brutally murdered, their bodies dumped in the swamps of the Crow River Game Preserve.

Even when all the leads had petered out and the trail had grown cold, Tidwell stayed on the case, poring over old files, piecing together scraps of information.

Interviews in the *Charleston Post and Courier* spoke of Tidwell's "eerie obsession" and his "uncanny knack" for creating a profile of the killer.

And Tidwell had finally nailed the Crow River Killer. His persistence had paid off big time.

"Oh, oh," said Drayton in a low voice.

Theodosia looked up to see Burt Tidwell's big form

looming in the doorway. He put a hand on the lower half of the double door and eased it open.

"Good morning!" Tidwell boomed. He seemed jovial, a far cry from his bristle and brash of the previous evening. "You open for business?"

"Come in, Mr. Tidwell," said Theodosia. "Sit with us and have a cup of tea." She remained seated while Drayton and Haley popped up from their chairs as if they'd suddenly become hot seats.

Burt Tidwell paused in the middle of Theodosia's small shop and looked around. His prominent eyes took in the more than one hundred glass jars of tea, the maple cabinet that held a formidable collection of antique teapots, the silk-screened pastel T-shirts Theodosia had designed herself with a whimsical drawing of a teacup, a curlicue of rising steam, and the words Tea Shirt.

"Sweet," he murmured as he eased himself into a chair.

"We have Assam and Sencha," Drayton announced, curiously formal.

"Assam, please," said Tidwell. His eyes shone bright on Theodosia. "If we could talk alone?"

Theodosia knew Haley had already escaped to the nether regions of the back offices, and she assumed Drayton would soon follow.

"Of course," said Drayton. "I have errands to run, anyway."

Tidwell waited until they were alone. Then he took a sip of tea, smiled, and set his teacup down. "Delicious."

"Thank you."

"Miss Browning," Tidwell began, "are you aware our hapless victim of last evening is Hughes Barron, the real estate developer?"

"So I understand."

"He was not terribly well liked," said Tidwell, smiling.

"I didn't know that."

"Miss Browning, it saddens me to be the bearer of such news, but Mr. Barron's death was no accident." He paused, searching out Theodosia's face. "We are looking at a wrongful death. Even as we speak, a sample of the tea that Hughes Barron was drinking last night has been dispatched to the state toxicology lab."

Theodosia's heart skipped a beat, even as she willed herself to remain calm. Do not let this man rattle or intimidate you, she told herself. *You* had nothing to do with Hughes Barron's death. Surely this would soon reveal itself as one big misunderstanding.

On the heels of that came the realization that she had spent nearly a dozen years in advertising, where everything had run in panic mode. Everything a crash and burn involving millions of dollars. Could she keep her cool? Absolutely.

"Perhaps you'd better explain yourself," was all Theodosia said. *Better to play it close to the vest,* she thought. *Find out what this man has to say.*

Burt Tidwell held up a hand. "There is concern that whatever liquid was in Hughes Barron's teacup severely compromised his health. In other words, his beverage was lethal."

Now amusement lit Theodosia's face. "Surely you don't believe it was my tea that killed him."

"I understand you served a number of teas last night."

"Of course," said Theodosia lightly. "Darjeeling, jasmine, our special Lamplighter Blend. You realize, of course, everyone who stopped by the garden—and we're talking probably two hundred people—sampled our teas. No one else is dead."

She took another sip of tea, blotted her lips, and favored Tidwell with a warm yet slightly indulgent smile. "Frankly, Mr. Tidwell, if I were you, I'd be more concerned with *who* Hughes Barron was sitting with in the garden last night rather than which *tea* he drank."

"Touché, Miss Browning," Tidwell replied. He reclined in his chair, swiped the back of his hand against his quivering chin, and let fly his curve ball. "How long has Bethany Shepherd worked for you?"

So that's where this conversation was going, thought

Theodosia. "Really just a handful of times over the past few months," she replied. "But surely you don't consider the girl a suspect."

"I understand she had words with Hughes Barron last week at a Heritage Society meeting."

"Bethany recently obtained an internship with the Heritage Society, so I imagine she spends considerable time there."

"Rather harsh words," said Tidwell. His eyes bored into Theodosia.

"A disagreement doesn't make her a murderer," said Theodosia lightly. "It only means she's a young woman blessed with gumption."

"We have her at the police station now."

"Indeed."

"Taking a statement. Very pro forma."

"I assume her lawyer is with her?"

"Do you think she needs one?" Tidwell arched a tufted eyebrow.

"Not the issue."

"Pray tell, what is?"

"She's *entitled* to one," replied Theodosia.

CHAPTER 5

❋❋❋

"*P*OISON!" EXCLAIMED HALEY.

"Sshh!" Drayton held a finger to his lips. "The customers," he mouthed in an exaggerated gesture, although a couple patrons had already turned in their chairs and were staring inquisitively at the three of them clustered at the counter.

"Tidwell thinks someone *poisoned* Hughes Barron?" said Haley in a low voice, her eyes wide as saucers.

"That's his notion so far," said Theodosia. "He's already sent the contents of Hughes Barron's teacup to the state toxicology lab."

"What absolute rubbish!" declared Drayton. "We had nothing to do with the man's demise. Are you sure those paramedics checked the man's heart? Big fellow like that might've had a bad ticker."

"I'm sure they'll perform an autopsy and clear everything up eventually," said Theodosia.

"The problem is," said Drayton, "what do we do in the short term?"

Damage control, Theodosia thought to herself. *That was our PR department's job when I was still at the agency. They'd get a positive spin working before anything negative could grab hold.*

"Your point is well taken," said Theodosia. "As outrageous as the notion is that our tea killed the man, Hughes Barron's death is fertile ground for wild rumors."

"Rumors that could cast a veil of suspicion over all of us," added Haley.

"Actually," said Theodosia as she stared into the worried eyes of her two dear employees and friends, "I'm more concerned with Bethany right now. Tidwell has her down at the police station."

Haley's eyes welled with tears, and she bit her lip to keep from bursting into sobs. "Just who *is* this man, Hughes Barron? I've never even heard of him before!"

"Well," said Drayton, his dark eyes darting from side to side, "I don't mind telling you that Church Street is positively buzzing about him today." His back to the customers, Drayton edged closer to the small counter and faced Theodosia and Haley.

"I spoke earlier with Fern Barrow at the Cottage Inn. She had heard about the disturbance at last night's Lamplighter Tour and seemed to know quite a bit about our Mr. Hughes Barron."

"Really?" said Theodosia, intrigued.

"Apparently, he was born and raised in Goose Creek, just north of here, but lived in California most of his life. Santa Monica. Fern said Hughes Barron made a tidy profit out there as a real estate developer. Mostly condos and strip malls." Drayton rolled his eyes as though he were talking about organized crime.

Theodosia flashed on her conversation with Delaine yesterday afternoon. "God knows what sins a developer with Barron's reputation might wreak," she had said.

"Anyway," continued Drayton, "Hughes Barron moved back to the Charleston area about two years ago. He bought a beachfront home on the Isle of Palms. You know, Theo, near Wild Dunes?"

Theodosia nodded.

"Since he's moved back, Hughes Barron's big hot project has been developing some truly awful time-share condominiums," said Drayton. "Out on Johns Island."

Johns Island was a sleepy agricultural community known mostly for its large bird refuge.

"That couldn't have been terribly popular," said Theodosia.

"Are you kidding? He was almost *pilloried* for it!" said Drayton. "He was picketed and protested before the bulldozers scooped a single shovel of dirt. The people who opposed the development kept the pressure going all through the construction phase, too. But, of course, the condos were built anyway. They weren't able to block it." Drayton sighed. "Hughes Barron must have had powerful connections to get that land rezoned. We're talking statehouse level, of course,"

"I do remember hearing about that development," said Theodosia. "And you're right. There was major opposition from environmental groups as well as the local historical society."

"Nothing they could do, though." Drayton sighed again.

"Excuse me," called a woman seated at one of the tables. "Could we please get a little more tea here?"

"Certainly, ma'am." With a quick rustle and a cordial smile, Haley flitted across the tea room. Besides refilling the teapot, she brought a fresh pitcher of milk and, much to the delight of the party of three women, also produced a plate of caramel-nut shortbread. On the house, of course.

"Drayton." Theodosia slid the cash register drawer closed. Something was bothering her, and she had to know the full story.

Drayton Conneley had pulled a little step stool out from beneath the counter. Now he was balanced on it, stacking jars of creamed honey from the local apiary, DuBose Bees. He peered down at Theodosia in midstretch. "What's needling you?" he asked.

"Did Bethany really have words with Hughes Barron at a Heritage Society meeting?"

Drayton's mouth opened as if he meant to speak, then he seemed to think better of it. To say anything from his lofty perch would be to broadcast trouble they didn't need right now. Drayton held up an index finger and clambered down.

"Let me put this in perspective," he said.

Theodosia looked out over the tea room, where all her customers seemed content and taken care of, and nodded.

"I'm not sure how clued in you are about this," said Drayton, "but Hughes Barron had recently become a new board member at the Heritage Society."

"So it would seem."

"I don't have exact details on who sponsored him or what the final vote was on accepting him, because, as you recall, I was up in Boston when all that took place."

Theodosia nodded. Drayton had been at Chatham Brothers Tea Wholesalers on a buying trip.

"Suffice it to say, however, that Hughes Barron was voted in by a small margin, and Timothy Neville, our board president, was *extremely* displeased. Well," continued Drayton, "last week, this past Wednesday evening to be exact, was our most recent board meeting. Because I had never met Hughes Barron before, I decided it was only fair to reserve judgment on the man. I wasn't privy to his background or what his motivations for joining the Heritage Society were. For all I knew, they could have been totally altruistic. So I maintained an open mind. Until, of course, Hughes Barron got up to speak and jumped on his own personal bandwagon concerning new development in the historic district." Drayton suddenly looked unhappy. "That's when it all started."

"When what started?" asked Theodosia.

"I'm afraid we got into a row with Hughes Barron," confessed Drayton.

"Who did?" asked Theodosia. "All of you?" She knew any kind of new development in the historic district was one of Drayton's pet peeves. He himself resided in a 160-year-old home once occupied by a Civil War surgeon.

"Timothy Neville, Joshua Brady, and me. Samantha and Bethany threw their two cents in as well. But mostly it was Timothy. He had a particularly ugly go-round with Hughes Barron." Drayton lowered his voice. "You know how cantankerous and judgmental Timothy can be."

Indeed, Theodosia was well aware of Timothy Neville's fiery temper. The crusty octogenarian president of the Heritage Society had a reputation for being bull-headed and brash. In fact, she had once seen Timothy Neville berate a waiter at the Peninsula Grill for incorrectly opening a bottle of champagne and spilling a few drops of the French bubbly. She had always felt that Timothy Neville was entirely too full of himself.

"So Timothy Neville took off on Hughes Barron?" said Theodosia.

"I'd have to say it was more of a character assassination." Drayton looked around sharply, then lowered his voice an octave. "Timothy denounced Hughes Barron as a Neanderthal carpetbagger. Because of that condo development."

"Just awful," said Theodosia.

Drayton faced Theodosia with sad eyes. "I agree. A gentleman should never resort to name-calling."

"I meant the condos," Theodosia replied.

CHAPTER 6

❧❧❧

$\mathcal{T}$HEODOSIA STARED AT the storyboards propped up
against the wall in her office. Jessica Todd, president
of Todd & Lambeau Design Group, had brought in three
more boards. Now there were *six* different Web site designs for her to evaluate.

As her eyes roved from one to the other, she told herself
that all were exciting and extremely doable. Any one . . .
eeny, meeny, miney, moe . . . would work beautifully at
launching her tea business into cyberspace.

Ordinarily, Theodosia would be head over heels,
champing at the bit to make a final choice and set the
wheels in motion. But today it seemed as if her brain was
stuffed with cotton.

Too much had happened, she told herself. Was happen-
ing. It felt like a freight train gathering momentum. Not a
runaway train quite yet, but one that was certainly rum-
bling down the rails.

Bethany had phoned the tea shop a half hour ago, and
Haley, stretching the cord to its full length so she could
talk privately in the kitchen, had a whispered conversation
with her. When Haley hung up, Theodosia had grabbed a

box of Kleenex and listened intently as Haley related Bethany's sad tale.

"She's finished at the police station for now," Haley had told her. "But one of the detectives, I don't know if it was that Tidwell character or not, advised her to get a lawyer." Haley had snuffled, then blown her nose loudly. "Do you know any lawyers?" she'd asked plaintively.

Theodosia had nodded. Of course she did. Her father's law firm was still in business. The senior partner, Leyland Hartwell, always a family friend, was a formidable presence in Charleston.

Jessica Todd impatiently tapped a manicured finger on her ultraslim laptop computer. Hyperthyroidal and superslim herself, wearing an elegant aubergine-colored suit, Jessica sat across the desk from Theodosia. She was anxious to get Theodosia's decision today.

As President of Todd & Lambeau, Jessica had distinguished herself as one of the top Internet marketing gurus in Charleston. And today she was fairly jumping out of her skin, eager to implement her graphic design ideas, Web architecture, and marketing strategies for the Indigo Tea Shop's new Web site.

"Would you like a cup of tea, Jessica?" Theodosia asked, stalling. Decisions weren't coming easily.

"That's the fourth time you've asked," Jessica replied somewhat peevishly. She shook her head and ran long fingernails through her sleek, short helmet of dark hair. "Again, no thank you."

"Sorry," murmured Theodosia.

Jessica reached over and plucked up a board that featured a montage of teapots and tea leaves, set against a ghosted background of green terraced slopes, one of the old Chinese tea plantations.

"If we could just revisit this concept for a moment," said Jessica, forging ahead, "I believe you'll find it meets all criteria we established. Dynamic graphics, intuitive user interface. Look at the global navigation buttons. Online Catalog, Tea Tips, Tea Q&A, and Contact Us. Here, I'll show you how it works on the laptop."

"Jessica . . ." Theodosia began, then stopped. There was no way she could focus on this when she was so concerned about Bethany and the events of last night. She knew better than to make critical business decisions when her mind was somewhere else.

"I'm sorry," said Theodosia standing up. "We're going to have to do this another time."

"What?" sputtered Jessica.

"Your designs are perfectly lovely. Spectacular, in fact. But I need to live with them for a few days. And it's only right to share them with Drayton and Haley, get a consensus."

"Let's call them in now."

"Jessica. Please."

"All right, all right." Jessica Todd snapped her laptop closed, gathered up her attaché case. "Call me, Theodosia. But don't wait too long. We're hot into a pitch right now for a new on-line brokerage. And if it comes through, *when* it comes through, we're all going to be working twenty-four/seven on it."

"I hear you, Jessica."

Walking Jessica to the door, Theodosia thought back on her own career in advertising. *I was like that,* she told herself. *Nervous, nuts. Slaving evenings and weekends, caught in the pressure cooker. What had Jessica called it? Working twenty-four/seven. Right.*

Breathing a sigh of relief, feeling enormously grateful for her serene little world at the tea shop, Theodosia surprised Haley just as she was dusting a fresh pan of lemon bars with powdered sugar.

"I'm going to do deliveries today," Theodosia announced.

"*You* are? Why is that?" asked Haley.

"Can't sit still, don't want to sit still."

"I know the feeling," said Haley. She reached under her wooden baker's rack and pulled out a large wicker hamper.

"Okay, lucky for you it's the milk run. Only two deliveries. A half-dozen canisters of jasmine and English breakfast teas for the Featherbed House and some of Drayton's special palmetto blend for Reverend Jonathan at Saint Philip's."

Once outside, Theodosia walked briskly in the direction of the Featherbed House. The sun shone down warmly. The breeze off the Cooper River was light and tasted faintly salty. White, puffy clouds scudded overhead. But what should have been a glorious day to revel in went relatively unnoticed by Theodosia, so preoccupied was she by recent events.

Why on earth were they pressing Bethany so hard? she wondered. Surely the police could see she was just a young woman with no ax to grind against anyone. Especially a man like Hughes Barron. Burt Tidwell was no fool. He, of all people, should be able to see that.

Theodosia sighed. Poor Bethany. The only thing she'd been up to lately was trying to rebuild her life. And she'd seemed to have been going about it fairly successfully.

Only last week Theodosia had overheard Bethany speaking glowingly to Drayton about her internship at the Heritage Society. How she'd been chosen over six other candidates. How she was so impressed by the many volunteers who donated countless hours and dollars. How the Heritage Society had recently staged a black-tie dinner and silent auction and raised almost $300,000 to purchase the old Chapman Mill. Abandoned and scheduled for demolition, the historic old mill would now live on in Charleston's history.

As Theodosia turned the corner at Murray Street, the rush of wind coming off Charleston Harbor hit her full on. It blew her hair out in auburn streamers, brought a rosy glow to her cheeks and, finally, a smile to her face.

The Battery, that stretch of homes and shore at the point of land where the Ashley and Cooper Rivers converged and the Atlantic poured in to meet them, was one of Theodosia's favorite places. Originally known as Oyster Point because it began as a swampy beach strewn with oyster shells, The Battery evolved into a military strong point and finally into the elegant neighborhood of harborside homes and parks it is today. With its White Point Gardens, Victorian bandstand, and no fewer than twenty-six cannons and monuments, The Battery held a special place in the hearts of every Charlestonian.

Perched on The Battery and overlooking the harbor with a bird's-eye view of Fort Sumter, the Featherbed House was one of the peninsula's premier bed-and-breakfasts. It featured elegantly furnished rooms with canopied beds, cypress paneling, and twelve-foot-high hand-molded plaster ceilings. And, of course, mounds of featherbeds just as the name promised. A second-story open-air bridge spanned the backyard garden and transported delighted visitors from the main house to a treetop dining room in the renovated hay loft of the carriage house.

In the cozy lobby, filled with every manner of ceramic goose, plush goose, and needlepoint goose, Theodosia stopped to chat with owners Angie and Mark Congdon. They were a husband and wife team who had both been commodity brokers in Chicago and fled the Windy City for a more temperate climate and slower pace.

Changes and reevaluations, mused Theodosia as she hurried back down the street toward Saint Philip's. *Lots of that going around these days.*

Saint Philip's Episcopal was the church for whom Church Street was named. It was a neoclassical edifice that had been drawing communicants for almost 200 years. When the bells in the tall, elegant spire chimed on Sunday mornings, the entire historic district knew that the Reverend Jonathan's service was about to begin.

Theodosia stepped through a wrought iron archway into the private garden and burial ground.

"Good morning!" a voice boomed.

Theodosia halted in her tracks and looked around. She finally spotted Reverend Jonathan, a small, wiry man with short silver hair, on his hands and knees underneath a small oak tree.

"This tree didn't fare well in the last big storm," said Reverend Jonathan as he pulled a metal cable tight around a wooden stake. "I thought if I shored it up, it might have a chance to catch up with its big brothers."

The "big brothers" Reverend Jonathan referred to were the two enormous live oaks that sat to either side of the parish house.

"You've worked wonders here," said Theodosia. Under Reverend Jonathan's watchful eye, the garden and historic burial ground had evolved from a manicured lawn with a few shrubs and memorial plaques to a hidden oasis filled with a delightful profusion of seasonal plants, flowering shrubs, stepping stones, and decorative statuary.

Reverend Jonathan straightened up and gazed about with pride. "I love getting my hands dirty. But I have to admit there's always something needs fixing. Next big project is some restoration work on our beloved church's interior arches."

Even though he had well over 1,500 communicants to minister to, dozens of committees to juggle, and fund-raising to tend to, Reverend Jonathan was a tireless worker. He always seemed to find time for hands-on gardening and maintenance of the historic church.

"That's the thing about these grande dame buildings." He grinned. "Patch, patch, patch."

"Mm," said Theodosia as she handed Reverend Jonathan his canisters of tea. "I know the feeling."

On her return trip to the Indigo Tea Shop, Theodosia's thoughts turned once again to Hughes Barron's death. Although she felt saddened that a human life had ended, it prickled her that the investigators seemed to be overlooking the obvious. If someone had been sitting at that far table with Hughes Barron, wouldn't *that* person have had the perfect opportunity to slip something toxic into the man's tea?

On a hunch, Theodosia jogged over toward Meeting

Street, where Samantha Rabathan lived. Samantha had been the chairperson for last night's event, she reasoned. Maybe Sam would have a list of attendees. That might be a logical place to start.

As luck would have it, Samantha was outside, bustling about on her enormous veranda, tending to the heroic abundance of plant life that flourished in her many containers and flower boxes. A divorcée for almost ten years, Samantha's only avocation seemed to be gardening. If Reverend Jonathan was the patron saint of trees and shrubs, Samantha was the guardian angel of flowers.

Samantha changed her flower boxes seasonally, so they might contain flowering bulbs, English daisies, clouds of wisteria, or miniature shrubs. Her trellises, usually hidden under mounds of perfect pink climbing roses, were legendary. Her backyard garden, with roses, star jasmine, begonias, and verbena clustered about a sparkling little pool, and tangled vines creeping up a backdrop of crumbling brick, was a must-see on the annual Garden Club Tour. And Samantha's elegant floral arrangements always garnered blue as well as purple ribbons at the annual Charleston Flower Show.

"Samantha!" Theodosia waved from the street.

"Hello," Samantha called back.

She was wearing her Mr. Green Jeans garb today, Theodosia noted. Green coveralls, green gloves, green floppy cotton hat, to go with her green thumb.

Most people in the neighborhood regarded Samantha as a bit of a hothouse plant herself. A delicate tropical flower with fine yellow hair and alabaster skin who shunned the sun. Close friends knew she was merely trying to prolong her facelift.

"How are you feeling today?" asked Theodosia. She shaded her eyes and gazed up at the porch with its trellises of ivy and trumpet vine and window boxes with overflowing ramparts of crape myrtle and althaea.

Samantha grinned sheepishly and fanned a gloved hand in front of her face. "Fine, really fine. Just too much excitement last night. I can't believe I actually fainted over that poor man. How embarrassing. Oh, well, at least it proves I'm a true Southern lady. Got the vapors. All so very *Gone With the Wind*," she added in an exaggerated drawl.

"Samantha . . ." began Theodosia.

But Samantha gushed on. "What a gentleman Drayton was to come to my aid. I must remember to thank him." She aimed her pruning shears toward a pot of cascading plumbago, snipped decisively, and laid a riot of bright blue flowers in her wicker basket. "I know. I shall put together one of my special bouquets. Drayton is a man of culture and refinement. He will appreciate the gesture."

"I'm certain he will, Samantha," said Theodosia.

"Theodosia." Samantha peered down from her veranda. "The sun is almost overhead. Do take care."

Theodosia ignored her warning. "Samantha, is there any way to connect people's names with the Lamplighter Tour tickets that were purchased?"

Samantha considered Theodosia's question. "You're asking me if we wrote down guests' names?"

"Did you?" asked Theodosia hopefully.

Samantha shook her head slowly from side to side. "No, we just sold the tickets and collected the money. Nobody has ever bothered to keep track of who bought what or how many. Usually our biggest concern is trying to outsell the Tradd Street tour. You know, they have an awful lot of volunteers out pounding the streets. This year they even placed printed posters in some of the B and Bs!"

Theodosia put a hand to her head and smoothed back her hair. This was what she'd been afraid of. No record keeping, just volunteers selling tickets wherever they could.

"But you know," added Samantha, venturing toward the sunlight, "if we offered a drawing or door prize in conjunction with the Lamplighter Tour, that would be an extra incentive to buy a ticket! And then, of course, we'd have to record people's names and addresses and phone numbers, that sort of thing." She wrinkled her nose in delicious anticipation. "A drawing! Isn't that a marvelous idea? I can't wait to propose it for next year's Lamplighter Tour."

Samantha snipped a few more stems of plumbago, then smiled brightly at Theodosia. "Theodosia, would *you* be interested in donating one of your gift baskets?"

CHAPTER 7

✺

CANE RIDGE PLANTATION was built in 1835 on Horlbeck Creek. It included a fanciful Gothic Revival cottage replete with soaring peaks and gables, steeply pitched shingled roof, and broad piazza extending around three sides. Set high on a vantage point overlooking a quiet pond and marshland, it had been a flourishing rice plantation in its day, with acres of flat, low fields that stretched out to meet piney forests.

Theodosia's father, Macalester Browning, and her Aunt Libby had grown up at Cane Ridge, and Theodosia had spent countless summers there. She always returned to Cane Ridge when her heart was troubled or she was in need of clearing her head.

"The cedar waxwings are here, but the marsh wrens have not yet arrived." Libby Revelle, Theodosia's aunt, scanned the distant marsh as she stood on the side piazza, a black cashmere shawl wrapped around her thin but firmly squared shoulders.

Tiny but elegant in her carriage, the silver haired Libby Revelle was a bird-watcher of the first magnitude. With her binoculars and Peterson's *Field Guide to Eastern*

Birds, she was able to identify shape of bill, tail patterns, and wing bars much the same way aviation aficionados delighted in identifying aircraft.

Theodosia hadn't intended on stopping at Aunt Libby's and staying for lunch. She had driven out to the low-country with every intention of visiting the Charleston Tea Plantation. Owners Mack Fleming and Bill Hall were good friends, and she was anxious to inspect the tea from their final harvest of the season.

But driving out the Maybank Highway in her Jeep Cherokee, Theodosia had felt a sudden longing for the old plantation, a desire to return to a place where she had always felt not only welcome, but also comfortably at home. And so, when she neared the turnoff for Rutledge Road, she pointed her red Jeep down the bumpy, gravel road that led to Cane Ridge and Aunt Libby.

Jouncing along, Theodosia had felt a certain peacefulness steal over her. The live oaks, dogwoods, and enormous hedges of azaleas closed in on the road in a comforting way. Through the forest's dense curtain were distant vine-covered humps, tell tale remnants of old rice dikes. And as she bumped across a rickety bridge, black water flowed silently beneath, conjuring images of youths in flat-bottomed bateaus.

Theodosia downshifted on her final approach, thankful for four-wheel drive. She'd purchased her Jeep just a year ago, against Drayton's advice, and was totally in love with it.

Drayton, ever mindful of image, had argued that the Jeep was "not particularly ladylike."

Theodosia had countered by pointing out that the Jeep was practical. "Perfect," she'd told him, "for transporting boxes and gift baskets. And if I want to go into the woods and pick wild dandelion or wild raspberries for flavoring teas, the Jeep's ideal. I can jounce down trails and even creek beds and not worry about getting stuck."

Drayton had dramatically put a hand to his forehead and sighed. "You had to buy red?"

Haley, on the other hand, had jumped in the passenger side and pleaded that they go "four-wheeling."

"Help me put out my buffet, will you?" asked Libby. "We've eaten our soup and sandwiches, and now it's our winged friends' turn."

"You stay here and enjoy the sun while I take the seed down," said Theodosia, glad to be of help.

Aunt Libby plied her winged visitors with a mixture of thistle, cracked corn, and black oil seed. Over the coming winter, Libby would go through at least eight hundred pounds of seeds.

Theodosia carried two pails overflowing with Libby's seed mixture to a fallen log on the edge of the marsh. A fifteen-foot length of gnarled oak, the tree trunk was peppered with hollow bowls and clefts, making perfect natural basins for birdseed.

Back on the piazza, Libby's heart expanded with pride as she watched this beautiful, accomplished woman, her niece. She loved Theodosia as a mother would a child. When Theodosia's mother died when Theo was only eight, she was only too happy to fill in wherever she could. She'd enjoyed attending Theodosia's various music recitals and class plays, sewing labels on Theodosia's clothes when she went off to camp, and teaching her how to whistle with two fingers in her mouth.

Then, when Theodosia's father passed away when she was twenty, she'd become her only real family. Even though Theodosia was living in a dorm at school, she'd gladly opened her house to her on holidays, hosted parties for Theodosia's friends, and gave her advice when she graduated and began job hunting.

And when Theodosia had decided to drop out of advertising and test her entrepreneurial spirit by buying the little tea shop, Libby had backed her one hundred percent.

"I was on my way to see Mack and Bill," Theodosia said as she came up the short flight of steps. The pails clanked down on the wooden porch.

"So you said," answered Libby. She sat in a wicker

chair, gazing out at a horizon of blue pond, waving golden grasses, and hazy sun.

Theodosia stared out at the old log she'd just replenished with seed, watched a striped chipmunk scamper out from a clump of dried weeds, snatch up a handful of fallen seeds, then sit back on its haunches to dine.

"We had some trouble in town last night," said Theodosia.

"I heard," said Aunt Libby.

Theodosia spun about. "What?" Libby, the sly fox, had sat through lunch with her, watched her fidget, and never said a word. Theodosia smiled wryly. Yes, that was Libby Revelle's style, the Aunt Libby she knew and loved. Don't push, let people talk in their own good time.

"What did you hear?" asked Theodosia. "And from who?"

"Oh, Bill Wexler came by, and we had ourselves a nice chat."

Bill Wexler had delivered mail in the low-country for almost twenty-five years. He also seemed to have a direct pipcline to everything that went on in Charleston, the low-country, and as far out as West Ashley.

"If people out here know, it's going to be all over town by the time I get back this afternoon," said Theodosia.

Libby nodded. "Probably."

Theodosia squinted into the sun, looking perplexed.

"Nothing you can do, dear," said Libby. "The only part you played in last night's little drama was a walk-on role. If folks are silly enough to think you're involved, that's their problem."

"You're right," agreed Theodosia. She eased herself down into the chair next to Libby, already deciding to stay the afternoon.

"But then, you're not worried about yourself, are you?" asked Libby.

"Not really," said Theodosia.

Libby reached a hand out and gently stroked Theodosia's hair. "You're my cat, always have been. Land on your feet, nine lives to spare."

"Oh, Libby." Theodosia caught her aunt's hand in hers and squeezed it gratefully. As she did, she was suddenly aware of Libby's thin, parchmentlike skin, the frailness of her tiny bones. And Aunt Libby's mortality.

CHAPTER 8

✖✖✖

TEAPOTS CHIRPED AND whistled and teacups clinked against saucers as Drayton bustled about the shop. Four tables were occupied, customers eager for morning tea and treats. Afterward, they would be picked up by one of the bright yellow jitneys that would whisk them away on their morning tour through Charleston's historic district, the open air market, or the King Street antiques district.

"Where's Haley?" Theodosia swooped through the doorway just as Drayton measured a final tablespoon of Irish breakfast tea into a Victorian teapot.

"Hasn't shown up yet," Drayton said as he arranged teapots, pitchers of milk, bowls of sugar cubes, and small plates of lemon slices on a silver tray, then deftly hoisted it to his shoulder.

"That's not like her," said Theodosia, pitching in. She was instantly concerned about Haley's absence since she was ordinarily quite prompt, usually showing up at the Indigo Tea Shop by 7:00 A.M. That's when Haley would heat up the oven and pour out batter she'd mixed up and refrigerated the day before. It was Haley's shortcut to fresh-baked scones, croissants, and benne wafers without having to get up at four in the morning.

While Drayton poured tea, Theodosia mustered up a pan of scones from the freezer and warmed them quickly in the oven.

"It won't matter that they've been frozen," Drayton murmured under his breath. "Scones are so amazingly heavy anyway, I don't think anyone will know the difference."

And Drayton was right. Served piping hot to their guests along with plenty of Devonshire cream and strawberry jam, the scones were actually ooed and ahed over.

"Have you noticed anything odd?" asked Theodosia. She stood behind the counter surveying the collection of customers who lingered at the tables.

Drayton glanced up from the cash register. "What do you mean?"

"I'm not seeing any of our regulars," said Theodosia.

Drayton gave her a sharp look. "You're right." His eyes searched out Theodosia's. "You don't suppose . . ."

"I'm sure they'll be in later," she said.

"Of course they will."

Forty minutes later, the early customers had all departed, tables had been cleared, floors swept, and teapots readied for the next influx.

"Now that I've got a moment to breathe, I'm going to phone Haley," said Theodosia. "I'm really getting worried."

The bell over the door jingled merrily. "Here we go," said Theodosia. "More customers." She turned toward the door with a welcoming smile, but it was Haley who burst through the door, not another throng of customers.

"Haley!" said Theodosia. "What's wrong?" Haley's ordinarily placid face projected unhappiness, her peaches-and-cream complexion blotchy. Her shoulders sagged, her eyes were puffy, and she'd been crying. Hard.

"They fired her!" cried Haley.

Theodosia flew across the room to Haley, put an arm

around her shoulder. "Come, dear. Sit down." She led Haley to the closest table and got her seated. "Drayton," Theodosia called, "we're going to need some tea. Strong tea."

Tears trickled down Haley's cheeks as she turned sad eyes on Theodosia. "They fired Bethany. From the Heritage Society."

"Oh, no," said Theodosia. "Are you sure?"

"Yes, they called her a little while ago and told her not to bother coming in."

"Who called her?" asked Theodosia.

"Mr. Neville," said Haley.

"Timothy?"

"Yes, Timothy Neville," said Haley in a choked voice.

"What happened?" Drayton set a pot of tea and three mugs on the bare table.

"Timothy Neville fired Bethany," said Theodosia.

He sat down, instantly concerned. "Oh, no."

"Can he do that, Drayton?" asked Theodosia.

Drayton nodded his head slowly, as if still comprehending Haley's words. "I suppose so. He's the president. As such, Timothy Neville wields an incredible amount of power. If he were firing someone from an executive position, he'd probably have to call a formal board meeting. At least it would be polite protocol to do so. But for an intern . . . Yes, I'm afraid Timothy Neville is empowered to hire or fire at will."

"Because she's not important enough," Haley said with a sniff.

"I didn't say that," said Drayton.

"What you all don't realize," cried Haley, "is that Bethany was going to use her internship as a stepping stone to a better job. You can't get hired by a good museum unless you have some kind of internship under your belt. And now Bethany's credibility is completely ruined!" She put her face in her hands and sobbed.

Drayton gently patted her arm. "There, there, perhaps

something can still be done." He gazed sadly at Theodosia.
His hangdog look implored her, *Can't you do something?*

Theodosia arched her eyebrows back at him. *What can
I do?*

"Can't you at least talk to him?" Drayton finally asked
out loud.

Haley's tear-streaked face tipped up toward Theodosia
and brightened. "Could you? Please? You're so good at
things like this. You're brave, and you know lots of important people. Please, you've just got to help!"

The pleading looks on Drayton's and Haley's faces
spoke volumes.

Theodosia sat back in her chair and took a sip of tea.
She had spoken with Timothy Neville once or twice over
the years. He had always been clipped and formal. She recalled him the other night at the Lamplighter Tour. Sitting
at one of the tables, almost holding court as he lectured
about the bronze bells that hung in the tower of Saint
Michael's and how they'd once been confiscated by
British soldiers.

"Of course, I'll talk to him," she said with outward
bravado, when what she really felt inside was *Oh, dear.*

CHAPTER 9

OUTRAGE MAKES MANY women belligerent and strident.
With Theodosia it only served to enhance her firm,
quiet manner. She strode down Church Street past Noble
Dragon Books, Bouquet Garni Giftware, and the Cotton
Duck clothing shop. Her thoughts were a jumble, but her
resolve was clear. Firing Bethany was unconscionable.
The girl was clearly not involved in anything that had to do
with Hughes Barron. This had been an incredible overre-
action by the Heritage Society and especially on the part of
Timothy Neville. She didn't know a whit about employ-
ment law, but she did know about being an employer.
Since Bethany's internship had been a paid internship, that
meant she was a regular employee. So just maybe the firing could be considered illegal. Particularly since it was
highly doubtful the Heritage Society could prove mali-
cious intent or lack of ability on Bethany's part.

Her zeal carried Theodosia past the Avis Melbourne
Home before she even realized it. When she suddenly became aware of just where she was, Theodosia slowed her
pace, then stopped. Standing just outside a heroic hedge of
magnolias, she gazed up at the lovely old home. It looked

even more magnificent by day. Stately Ionic columns presented an elegant facade on this predominantly Georgian-style house with its keen attention to symmetry and grace.

But this was where the murder took place, Theodosia reminded herself. This was where Hughes Barron was—dare she say it?—poisoned.

Theodosia turned back and walked slowly up the broad front walk. The lanterns and glowing jack-o'-lanterns of the other night were gone. Now the house gleamed white in the sunlight.

It really was a wedding cake of a house, Theodosia thought to herself. The columns, second-floor balustrade, and roof ornaments looked just like daubs of white frosting.

She paused at the front steps, turned onto the winding flagstone path that led through a wrought-iron gate, and walked around the side of the house. Within moments, shade engulfed her. Ever since she'd taken a botany class, when she had first purchased the tea shop, Theodosia had made careful observation of plants. Now she noted that tall mimosa trees sheltered the house from the hot Charleston sun, and dense stands of loquat and oleander lined the pathway.

As her footsteps echoed hollowly, she wondered if anyone was home. Probably not. The Odettes, the couple who called this lovely mansion home, owned a travel agency. They were probably at their office or off somewhere leading a trip. Come to think of it, she hadn't even seen the Odettes the night of the Lamplighter Tour. Heritage Society volunteers had supervised the event, helping her get set up in the butler's pantry, and they had guided tour guests through the various downstairs rooms and parlors.

As she rounded the back corner of the house and came into full view of the garden, Theodosia was struck by how deserted it now looked. Two days ago it had been a lush and lavish outdoor space, darkly elegant with sweet-scented vines and twinkling lanterns, filled with the chatter and laughter of eager Lamplighter Tour guests. Then, of course, had come the gruff and urgent voices of the various police and rescue squads echoing off flagstones and brick walls. But now the atmosphere in the garden was so very still. The tables and chairs were still there, the fountain splattered away, but the mood was somber. *Like a cemetery,* she thought with a shiver.

Stop it, she chided herself, *don't let your imagination run wild.*

Theodosia walked to the fountain, leaned down, and trailed a hand in the cool water. Thick-leafed water plants bobbed on the surface, and below, copper pennies gleamed. *Someone threw coins in here,* she mused. *Children, perhaps. Making a wish. Or Lamplighter Tour guests.* She straightened up, looked around. It really was a beautiful garden with its abundant greenery and wrought-iron touches. Funny how it had seemed so sinister a moment ago.

Theodosia walked to the far table—the table where Hughes Barron had been found slumped over his teacup. She sat down in his chair, looked around.

The table rested snug against an enormous hedge that ran around the outside perimeter of the garden. Could someone have slipped through that hedge? Theodosia reached a hand out to touch the leaves. They were stiff, dark green, packed together densely. But down near the roots there was certainly a crawl space.

She tilted her head back and gazed at the live oak tree overhead. It was an enormous old tree that spread halfway across the garden. Lace curtains of Spanish moss hung from its upper branches. Could someone have sat quietly in the crook of that venerable tree and dropped something in Hughes Barron's tea? Yes, she thought, it was possible. Anything was possible.

CHAPTER 10

TIMOTHY NEVILLE LOVED the Heritage Society with all
his being. He possessed an almost religious fervor for
the artifacts and buildings they worked to preserve. He displayed uncanny skill when it came to restoration of the society's old documents, doing most of the painstaking
conservation work himself. He worked tirelessly to recruit
new members.

But, most of all, Timothy Neville reveled in Heritage
Society politics. Because politics was in his blood.

Descended from the original Huguenots who fled religious persecution in France during the sixteenth century,
his ancestors had been fiery, spirited immigrants who'd
settled in the Carolinas. Those hardy pioneers had eagerly
embraced the New World and helped establish Charles
Town. Fighting off the governance of the English crown,
surviving the War Between the States, weathering eco-
nomic downturns in rice and indigo, they were an independent, self-assured lot. Today they were regarded as the
founding fathers of Charleston's aristocracy.

"Miss Browning." Timothy Neville inclined his head
and pulled his lips back in a rictus grin that displayed two

rows of small, sharp teeth. "Come to plead the case of the young lady?"

Standing in the doorway of Timothy Neville's Heritage Society office, peering into the dim light, amazed by the clutter of art and artifacts that surrounded him, Theodosia was taken aback. How on earth could Timothy Neville have known she wanted to talk with him about Bethany? She was certain Bethany hadn't said anything about the two of them being friends. In fact, Bethany hadn't ever really been formally employed by her. And this morning Haley had certainly been far too upset and frightened to place any phone calls.

Timothy Neville pointedly ignored her and turned his attention back to the Civil War–era document he was working on. It was badly faded and the antique linen paper seriously degraded. *An intriguing challenge,* he thought to himself.

Instead of answering him immediately, Theodosia took this opportunity to study Timothy Neville. Watching him in the subdued light, his head bent down, Theodosia was struck by what an unusual-looking little man Timothy Neville was. High, rounded forehead, brown skin stretched tightly over prominent cheekbones, a bony nose, and small, sharp jaw.

Why, he was almost simian-looking, thought Theodosia. Timothy Neville was a little monkey of a man.

As if reading her mind, Timothy Neville swiveled his head and stared at her with dark, piercing eyes. Though small and wiry, he always dressed exceedingly well. Today he was turned out in pleated gray wool slacks, starched white shirt, and dove gray jacket.

Theodosia met his gaze unfalteringly. Timothy Neville had been president of the Heritage Society for as long as she had been aware there was a Heritage Society. She figured the man had to be at least seventy-five years old, although some folks put him at eighty. She knew that, besides being a pillar in the Heritage Society, Timothy Neville also played second violin with the Charleston

Symphony Orchestra and resided in a spectacular Georgian-style mansion on Archdale Street. He was exceedingly well placed, she reminded herself. It would behoove her to proceed carefully.

He finally chose to answer his own question. "Of course that's why you're here," he said with a sly grin. And then, as though reading her mind, added, "Last week Drayton mentioned that the girl was living with one of your employees. In the little cottage across the alley from you, I believe."

"That's right," said Theodosia. Perhaps this was going to be easier than she'd initially thought. Neville was being polite, if not a trifle obtuse. And Drayton was, after all, on the board of the Heritage Society. She herself had once been invited to join. Maybe this misunderstanding could be easily straightened out. Maybe the Heritage Society had just panicked, made a mistake.

"Nothing I can do," said Timothy as he bent over his document again.

"I beg your pardon?" said Theodosia. The temperature in the room suddenly seemed to drop ten degrees. "I realize Bethany was . . . is . . . only an intern with the Heritage Society. But I'm afraid she was let go for the wrong reason. For goodness sake, she was Hughes Barron's *waitress.* The girl had nothing to do with the man's untimely death."

"I don't give a damn about the girl or the man's death!" Timothy Neville's dark eyes glittered like hard obsidian, and a vein in his temple throbbed. "But as far as untimely goes, I'd say it was *extremely* timely. Opportunistic, in fact." He gave a dry chuckle that sounded like a rattlesnake's warning. "Not unlike the man himself."

Timothy suddenly jumped up from his chair and confronted Theodosia. Although he was four inches shorter than her, he made up for it with white-hot fervor.

"Hughes Barron was a despicable scoundrel with a callous disregard for historical preservation!" he screamed, his brown face suddenly contorting and turning beet red.

"The man thought he could come to our city—*our* city, for God's sake—and run roughshod over principles and ideals we hold dear."

"Look, Mr. Neville, Timothy . . ." Theodosia began.

He pointed a finger at her, continuing his tirade. "That evil man had even been planning something for *your* neck of the woods, young lady! That's right!"

Timothy Neville bounced his head violently several times, and Theodosia felt a light spray hit her face. She took a step back.

"Property on your block!" screamed Timothy Neville. "You think you're immune? Think again!"

Theodosia stared with fascination at this little man who was clearly, almost frighteningly, out of control. She wondered if such a neurotic, brittle man could get so overwrought concerning historical buildings, could he also commit murder?

CHAPTER II

❦

WONDERFUL SMELLS EMANATED from the kitchen, a sure sign that Haley had regained her balance and slipped back into her usual routine.

"It's me," called Theodosia as she let herself into her office and pulled the back door closed behind her.

Haley popped her head around the doorway like a little gopher. "Successful meeting?" Her face glowed from the heat of the kitchen, and her mood seemed considerably improved. Theodosia thought she looked 200 percent better than she had a few hours ago.

"I'd say so."

Now Drayton appeared. "You saw Timothy," he said eagerly.

"Yes."

"Were you able to reason with him?" he asked.

Still vivid in Theodosia's mind was the sight of Timothy Neville in the throes of a hissy fit. "Not exactly," she replied.

"So you *didn't* get Bethany's job back?" asked Haley.

"No," said Theodosia. "Not yet."

Haley's smile sagged.

"I don't understand," said Drayton. "You said it was a success."

"It was, in a way. Timothy was kind enough to reveal his true character."

Drayton and Haley stared at each other. They were uncertain as to what exactly Theodosia meant by this. And Theodosia, seeing their disappointment, had no intention of giving them a blow-by-blow description of Timothy Neville's incredibly obnoxious behavior.

"Drayton, Haley," said Theodosia. "I need to make a phone call. Trust me; this isn't over. In fact, we've only just scratched the surface."

"Now, what do you suppose she meant by all that?" Haley asked Drayton as they went out into the tea room, shaking their heads.

Flipping through her hefty Rolodex, Theodosia found the number she wanted. *Step one,* she thought to herself. *Sure hope he's in.*

"Leyland Hartwell, please. Tell him it's Theodosia Browning."

As Theodosia waited for Leyland Hartwell to come on the line, her eyes searched out the pale mauve walls of her little office. Along with framed tea labels and opera programs, Theodosia had hung dozens of family photos. Her eyes fell on one now. A black-and-white photo of her dad on his sailboat. Looking suntanned, windblown, relaxed. He'd been a member of the Charleston Yacht Club and had once sailed with a crew of three others in the 771-mile Charleston-to-Bermuda Race. He had been an expert sailor, and she had loved sailing with him. Handling the tiller, throwing out the spinnaker, thrilling to the exhilarating rush of sea foam when they heeled over in the wind.

"Theodosia!" Leyland Hartwell's voice boomed in her ear. "What a pleasant surprise. Do you still have that Heinz fifty-seven dog?"

"The Dalbrador," she said.

"That's the one. Ha, ha. Very clever. What can I do for you, my dear?"

"I'm after some information, Leyland. Your firm still handles a considerable amount of real estate business, am I correct?"

"Yes, indeed. Mortgages, title examinations, deeds, foreclosures and cancellations, zoning, leases. You name it, we've got our fingers in the thick of things."

"I'm trying to gather information on a real estate developer by the name of Hughes Barron. Do you know him?"

"Heard of him," said Leyland Hartwell. There was a pause. "We're talking about the fellow who just died, right?"

"Right," said Theodosia. *And please don't ask too much more,* she silently prayed.

"Lots of rumors flying on that one," said Leyland Hartwell. "I was at Coosaw Creek yesterday afternoon playing a round with Tommy Beaumont. He told me Barron died of a heart attack. Then later on a fellow at the bar said he heard a rumor that Barron had been poisoned. Arsenic or something like it."

"I really wanted to know about his business dealings," said Theodosia.

Theodosia heard a rustle of paper, and then Leyland Hartwell spoke to her again.

"Business deals. Gotcha. Is this time-sensitive?"

"I'm afraid so."

"No problem. I'll put one of my people on it and light a fire. We'll find out what we can. Say, do you still sell that lemon mint tea with the real lemon verbena?"

"We certainly do."

"Mrs. Hartwell surely does love that stuff on ice. Awfully refreshing."

Theodosia smiled. Leyland Hartwell was devoted to his wife and always referred to her as Mrs. Hartwell. "Good, I'll send some over for her."

"Aren't you a love. One of my fellows will be back to you soon. Hopefully first thing tomorrow."

CHAPTER 12

CLICK, CLICK, CLICK. Earl Grey took long, easy strides as his toenails hit the blue vinyl runner that ran down the center hallway of the O'Doud Senior Home. Head erect, ears pitched forward, he was spiffily outfitted in his blue nylon vest emblazoned with his therapy dog patch.

"Hello there, Earl." Suzette, one of the regular night nurses who had worked there a good fifteen years, greeted him with a big smile as he passed by. As an afterthought, Suzette also acknowledged Theodosia. "Hello, ma'am," she said.

Earl Grey and Theodosia were both officially on duty, but Theodosia had long since gotten used to playing second fiddle. Once they set foot in the door, it was strictly Earl Grey's show. And everyone, from head nurse to janitor, tended to greet Earl Grey first. It was as though *he* was the one who'd driven over for a visit and allowed Theodosia to tag along.

That was just fine with Theodosia. In fact, downplaying her role was the whole idea behind therapy dog work. You wanted the dog to approach residents first, in the hallways or recreation room, or even in a resident's private room.

Let the residents themselves decide their level of interaction.

Sometimes, if a person was lying in bed, sick or infirm, they'd just smile at Earl Grey. Often he'd have a calming influence on them, or he'd be able to cheer them with his quiet presence. It was at times like those that Theodosia thought they might be remembering some lovable dog they'd once enjoyed as a pet. Earl Grey, uncanny canine that he was, seemed to understand just when a resident had gained that certain comfort level with him. When he thought the time was right, he'd rest his muzzle on the edge of their bed and give them a gentle kiss.

One elderly man who was blind and confined to a wheelchair, severely limited in his activities, enjoyed tossing a tennis ball for Earl Grey. Earl Grey would bump and bounce his way down the hallway, painting an audio picture for the man, then bring the tennis ball back to him and snuggle affectionately in the man's lap.

Then there was the foursome of fairly active women who never failed to have a plate of treats for Earl Grey. They either coaxed relatives into bringing dog biscuits in for them, or they baked "liver brownie cake," a strange concoction of beef liver and oatmeal. Theodosia thought the liver brownie cake *looked* a great deal like liver pâté but tasted like sawdust. Earl Grey, on the other hand, found it a gourmet delight.

These experiences were all enormously rewarding for Theodosia, and sometimes, driving home at night, her eyes would fill with tears as she remembered a certain incident that had touched her heart. She'd have to pull the car over to the side of the road, search for her hanky, and tell Earl Grey, once again, what a truly magnificent fellow he was.

CHAPTER 13

LEYLAND HARTWELL WAS as good as his word. The next morning, the phone rang bright and early.

"Miss Browning?"

"Yes?" answered Theodosia.

"Jory Davis here. I'm an associate with Ligget, Hume, Hartwell. Leyland Hartwell wanted me to call you concerning information we gathered for you. He also wanted me to assure you he would've phoned personally, but he was called into an emergency meeting." There was a slight pause. "Miss Browning?"

"Yes, Mr. Davis. Please go on."

"Anyway, that is why I am the bearer of this information."

"It was kind of you to help out on this matter."

"My pleasure." Jory Davis cleared his throat. "Hughes Barron, the *late* Hughes Barron, was a real estate developer of the worst kind. Realize, now, this is me editorializing."

Theodosia had been hunkered down in her office like a hermit crab, pondering what to do next about Bethany, about business, and now this pleasant man with the rich, deep voice was able to coax a smile out of her. She had seen the name Jory Davis mentioned several times in the business section of the newspaper and in the Charleston Yacht Club's newsletter but had never met him. Now, however, she was intrigued.

Jory Davis continued as though he were giving a final summation before a jury. "Barron's track record in California includes not paying contractors, defaulting on mortgages, and fraudulent activity regarding low-interest loans for senior housing that was never built. Obviously, there are more than a few people and government agencies in California who are . . . were . . . pursuing Hughes Barron."

Theodosia's silver pen bobbed as she jotted down notes.

"We also did a search of local city and county records and found that Hughes Barron has a silent partner, a Mr. Lleveret Dante. Not surprisingly, this Mr. Dante is currently under indictment by the state of Kentucky for a mortgage-flipping scam and, apparently, had Hughes Barron serving as front man for the pair here in Charleston. Their corporate name is Goose Creek Holdings, a nod to the area north of here where Mr. Barron grew up. Corporate offices for Goose Creek Holdings are located at 415 Harper Street. Stop me if you already know any or all of this, Miss Browning," said Jory Davis rather breathlessly.

Theodosia was impressed. Jory Davis had seemingly thrown himself headlong into researching Hughes Barron for her.

"This is enormously enlightening," said Theodosia. "And highly entertaining," she added.

"Good," said Jory Davis. "Now that I know I have such an appreciative audience, I'll continue. Goose Creek's first real estate project was a time-share condominium on nearby Johns Island known as Edgewater Estates. Edgewater Estates still has a lawsuit pending by the Shorebird Environmentalist Group, but their lawyers have been stalling on it. Early on, this Shorebird Group succeeded in obtaining a court order to stop the development but then lost when it was overturned by a higher court. Goose

Creek Holdings also owns undeveloped land in West Ashley and Berkeley County. But it's just raw property, no condos or strip malls yet." There was a rustle of papers. "That's pretty much a quick overview on Hughes Barron, the Cliffs Notes version, anyway. I have a sheaf of papers that includes a little more in-depth information. On the lawsuits as well as the condos and property holdings. I'm sure you'll want to take a look at it."

"Mr. Davis," said Theodosia, "your fact-finding has been extremely helpful. I can't thank you enough."

"Please, call me Jory. Miss Browning, I understand your father used to be a senior partner at our firm."

"Yes, he and Leyland started the practice back in the midseventies."

"You're family, then, aren't you?"

Theodosia couldn't help but smile. "What a kind way to put it."

"Miss Browning, like I said, I've got some background information for you. I can drop these papers in the mail for you, or perhaps we could meet for a cup of coffee?"

"I own a tea shop."

Jory Davis never missed a beat. "Cup of tea. Better yet."

Theodosia chuckled. She liked this hot-shot attorney who had started out so curiously formal and then veered toward not quite hitting on her, but darn close to it.

"The Indigo Tea Shop," said Theodosia. "On Church Street. Drop by anytime."

CHAPTER 14

LOCATED SOUTHWEST OF Charleston, Johns Island is a big boomerang-shaped piece of land. It is only technically an island in that it is surrounded by waters that include the Stono River, Intracoastal Waterway, Kiawah River, and Bohicket Creek. For many years, Johns Island was a sleepy, rural backwater. Farms dotted the landscape, and a few charming villages served as small bedroom communities for Charleston.

But all that began to change a few years before, as home prices in Charleston escalated, the economy boomed, and the entire Charleston area began to strain its boundaries.

Real estate developers eyed the still-affordable rolling farms of Johns Island as prime targets for development and began to snatch up properties. Long-time Johns Island residents suddenly saw their rural utopia and relaxed way of life about to be threatened. Tensions ran high.

In stepped Hughes Barron, thought Theodosia, as she maneuvered her Jeep Cherokee through light midmorning traffic on the Maybank Highway. Jory Davis's call this morning had made her, as they say, curiouser and curiouser. So she had jumped into her Jeep, rolled back the canvas cover, and was now enjoying the exhilaration of an open-air ride.

She knew Hughes Barron had been one of the first developers to pounce on property out there. It wasn't exactly prime oceanfront, but the Atlantic Ocean did flow in between Kiawah and James Islands and create some wonderful tidal rivers and marshes.

Exiting Maybank, Theodosia followed Rivertree Road for a good five miles, then hung a right on Old Camp Road. Those were the directions she'd gotten earlier when she'd phoned the sales office at Hughes Barron's so-called Edgewater Estates. But right now she was seeing only pastoral vistas and farmland. Just when she thought she must have gotten off course and was prepared to turn around, an enormous, colorful billboard rose up out of a field of waving, yellow tobacco.

Edgewater Estates, the sign proclaimed in painted pinks and greens. Time-Share Condominiums. Own A Piece Of History. Deluxe 1, 2, and 3 Bedrooms. Developed By Goose Creek Holdings.

Theodosia wondered just what piece of history it was that came part and parcel with your Edgewater Estates time-share condo. What had the greedy developer, Hughes Barron, been referring to?

The archaeological remains of the Cusabo Indians who had lived here 400 years ago?

The barely visible ruins of an old Civil War fort? Constructed of crushed lime and oyster shells, an amalgam known as tabby, the old fort had begun to crumble even before the turn of the last century.

How about the 900 acres set aside by the Marine Resources Department?

No matter, she told herself. She wasn't here today to do a consumer confidence check on Goose Creek Holdings. She was here because, armed with information Jory Davis had provided, her curiosity was running at a fever pitch. Everything she'd heard about Hughes Barron told her the man was definitely not Mr. Popularity. He had to have made enemies. Lots of them. When land was at stake, or multimillion-dollar real estate deals, that's when people got very, very serious. And sometimes very, very nasty.

Swinging into the entrance of Edgewater Estates, a circular, white-crushed-rock drive that wound around a five-tiered fountain, Theodosia hated the place on sight. The building wasn't just the antithesis of Johns Island. Rather, it looked more like a retirement village in south Florida.

Edgewater Estates Time Share Condominiums was big, sprawling, and gaudy. Stone cherubs and doves flanked the building's main entrance, while the building itself was painted what could only be described as tropical green. Accents of white shutters and false balustrades completed the garish touches.

It's like a bad leisure suit, thought Theodosia as she slid her Jeep into the slot marked Visitor Parking. *Overly casual combined with bad design. Always a disastrous marriage.*

Hughes Barron or, more likely, his architect, had borrowed drips and drops from Charleston architecture. Unfortunately, they seemed to have thrown out what was true and good and classic and reconstituted it into something overblown and commercial.

My God, Theodosia thought to herself, *it's a good thing I didn't have to create sales materials for this real estate project! Granted, I had my fair share of turkey accounts at the ad agency. Some awful children's toys that were supposed to be educational but weren't. A shopping mall. A line of instant soup mixes that never thickened and had a chalky undertaste. But never, never anything this bad.*

"Good morning. Welcome to Edgewater Estates." A perky young woman, probably no older than twenty-six, in a bright yellow suit smiled at Theodosia from the other side of a white marble counter. "This is our sales office, such as it is." The girl spread her arms in a theatrical gesture. "We're already sixty percent sold, so the office we *were* using is now the recreation room. But you are *so* in luck. We also have several resales that have just come available, and some of them have ocean views." The young girl halted her pitch, appraised Theodosia quickly, then added, "You *are* looking for a time-share condo, aren't you?"

"Absolutely," declared Theodosia. "And I've heard wonderful things about Edgewater Estates."

The girl beamed. "We like to think we're the premier time-share property on Johns Island."

Theodosia wanted to tell the girl they were the *only* time-share property right now. And if the island's residents woke up and learned their lesson, they'd probably remain the only one. But she held her tongue. Better to play it cool, gather as much information as possible. You never knew when something interesting would pop up in conversation.

The real estate agent stuck out her hand. "I'm Melissa Chapman, sales associate."

Theodosia shook the girl's hand and smiled convincingly. "Theodosia Browning, prospective buyer." Theodosia fingered one of the oversized glossy catalogs that lay on the counter between them. "These are your sales brochures?"

"Oh, yes, help yourself." Melissa thrust one of the colorful brochures into Theodosia's hands. "There are four different floor plans available. Do you know what you're looking for?"

"Probably a two bedroom," said Theodosia.

"Our most requested model," enthused the girl. "And what about time of year? Obviously, summer is wildly popular and carries a premium charge. We only have a few blocks of time left. Late August, I believe. But what many people don't realize is that right now, October, November, is absolutely perfect out here. And the price is a good seventy percent below a summer slot." Melissa widened her eyes in mock surprise. "Interested?"

"Very," said Theodosia. "Can I take a look at some of the units?"

"I'll get my keys." Melissa smiled.

CHAPTER 15

❧

TACKY, TACKY, TACKY. Theodosia chanted her mantra as she gunned the Jeep's engine and zipped across a narrow wooden bridge. Loose boards clattered in her wake, and gravel flew as she hit the dirt road on the other side.

To her point of view, the condos had been awful. First off, they'd all had that new-apartment smell. Whatever it was, paint, carpet, adhesive, Sheetrock, every unit she'd looked at had caused her nose to tickle and twitch. On top of that, the condos felt stifling and claustrophobic. And it wasn't just their size, she told herself. Her apartment above the tea shop was small, but it was *cozy* small. Not *cramped* small. Why, the two-bedroom unit Melissa had been so proud of hadn't really been two bedrooms at all. The so-called second bedroom had been an alcove off one end of the living room with cheap vinyl accordion doors that pulled across!

Raised as she had been in homes with stone foundations and heavy wood construction that had withstood wars as well as countless hurricanes, Theodosia was exceedingly leery of these new slap-dab structures. What would happen when a September hurricane boiled up in the mid-Atlantic and came bearing down on Edgewater Estates with gale-force winds? It would go flying, that's what, *Wizard of Oz* style. And the pieces probably wouldn't land in Kansas.

She gritted her teeth, making a face. *Shabby. Truly shabby.* Oh, well, this visit had certainly given her insight into the kind of developer Hughes Barron had been. The kind of developer his partner Lleveret Dante was. The worst kind, just as Jory Davis had warned.

Cruising past a little beachfront café with a sign that read Crab Shack, Theodosia suddenly had a distant memory of her and her dad exploring the patchwork of water-ways out here, of pulling their boat up on a sand dune and sitting at one of the picnic tables to eat boiled crab and French fries. The memory flowed over her so vividly, it brought tears to her eyes.

She slowed the car, blinked at the passing scenery, and slammed on the brakes.

Five hundred yards down from the Crab Shack was a small, whitewashed building with a blue and white sign that carried the image of a long-legged bird. The sign said Shorebird Environmentalist Group.

Shorebird Environmentalist Group.

She scanned her memory. Wasn't that the group that had sued Edgewater Estates? Sure it was. Jory Davis had told her about the environmentalists losing their case in court. And Drayton had confided earlier that they'd mustered nearby residents and picketed the Edgewater Estates while it was under construction. Probably their outrage still hadn't abated. Well, that was good for her. It gave her one more source to draw upon.

Tanner Joseph glanced up from his iMac computer and the new climate modeling program he was trying to teach himself and gazed at the woman who'd just stepped through his door. Lovely, was his first impression. Perhaps a few years older than he was, but really lovely. Great hair plus a real presence about her. Was she old money, per-haps?

Growing up in a steel mill town in Pennsylvania, Tanner Joseph was always painfully aware of class distinction. Even though he'd graduated from the University of Minnesota with a master's degree in ecology, most of the time he still felt like the kid from the wrong side of the tracks.

"Good afternoon," he greeted Theodosia.

Theodosia surveyed the little office. Three desks, one occupied. But all outfitted with state-of-the-art computers and mounded with reams of paper. A folding table set against the wall seemed to be the repository for the Shorebird Environmentalist Group's brochures, literature, and posters. Surprisingly well-done paintings hung on the walls, depicting grasses, birds, and local wildlife, executed in a fanciful, contemporary style, almost like updated Chinese brush strokes.

To Theodosia, the organization appeared viable but understaffed. Probably just a director and a couple assistants and, hopefully, a loyal core of volunteers.

She walked over to the desk where the young man who'd greeted her was sitting and stared down at him. He was good-looking. Blond hair, tan, white Chiclet teeth. Haley would have thought him "hunky."

"I'm interested in finding out about the Shorebird Environmentalist Group," she said.

Tanner Joseph clambered to his feet. It wasn't every day a classy-looking lady came knocking at his door. And classy-looking ladies, more often than not, had access to the kind of funding that could help bootstrap a struggling, little nonprofit organization like his.

"Tanner Joseph." He stuck out his hand. "Executive director."

"Theodosia Browning." She shook hands with him. "Nice to meet you."

"First let me give you one of our brochures." Tanner Joseph handed her a small, three-fold brochure printed on recycled paper.

Theodosia flipped it open and studied it. The brochure was well-written and beautifully illustrated. The same artist who had done the paintings on the wall had also illustrated the brochure. Short subheads and bulleted copy documented four different projects the Shorebird Environmentalist Group was currently involved in. The information was interesting, punchy, and easy to digest.

"Listen," Tanner Joseph said. The whites of his eyes were a distinct contrast to his deep suntan. His hands fidgeted with the front of his faded green T-shirt that proclaimed Save the Sea Turtles. "I was about to step out for a bite to eat. At the Crab Shack just down the road. If you'd like a lemonade or something and don't mind watching me eat, I could fill you in there."

"Perfect," exclaimed Theodosia.

CHAPTER 16

✺

TURNS OUT, THE Crab Shack *was* the exact same place where she and her dad had eaten, a quaint little roadside shack where you studied the hand-painted menu on the side of the building, then went to the window and ordered your food. All dining was outdoors, at sun-bleached wooden picnic tables with faded blue umbrellas. Because of her fond memory and the fact that it was almost noon, Theodosia ended up ordering crab cakes and a side of cole slaw. She and Tanner Joseph sat on wobbly wooden benches, enjoying the sun, salty breezes, and surprisingly tasty food.

Throughout lunch, Tanner spoke convincingly about the mission of the Shorebird Environmentalist Group, how they were dedicated to the preservation of coastlines and natural marshes, as well as nesting grounds and marine sanctuaries. He also filled her in on his credentials, his degree in ecology and his graduate work in the dynamics of ecosystem response.

"What does one actually *do* with a degree in ecology?" asked Theodosia out of curiosity. "What avenues are open?"

Tanner Joseph shrugged. "Today, you can go any number of ways. Work for the Forest Service, the EPA, or Department of Natural Resources. Go private with literally thousands of corporations to choose from, including groups like the Nature Conservancy or Wilderness Society. Or"—he spread his arms wide and grinned—"you can work for a struggling little nonprofit organization. Try to drum up public interest, writing brochures, illustrating them—"

"Those are your drawings?" Theodosia interrupted.

"One of my many talents." Tanner Joseph smiled. "And duties. Along with writing dozens of grant requests to various foundations in hopes of getting a thousand dollars here, two thousand dollars there. That is, if I'm lucky enough to touch a responsive chord with a sympathetic foundation director."

"Sounds tough," said Theodosia.

"It is." Tanner Joseph popped a French fry in his mouth. "But I wouldn't trade it for the world. After grad school, I spent a year in the Amazon studying land surface–atmosphere interaction. It was amazing how just building a one-lane dirt road through an area of jungle severely impacted the ecosystem. I was able to observe all the effects first-hand. I understand now how important it is for a community to plan and manage growth. It's okay to think big, but it's generally more prudent to take small steps."

"What about the newly expanded road out here? It makes the commute a lot easier to Johns Island from Charleston proper."

"Sure it does. But it's also probably a mistake," said Tanner Joseph, "although no one thought so at the time of construction. But think about it. There are hundreds of acres of saltwater marshes out here and almost a dozen species of wildlife on the yellow list, the nearing endangered list."

"And the Edgewater Estates?" asked Theodosia.

Tanner Joseph grimaced, set his crab salad sandwich down, and gazed intently at Theodosia. "You just touched a raw nerve. Our group was opposed to that development from the outset. Everything about it was fraudulent. The developers lied to the eighty-two-year-old farmer who sold them the land. And the shark lawyers who represented Goose Creek Holdings pressured the local town council for some fast zoning changes. We think they had two council members in their pocket."

"You fought a good fight," said Theodosia. "Got lots of press from what I hear."

Tanner Joseph snorted angrily. "Not good enough. We lost, and the damn thing got built. Right on twenty-five acres of prime snowy egret nesting ground." He shook his head with disgust. "To make matters worse, the place is a monstrosity." He peered at Theodosia sharply. "Have you seen it?"

Theodosia nodded.

Tanner Joseph picked up his sandwich again, held it in both hands like an offering. "Do you believe in karma, Miss Browning?"

Theodosia brushed back a ringlet of hair and smiled. "Some things do seem to have a way of coming full circle."

"Well," he said, staring at her intently, "Edgewater Estates turned out to generate some very *bad* karma for one of its developers. The so-called money man, Hughes Barron, died three days ago." The statement hung in the air as Tanner Joseph narrowed his eyes and smiled a tight, bitter smile. "It looks as though cosmic justice may have been at work, after all."

CHAPTER 17

✜

$\mathcal{D}$ELAINE DISH WAS sitting at a quiet table in the corner when Theodosia returned to the tea shop. The owner of Cotton Duck Clothing, Delaine had arrived at the Indigo Tea Shop earlier, insisting to Haley and Drayton that she simply *had* to speak with Theodosia. Told that Theodosia would probably be back shortly, Delaine sat pensively, sipping a cup of tea, waving Haley off every time she advanced with a muffin or cookies.

"She's been here almost forty minutes," whispered Drayton as Theodosia brushed past him. "Didn't say what she wanted, just that she wants to talk to you."

"Delaine." Theodosia slid into the chair across the table from her shopkeeper neighbor. "What's wrong?"

Delaine Dish's heart-shaped face was set in a look of serious repose. Raven hair that normally fell almost to her waist was plaited into a single, loose braid, making her face seem all the more intense. Her violet Liz Taylor eyes flashed.

"Do you know what's being said out there on the street?" she began.

No, thought Theodosia, *but I'll bet you do.* "What's that, Delaine?" she said.

"There are rumors flying, literally *flying,* about what happened the night of the Lamplighter Tour."

"I am aware of some talk, Delaine. But I'm sure they are petty words spoken by a very few."

"Dear, dear Theo." Delaine reached across the table and grasped Theodosia's hand. "Always giving people the benefit of the doubt. Always such a positive outlook. Sometimes I think you should be put up for canonization."

"I'm no saint, Delaine. Believe me, if someone offends me or hurts someone close to me, I'll fire back. Have no fear."

Delaine's fingernails only dug deeper into Theodosia's hand. "Didn't I warn you?" she spat. "Didn't I tell you Hughes Barron was up to no good?"

"As I recall, you told me he put in an offer on the Peregrine Building next door."

"Yes. Hughes Barron and his partner, Lleveret Dante."

Theodosia stared at Delaine. She was obviously upset over something. Maybe if she gave Delaine some space, she'd spit out whatever was bothering her.

"Cordette Jordan stopped by the Cotton Duck this morning. You know, Cordette owns Griffon Antiques over on King Street?"

"Okay," said Theodosia.

"And, of course, we started chatting. Hughes Barron's mysterious death *is* a fairly hot topic of conversation right now. I mean, how many people just fall over dead in a beautiful garden while sipping tea?"

"You don't really believe he died from sipping tea, do you?" said Theodosia.

"No, of course not. And I didn't mean to imply it was *your* tea, Theodosia. It's just that . . . Oh, Theo . . . A lot of people are curious. I mean, the police are playing it very close to the vest and haven't released any information about cause of death. And the man *was* fairly dastardly in his business dealings. Who *knows* what really happened!"

Delaine pulled a linen hanky from the pocket of her perfect beige smock dress and touched it to her cheek.

"What was it you and Cordette were chatting about?" asked Theodosia, trying to gain some forward momentum in the conversation.

"Oh, that," said Delaine. She swiveled her head and scanned the tea room. When she was satisfied that the few patrons who were sitting there sipping tea and munching scones were probably tourists and completely uninvolved, she leaned toward Theodosia. "This is very interesting. Cordette told me that Hughes Barron and Lleveret Dante have their office in her building. One floor above her antique shop."

"Really," said Theodosia.

"It gets better. Cordette also told me she overhead the two men in the throes of a terrible argument last week. It was when she went up to use the ladies' room. The ladies' room is on the second floor, so Cordette would have been on the same floor as their offices. Anyway, and these are Cordette's exact words: She said the two men were having a *knock-down, drag-out fight.*"

As Delaine talked, Theodosia scanned her memory. King Street was definitely *not* the address Jory Davis had given her for Goose Creek Holdings. She was sure of that. So what had Cordette really heard, if anything? Had the two men really been there that day, locked in some kind of argument? Or had Delaine heard pieces of this, fragments of that, and put it all together in one big, juicy story as she was wont to do?

"Delaine." Theodosia pried Delaine's tiny but firm paw off her own. Embroiled as she was in Hughes Barron's death, she decided to give Delaine the benefit of the doubt. "Did Cordette say what Hughes Barron and Lleveret Dante were arguing about?"

Delaine studied her ring intently, trying to recall. It was a giant, pearly moonstone that Theodosia had often admired, and now Delaine twisted it absently.

"Something about buying or selling and one of them

wanting to renege or rescind," said Delaine. "Or maybe it was revenge," she added.

Not terribly enlightening, thought Theodosia. Even if Cordette Jordan's story about the loud argument *was* true, the two men could have been fighting about anything. Money, property, their long distance phone bill.

Theodosia patted Delaine's hand. "You're a dear to try to help. Thank you."

Delaine blinked back tears. "You mean the world to me, Theodosia. I mean it. When my Calvin passed on, you were the only one who really understood."

Calvin had been Delaine's fourteen-year-old calico cat. When he died last spring, Theodosia had sent a note expressing her condolences. It was what she would have done for anyone who was sad or emotionally distraught.

After Delaine had departed, Theodosia fixed herself a small pot of dragon's well tea. Technically a Chinese green tea, dragon's well yields a pale gold liquor that has a reputation for being both refreshing and stimulating. Because of the tea's natural sweetness and full-bodied flavor, milk, sugar, or even lemon is rarely taken with it.

"We need to talk about the holiday blends."

Theodosia looked up to find Drayton staring intently down at her.

"Absolutely," she replied. "Now?"

"Only if you're not too distracted," said Drayton. "I know a lot of things are weighing heavily on your shoulders right now. And haven't Haley and I helped enormously by putting added pressure on you to try to salvage Bethany's job at the Heritage Society?" Drayton rolled his eyes in a self-deprecating manner.

"Drayton, nothing would make me happier than to focus on what I love best. Which is the Indigo Tea Shop and the wonderful teas you continue to blend for us."

An enormous grin split Drayton's face as he plopped down next to Theodosia. He balanced his glasses on the tip of his nose, flipped open a leather binder, and wiggled his eyebrows expectantly.

Theodosia rejoiced inwardly at this show of unbridled enthusiasm. Drayton was in his element. Blending tea was his passion, and every autumn, Drayton blended three or four special teas in honor of the upcoming holidays.

"You realize we're starting late," said Drayton.

"I know. Somehow, with our initial work on the Web site and taking part in the Lamplighter Tour, things fell through the cracks. But if we need to jump-start things," said Theodosia, "we could repackage the Lamplighter Blend."

Drayton managed a pained expression. "We'd have to. It hasn't exactly been a top seller since . . ." His voice trailed off. "Let me put it this way. Even when we had a display of the Lamplighter Blend, nobody bought any. People seemed to view it more as a curiosity. Except for one woman who came in and bought a pound." Drayton paused dramatically. "She said she was thinking about killing her husband."

"Goodness!" exclaimed Theodosia unhappily. "Delaine might be right after all. Rumors are flying!"

Drayton nodded sagely. "They certainly are."

"Tell you what," said Theodosia. "Let's just start from scratch as usual. You've obviously put a lot of thought into the holiday blends, and I'm dying to hear your ideas."

Drayton picked up his notebook. "This year," he began, "I suggest we use an Indian black tea as our base. I'd recommend Kahlmuri Estates. It's well-balanced and rich but highly complementary to added flavors."

At the top of one of the pages in his notebook, Drayton had written Kahlmuri Estates black tea.

"I like it." Theodosia nodded.

"Okay," said Drayton, pleased. "Now for the tricky part. I've come up with four suggested holiday blends."

Theodosia inclined her head toward Drayton's notebook, following along as he read aloud his notations. For the moment, all thoughts of the disastrous events at the Lamplighter Tour were pushed from her head.

"Apple," said Drayton, tapping his notebook. "Apple

pies, cider, and dried potpourris are a holiday staple, so let's add it to our black tea as well. The aroma will impart a sweet, crisp fragrance and make a delightful beverage for holiday parties. More sophisticated than apple cider, but still warming and flavorful."

"Have you got a name for it?" asked Theodosia.

"That's your province, isn't it?" Drayton grinned. "Or have you left your advertising and marketing days behind?"

"I don't think you ever stray far from that," said Theodosia. "Seems like most decisions made in business these days are marketing-related."

"Including naming these teas and creating labels." Drayton smiled slyly.

"You come up with the blends, and I'll take care of the rest."

"Deal," said Drayton. "Okay, then. Next holiday blend, black currant. This should be a big, fruity berry flavor. Great for afternoon holiday teas, pleasing with desserts."

Theodosia smiled. Dear Drayton. He had thrown himself headlong into this project and, like everything he attempted in the realm of tea, wine, or the culinary arts, it would be a rousing success.

"Next," said Drayton, "I want to do an Indian spice. Overtones of cardamom with various spices to be determined. We'll aim for a slightly heady, intoxicating fragrance."

"Sounds heavenly," said Theodosia.

"For my final tea, I pulled out all the stops. A cranberry blend. Heavy on the cranberry with an accent of dried oranges and a nip of orange flavoring. Tangy, tart, perfect for the crisp days ahead. Very complementary with holiday dinners."

"You were thinking of getting your dried cranberries from the Belvedere Plantation in the low-country?" asked Theodosia.

Drayton tapped his black Mont Blanc pen against the page. "They're the best."

Theodosia retired to her office where she brainstormed on names for Drayton's tea blends for the rest of the afternoon. By the time long shadows dappled her windows and Earl Grey rose from his rug and stretched, ready for his late afternoon walk, she had devised quite a few names.

Drawing upon her advertising background, she had come up with a list she thought might intrigue holiday shoppers. For the apple tea blend she liked the name Applejack. It was casual and fun. She had pondered the name Black Magic for the black currant tea, but finally settled on Au Currant. It sounded punchier and a little more elegant.

On the Indian spice blend, Theodosia decided to be straightforward and name it exactly that, Indian Spice. She knew from past experience that a good, descriptive name would usually outshine an overly clever one.

And for the cranberry orange tea, she went with Cooper River Cranberry, a tribute to the nearby Cooper River that contributed to the vast, wet cranberry bogs.

Pleased with her efforts, Theodosia's thoughts turned toward the visual elements: packaging and labels. Because these were holiday teas, she decided to purchase gold-colored tea tins. They were festive looking and easily obtained from several manufacturers.

That left the labels. She would have to devise colorful labels for each of Drayton's blends.

Her first thought was to call Todd & Lambeau, the group that was working on the graphics for her Web site. They were good commercial designers, but somehow their brand of design felt a little too slick. Wouldn't it be nicer to convey a more intimate, boutique feel for these holiday tea blends?

She had a friend, Julia, who was a highly skilled calligrapher. Julia did posters for the Charleston Museum, the symphony, wedding invitations, all manner of other things. Julia's calligraphy might be well suited for this project. But, she still needed a talented illustrator to convey the essence of the holiday teas on a label.

Then she remembered the paintings she'd seen that

morning at the Shorebird headquarters. The free-spirited, slightly whimsical illustrations Tanner Joseph had created also somehow embodied an Eastern spirit. Would that style work for her tea labels? The thought intrigued her and began to grow on her.

Most tea labels were what Drayton called "flowers and bowers." They were fussy and floral. But Tanner Joseph's drawings had an elegance to them. The style was slightly Asian, which would be perfect. And, if her memory served her correctly, Tanner Joseph also did lovely brush-stroke calligraphy!

The notion excited Theodosia, and she vowed to call Tanner Joseph first thing the next day. She hoped he'd take on the project. Even though the tea shop didn't have a huge budget for graphics, Tanner Joseph might view this commercial assignment as a welcome windfall.

The light flickered on and off above her head.

"Time to lock up," called Haley. She stood in the doorway, a book bag slung over one shoulder. "You've been hard at it all afternoon. Did you get lots done? Drayton said you were working on the holiday teas."

Theodosia stretched both arms over her head and groaned. "I think so. You're off to class?"

"Literature in contemporary society. Tonight we're studying Cormac McCarthy."

But still Haley stood there, quietly looking at Theodosia.

"What?" said Theodosia. She knew something was brewing behind the girl's furrowed brow. She beckoned to Haley. "Come."

Haley stepped closer to Theodosia's desk. "It's Bethany," she said, her face flushed pink with embarrassment. "Without her job, with nothing to do, she's . . ." Haley left her sentence unfinished, dropped her head shyly.

"What if . . ." said Theodosia slowly, "what if Bethany came and helped out for a while? Poor Drayton's going to be awfully busy supervising the blending of the holiday teas. You'll have extra baking to do . . ." Theodosia looked at Haley as though the thought had just occurred to her. "Do you think Bethany would come back and lend a hand in the tea shop again? Of course, you'll have to give her a refresher course in brewing tea. And that old cash register is a bear to use—"

Haley's face broke into a wide grin. "It's not a problem. She can do it, I know she can. But are you sure that . . . ?"

"Am I sure we need help?" Theodosia threw her arms up in mock despair. "Thanksgiving is three weeks away, and Christmas and New Year's will be upon us in no time." She placed her palm on her chest. "I *still* haven't gone out and found those extra sweetgrass baskets. And the Web site . . . Well, the delay on that project is decidedly my fault. I haven't made the necessary decisions on graphics and Web architecture. Yes, Haley. To answer your question, I'm sure, in a matter of days, we'll be swamped!"

CHAPTER 18

THEODOSIA PULLED THE head off the ceramic Scooby-Doo cookie jar and measured out two cups of dried kibbles for Earl Grey. She poured it into his metal dish, topped it with a tablespoon of olive oil for his coat, and set it down on the yellow rug next to his water dish.

Earl Grey responded as he always did. He gave Theodosia a look that somehow conveyed his doggy thank you, then went facedown into his dinner.

Theodosia did not go facedown. Rather, she stood in front of the open refrigerator, pondering supper. An oatmeal and raisin cookie, eaten at four o'clock, had left her relatively satisfied. Still, if she didn't eat now, she'd be hungry later on.

She stuck her head farther inside the refrigerator, investigating. There was some leftover pasta, a couple pieces of cold chicken, fresh hamburger. Nope, nothing tripped her trigger yet. She knew the freezer compartment contained lamb chops and maybe some frozen shrimp that could be quickly steamed and put on top of rice.

No, she thought, that would be fussy, and fussy was the last thing she needed right now. Now that decisions had been made regarding holiday teas, the conversation she'd had with Delaine earlier in the afternoon came back in her mind. Delaine was a dear, gentle soul who had shockingly good taste when it came to merchandising her clothing store, Cotton Duck. But Delaine also thrived on gossip and excitement and didn't always get her facts straight.

Theodosia pulled a small carton of cottage cheese from the refrigerator shelf. She dumped half of it onto a plate and grabbed a fork from the drawer and two bagel crisps from a glass jar on the counter.

Wandering into her living room, she eased herself down onto the couch, suddenly feeling a wave of relaxation flow over her. It was this apartment that ultimately contributed to her happiness and sense of well-being. Though small, it contained all the essential elements for a proper and genteel Charleston home. Fireplace, cove ceilings, bow windows, tiny balcony, French doors leading to a small but elegant dining room, and a cozy bedroom with a surprisingly ample closet for her many clothes.

She had decorated the place in what had become her own brand of Charleston shabby chic. The philosophy behind shabby chic appealed to her. It held that an item had to be both beautiful and functional. So that was what she strove for. Elegance married with practicality. It was a concept that worked well with the antique furniture and accessories she'd always been so passionate about, and which were easy to come by in Charleston antique shops and flea markets. Charleston was the mother lode when it came to English furniture, vintage fabrics, antique chandeliers, old prints, and silverware.

Aunt Libby had been amazingly generous, too, in helping to furnish her cozy abode, gifting her with a lawyer's bookcase, rocking chair, oriental rug, silver tea service, antique quilt, and some terrific old oil paintings. The paintings were dark, brooding seascapes in wonderfully ornate, gilded frames. Everyone who saw them tried to buy them from her.

Before she'd purchased the Indigo Tea Shop, she had

lived in a sleek, modern building. Lots of squared-off angles, floor-to-ceiling windows, black countertops, white walls. Very contemporary, very boring.

This was infinitely better.

Theodosia finished her cottage cheese and offered Earl Grey the last morsel of bagel crisp. He chewed thoughtfully, gazing at her with brown, intelligent eyes.

"Want to go for a ride?" she asked him.

Earl Grey's ears pricked forward, and his tail beat a syncopated rhythm on the pegged floor boards.

King Street, between Beaufain and Queen Streets, is often referred to as Charleston's antiques district. Here antiques aficionados will discover such shops as English Patina, with their fine collection of eighteenth- and nineteenth-century furniture, Perry's Estate Jewelry, and Helen S. Martin Antique Weapons. Down a narrow walkway at 190 King Street is Gates of Charleston, an eclectic little garden shop with wrought-iron planters, statuary, and quirky sundials.

It was 208 King Street that Theodosia was searching for as she cruised the picturesque street with its palm trees, white turreted buildings, and black wrought-iron touches. Since it was early evening, traffic was light, and she was able to drive slowly, scanning the numbers above the tall, narrow doorways as Earl Grey sat serenely in the passenger seat of the Jeep Cherokee.

208 King Street was where Griffon Antiques was located. The Griffon Antiques where Cordette Jordan had supposedly overheard an argument between Hughes Barron and his partner, Lleveret Dante, of Goose Creek Holdings. Of course, Jory Davis had told her that the two partners had their office at 415 Harper Street.

Okay, Theodosia told herself, *in about two minutes we're going to find out exactly who was right.*

She saw the sign for Griffon Antiques even before she could read the street address. A large, ornate, wooden sign with a griffon, that strange mythical eagle-cum-lion, painted in gold and black, hung out over the sidewalk from what appeared to be a four-story building. Theodosia took her foot off the accelerator, let the Jeep glide over to the curb, and studied the shop.

The large front windows were filled with English and French antique furniture. All genuine pieces, no reproductions. A hand-lettered sign hanging in the glass door said Sorry We Missed You, Please Return Tomorrow.

There was no Harper Street nearby. In fact, she wasn't even familiar with Harper Street. To the best of her knowledge, the next street up was Market Street. Sure, that had to be the sign for Market Street just ahead. Without bothering to pull into traffic, Theodosia eased the Jeep along the curb, up to the corner. She gazed up at the street sign.

It read Harper Street!

What?

She checked for traffic, then took the Jeep into a slow right turn. She found Harper Street wasn't really a street at all, just a narrow lane that seemed to lead to a small garden. She could venture in with the Jeep maybe twenty feet, then she'd have to back out.

Well, wasn't this interesting. There really *was* a Harper Street. And the reason it didn't sound at all familiar was because it wasn't really a through street. Harper Street was one of the myriad little lanes that snaked through the historic district and the antiques district, lanes that often didn't have names. Sometimes they were private and therefore not on official city maps. They could have their names changed at the whim of the property owner. These streets had probably been little passages that led to carriage houses at one time. Now they appeared on tourist walking guides that gift shops and B and Bs handed out.

"Sit tight," she told Earl Grey as she hopped out of the Jeep. Rounded cobblestones poked at the soft leather soles of her Todd loafers as she ambled down the little lane toward an arched doorway flanked by a pair of stone lions. She stopped in her tracks and looked up. Over the arched doorway was a sign that read Hayward Professional Building, 415 Harper.

A tingle of excitement ignited within her. So 208 King Street and 415 Harper were one and the same! The city might not be aware of it, but, knowing the tangled bureaucracy that ministered over Charleston, chances were the postal service did. That meant that the offices of Goose Creek Holdings were here, after all. And that maybe, just maybe, Delaine's secondhand story had been correct!

CHAPTER 19

✦✦✦

THERE WERE TWO Jory Davises listed in the phone book, but one lived over in West Ashley. So Theodosia figured the one she wanted had to be the one on Halsey, near the marina. Anyway, it certainly sounded like an area where the Jory Davis she'd spoken with this morning might reside.

"Hello?"

Same voice, same Jory Davis. Theodosia breathed a quick sigh of relief. "Mr. Davis? Hello, this is Theodosia Browning. Sorry to bother you at home, but you were so helpful this morning, and I have just a quick question for you."

"Uh-huh," said the voice, sounding slightly discombobulated and not at all the calm, efficient, buttoned-up lawyer he'd come across as earlier.

"I know this is out of the blue, but does buying-selling mean anything to you?" Theodosia asked.

There was a loud clunk on the other end of the line.

"Mr. Davis? Are you all right?"

In a moment, Jory Davis was back on the line. "Sorry, I dropped the phone. I'm in the kitchen trying to whip together a vinaigrette. I know it sounds kind of dorky, but I've got this bachelor's group coming to my place tonight. Four of us, all lawyers, who get together once a month for dinner. Kind of a boy's night out. Two of the fellows are divorced, so this is probably the only decent meal they get for a while. Anyway, long story short, tonight's my turn, and I'm hysterical. I was stuck at the office writing a legal brief until almost six-thirty, and now I'm halfway through this recipe and just found out I don't have any prepared English mustard. So, my question to you is this: Can I use plain old yellow mustard? Hot dog mustard?"

"I don't see why not," said Theodosia as she thought to herself, *Bachelor's group. Interesting.*

"And chives. It doesn't look good in the chives department, either. Problem?"

"Maybe you could pinch hit with a flavored olive oil. That would give your vinaigrette a little extra snap."

"Flavored olive oil," he muttered. "Yeah, I got some of that. Basil, I think. Awright, we're good to go."

Now there was the sound of a wire whisk swooshing against the sides of a glass bowl.

"What did you want to know about a buy-sell?" Jory Davis asked.

Theodosia inhaled sharply.

"Miss Browning?" said Jory. "You still there?"

"That's it!" exclaimed Theodosia. "A buy-sell. It's a kind of agreement, right?"

"A buy-sell agreement, correct," said Jory Davis matter-of-factly.

"Two partners would have this type of agreement?"

"They should. Although many don't plan ahead all that well."

"And one partner might want to *rescind* at some point in time?"

"Sure, it happens. But I still don't see where you're going."

"I didn't either," said Theodosia. "But I think I just arrived there anyway. Mr. Davis, thank you! Good luck with your dinner."

"That's it?" he asked.

"Oh," said Theodosia, "you're still bringing those papers by, right?"

CHAPTER 20

❧❦❧

KEEMAN," SAID HALEY, her hand resting on a glass jar filled with small black leaves. "From Anhui province in central China. See the leaves? Tiny but powerful. They yield a brilliant red liquor. Slightly sweet, so you don't need sugar. Gives off a delicious aroma, reminiscent of ripe orchids."

Bethany nodded. She'd shown up bright and early, eager to learn, ready to be put to work. Now she stood behind the counter, hair wound atop her head in a casual knot, small, oval, wire-rim glasses perched on her nose, looking every inch the career-minded young woman.

Haley pointed to another jar. "This one's Dimbulla from Ceylon. Also brews into a bright reddish, amber color. But it doesn't have quite the wake-up punch of the other, so we generally recommend it for midmorning or with afternoon snacks."

"Tea shop 101?" asked Theodosia as she breezed in and smiled at the two girls who looked like elegant butterflies, dressed almost alike in colorful cotton sweaters and long, gauzy, print skirts. She was pleased to see that silver teakettles had been filled with water and were beginning to steam atop their burners, fresh linens and silverware had been laid out, and all the tables sported freshly mounded sugar bowls and pitchers of cream.

Bethany pulled off her glasses and turned to Theodosia with merriment in her eyes. "It's all so fascinating. But complicated, too. And I still can't believe how many varieties of tea there are. Assam, Darjeeling, Earl Grey, Sencha, gunpowder, the list goes on and on. It's amazing! Plus, the tea is literally from every corner of the globe. China, Ceylon, India, Nepal, Japan, even Africa."

"Don't forget Turkey, Indonesia, and Russia. And, of course, our own wonderful South Carolina tea from the Charleston Tea Plantation," added Theodosia. "Their American Classic tea is a luxurious black tea that's descended from the original tea plants brought to America after the Revolutionary War."

"You're right!" exclaimed Bethany. "But I think Chinese teas are my hands down favorites because of their names. How quirky and creative to name a tea White Peony or Precious Eyebrows. Or even Temple of Heaven!"

"The Chinese have always had a profound and enduring passion for tea," declared Drayton as he arrived and caught the tail end of Bethany's remarks. "Good morning, good morning all." He bowed deeply to Haley and Bethany. "I hope our new apprentice is appropriately memorizing all our precious loose teas. Perhaps we shall plan a pop quiz for this afternoon."

"Don't you dare," Bethany said grinning. She turned toward Theodosia and lowered her voice slightly. "I can't thank you enough for having me here." Her brow furrowed, and her eyes suddenly glistened. "You don't know what it's been like." Bethany shook her head in confusion. "First everyone at the Heritage Society was so nice to me. It seemed like a perfect position. Then Mr. Neville . . ." Her throat constricted, and she was unable to finish for a few moments. "You just don't know," she managed to choke out.

"Perhaps I do," said Theodosia, patting her arm gently.

"But keep in mind the Chinese proverb: 'There is no wave without wind.'"

"That's lovely," said Bethany. She gazed at Theodosia with something akin to hero worship. "You're not afraid of anything, are you? You're very confident about making your place in the world."

"Sometimes I think the hard part is *finding* your place," said Theodosia as the bell over the front door tinkled merrily. "Now, why don't you put an apron on. . . . That's right." She smiled encouragingly at Bethany. "That white linen is lovely against your apricot sweater. . . . Go wait on our first customers."

Enthused, Bethany fairly scampered across the room.

"It's good to see Bethany with a smile on her face," said Drayton.

"Can you keep an eye on her?" asked Theodosia. "Give her a subtle assist if she gets stuck?"

"It would be my pleasure," said Drayton. "I've got a group from the Christie Inn coming in for a tea tasting at ten, but until then, I shall kibbitz to my heart's content."

Theodosia retreated to her back office, plopped herself down in her swivel chair, and gazed at the catastrophe that was her desktop.

While she had been out and about, getting dressed down by Timothy Neville, snooping at Edgewater Estates, and cruising King Street for a fix on Goose Creek Holdings, life had gone on. Mail had arrived. Messages had piled up. The Web site story boards she was supposed to make a decision on still sat staring up at her. And, of course, there were bills to be paid, paychecks to be written, overseas orders to be untangled.

But there was something else that took precedence, that had to be done. Let's see . . . Oh, yes! She had to phone Tanner Joseph.

After greeting him on the phone, Theodosia launched directly into her proposal. "I have what could be an intriguing project," she told him.

Tanner Joseph's voice conveyed both amusement and interest. "I'm already on the edge of my chair."

"I need some labels for small canisters of holiday tea that will be for sale in my shop. Your drawings came to mind. They're very good."

There was a long pause. "You really think so?"

"Yes, I do."

"And you're serious? This isn't just a crank call?" Tanner Joseph laughed. "You're actually asking if I want to design your tea labels?"

"Yes, but only if you have time. Unfortunately, we're in kind of a hurry-up mode. I'd need to get a finished product from you relatively fast."

"What's your idea of fast?"

"First we meet," said Theodosia. "I fill you in on the project, share a few ideas. If you agree to do the illustrations, then you have maybe three or four working days to do a few pencils. You know, black-and-white sketches. We meet again to go over them. If I like what I see, you proceed to color illustrations. You'd have another few days for that."

"You're on." Tanner Joseph fairly lunged at the offer. "Hey, I'm really flattered. For a guy with a degree in ecology, which is actually a very left-brain kind of thing, this is a dream come true. But, Miss Browning, I should come to your place. Your tea shop. Get a feel for what it's all about, what your customers might expect."

"How about this afternoon, say three o'clock?"

"Perfect," agreed Tanner Joseph.

Theodosia leaned back in her chair and took stock of things. Okay. One down, about forty more to go. She gazed in disgust at her desk. Make that fifty. Hmm.

"Excuse me." There was a soft knock at the door. "I'm serving tea to a bunch of divorced lawyers and was wondering what would be most suitable."

Theodosia glanced over, pleasantly surprised to find a tall, attractive man in a three-piece suit gracing her doorway. One of her eyebrows raised imperceptibly.

"You are the distinguished colleague from Ligget, Hume, Hartwell, I presume?"

Jory Davis flashed a crooked grin. "Guilty as charged."

"In that case, I highly recommend a Chinese varietal called Iron Goddess of Mercy."

The man in the doorway threw back his head and laughed, a deep, rich, easy laugh that gave Theodosia the perfect few moments to study him.

Jory Davis wasn't quite what she'd expected. He was attractive, yes, but in a slightly rugged and reckless way. Square jaw, curly brown hair, piercing blue eyes, probably midthirties. He was well over six feet tall, with broad shoulders and a tiny maze of lines at the corners of his eyes that probably meant he spent much of his free time out of doors. He also moved as though he was completely at ease with himself and wore his three-piece Brooks Brothers suit as if it had been cut just for him. Theodosia noted that Jory Davis wasn't exactly slick, but he was certainly *downtown*. She could picture him in a dark, clubby restaurant with leather booths, clinking glasses with other lawyers, celebrating a win. What she was having trouble picturing was Jory Davis in a kitchen with a wire whisk.

"Please come in, Mr. Davis." Theodosia stood and indicated the chair across from her. "Can I get you a cup of tea?"

"Call me Jory. And, no, I can only stay a moment." He remained standing and dug into his briefcase. "I'm due in court in fifteen minutes, but I wanted to drop off the rest of the information we ferreted out on Hughes Barron." He glanced up at her. "I hope you still want it."

"Of course."

He searched intently through the massive amount of papers in his oversized leather briefcase. Finally he grabbed a sheaf of papers and plopped it on her desk. "Here you go." His smile was dazzling, and his blue eyes sparkled.

Tinted contacts? she wondered. Or were his eyes really that blue?

"Thanks," she said. "How did your vinaigrette turn out?"

"Good. Great. Thanks to you." He stood gazing at her for a moment, then said, "Hey, this is a fun office. Lots of interesting eye catchers." His hand ever so gently touched a bronze head from a Thai temple that sat atop her desk, then moved on to an antique Spode teapot.

Funny, she thought, how very gently he ran his hand over that delicate china teapot.

"I meant it about the tea," said Jory Davis. "And that Iron Goddess sounded interesting. I admire strong women." He turned to study the framed opera programs and photos on her wall. "Hey, you sail! I keep a J-24 at the marina." He glanced back at Theodosia over his shoulder. "I'm decorating her this year for the Festival of Lights. You ought to sail with us."

Every Christmas, a fleet of fifty or so boats was decked out in holiday lights and set sail from Patriots Point. From there the colorful flotilla paraded around the tip of the peninsula, much to the delight of thousands of onlookers, and ended up at the Charleston Yacht Club.

"Let me think about it," said Theodosia, oddly pleased. "I sailed in the festival four years ago on Tom and Evie Woodrow's boat. It was a lot of fun."

"Well, then, you've just *got* to sail on my boat," said Jory Davis. "Woodrow's boat is a tub, compared to my J-24." He gathered up his briefcase and stuck out his hand. "Gotta go. Great meeting you."

"Nice meeting you," called Theodosia as Jory Davis disappeared through the doorway.

"Who was *that?*" asked Haley. She stood in the doorway wearing an expectant look on her face.

"A lawyer friend," replied Theodosia.

"I know that. He told me that earlier, when I showed him back here. I meant who is he to you?"

"Haley, did you need something?"

"Oh, right. Sorry. You've got a phone call."

"It's not Delaine, is it?"

"It's Burt Tidwell," whispered Haley. She put a finger to her mouth. Since Bethany was working out front, Haley obviously wanted to keep this phone call hush-hush. "Line two. Shall I close the door?" she asked.

Theodosia nodded to Haley as she picked up the phone and vowed not to let Burt Tidwell spoil her good mood.

"Mr. Tidwell," she said brightly.

"Miss Browning," he acknowledged gruffly.

"And how is your investigation proceeding?" She tossed him a leading question in hopes of getting a little feedback.

"Extremely well," Tidwell answered.

Theodosia slipped out of her loafers and wiggled her toes in the sunlight that spilled in through the leaded panes. *He has nothing,* she thought. *Diddly-squat, to use an inelegant term.* But she would humor him. Oh, yes, she would humor him and keep going with her own investigation. And she would surely play to what seemed to be a sense of vanity on his part concerning professional prowess.

"I trust you've gotten your lab results back," said Theodosia.

"I have indeed."

Damn, she thought. *This fellow is maddening.* "And . . ." she said.

"Exactly what I suspected. A toxic substance."

"A toxic substance," repeated Theodosia. "In the teacup."

"Yes."

"But not in the teapot." She could hear him breathing loudly at the other end of the line. Short, almost wheezy breaths. "Mr. Tidwell?" she said with more force.

"After forensic investigation by the state toxicology lab, it was determined that the teapot did not contain any toxic substance. Only the teacup."

"Would you care to share with me the nature of that substance?"

"It's still being analyzed."

"I'm sure it is."

"Miss Browning," said Tidwell, "did you know that Hughes Barron was looking at a property on your block?"

"The Peregrine Building," she replied.

"So you were aware of this?"

"I heard a rumor to that effect."

"His purchase could have impacted you, don't you think?"

"In what way?"

"Oh, a commercial development could change the character of your block. Might possibly affect business."

Theodosia caught her breath. "Mr. Tidwell, are you trying to imply that *I'm* a suspect?"

Now Burt Tidwell let go a deep, hearty laugh. "Madam, until I conclude an investigation, I consider everyone a suspect."

"Surely that can't be efficient."

"It is merely the way I work, madam. Good day."

Theodosia slammed down the phone. Of all the nerve! First he let it be known that Bethany was a suspect! Then to imply she might be! A cad. The man was truly a cad. Any grudging respect she had felt earlier had just flown out the window.

She stared at her desktop angrily. Then, with both hands, she pushed everything off to the left. Files began to topple, and she let them. One of the story boards slipped to the floor. Pink message slips that had been stacked in order of date and time were suddenly jumbled.

But she had just given herself a good expanse of wood on which to work. A place to start fresh, to think fresh. She set a piece of plain white paper in front of her. At the top of it she wrote the name, "Hughes Barron." Under that she wrote "Poison?"

Like the beginnings of a family tree, she jotted two names underneath. "Timothy Neville" and "Lleveret Dante." Because she didn't have another suspect, she put a third mark, a question mark, alongside the two names. Somehow it felt right.

She ruminated and read through the papers Jory Davis

had brought her until Drayton poked his head in some forty minutes later.

"Getting a lot done?"

"Yes," she lied. Then thought better of it. "No. Sit. Please." She indicated the tufted chair across from her desk.

Drayton sat down, crossed his legs, and gazed at her expectantly.

She fixed him with an intense stare. "How well do you know Timothy Neville?"

CHAPTER 21

ISS DIMPLE SMILED broadly at Theodosia. "Mr. Dauphine will just be a moment," she said. "He's on the phone. Long distance."

"Thank you," murmured Theodosia as she wondered why people always tended to be more patient when the person they're waiting for is talking long distance versus a local call. Strange that distance makes us polite, and nearness makes us impatient.

After her conversation with Drayton, she had made her way up four flights of stairs in the Peregrine Building to the office of Mr. Harold Dauphine, the owner. Theodosia knew the man had to be at least seventy-five years old. His plump secretary, Miss Dimple, couldn't be that much younger. Did they scoot up and down these stairs all day? she wondered. Could that be the key to longevity? Or, once they arrived for work in the morning, did they just perch up here, recovering from the effort?

"Miss Browning?" Miss Dimple was smiling at her. "Can I offer you a cup of coffee?"

"No, thank you."

Theodosia sat and marveled at the decor of the office.

The whole thing was like a throwback to the fifties. Gray metal filing cabinets, venetian blinds, an honest-to-goodness Underwood upright typewriter. You could film an old Perry Mason episode right here. She half expected to see Miss Dimple don a green eyeshade.

Theodosia thumbed through a dog-eared copy of *Reader's Digest*, skimming the "Quotable Quotes" section. She stared out the window and wondered about Hughes Barron's partner, Lleveret Dante, and she thought about Drayton's reaction to her suspicions about Timothy Neville.

As much as the look on Drayton's face had betrayed his skepticism about Timothy Neville, he'd still listened carefully to her.

"Well," Drayton had said after hearing her out, "it's interesting speculation, but it'd be another thing to prove. I certainly don't discount the fact that Timothy Neville has an abominable temper and is capable of causing harm. Most people have a dark side. And I certainly think you should find out more about this man, Lleveret Dante. Tell you what, why don't you come along with me tomorrow night? Timothy Neville is having a small concert at his home. One of the string quartets he plays in for fun. There will be people from the Heritage Society as well as people from the neighborhood that you undoubtedly know. You can listen to some good music, then have a jolly snoop in his medicine cabinet, if you like."

If Drayton had been pulling her leg, his serious demeanor hadn't betrayed the fact. So she'd agreed. She had to harness her enthusiasm, in fact, because tomorrow night would be, just as Drayton had said, the perfect opportunity to snoop. And she had a sneaking suspicion Timothy Neville wasn't the righteous pillar of the community that most people thought he was.

"Mr. Dauphine can see you now, Miss Browning."

Theodosia stood and smiled at Miss Dimple. The woman was aptly named, she thought. Even looked like a dimple. Round, sweet, slightly pink.

"Always nice to see a neighbor, Miss Browning." Mr. Dauphine struggled to his feet and shook her hand weakly.

"Nice to see you again," said Theodosia. She noted that Mr. Dauphine's office was just as antiquated as the reception area, right down to a rotary phone and an archaic dictation machine, what they used to call a *steno*.

"Of course," said Mr. Dauphine, "I don't come in every day like I used to. Been taking it a little slower." What should have been easy laughter segued into a hacking cough.

"Are you all right, Mr. Dauphine?" said Theodosia. "Can I get you something? A glass of water?"

Mr. Dauphine waved her off with one hand. "Fine, fine," he choked. Pulling a plastic inhaler from his jacket pocket, he shook it rapidly, depressed the button, and inhaled as best he could.

"Emphysema," Mr. Dauphine explained, tapping his chest. "Used to smoke." He helped himself to another puff from his inhaler. "You ever smoke?"

"No," she replied.

"Good girl. I'd advise you never to start." He looked at her and smiled. Despite his obvious frailties, Mr. Dauphine's eyes shone brightly, and his mind seemed quick. "Now," he said, "have you come to make an offer on my property as well?"

Theodosia tried not to betray her surprise. She'd come looking for information about Hughes Barron and Lleveret Dante, and Mr. Dauphine had just nicely opened up that conversational front.

"Not really," she told him lightly. "But I take it you've been under siege of late?"

Mr. Dauphine laughed. "I was, but not anymore. Fellow who wanted to buy this place died."

"Hughes Barron," she said. How interesting, she thought, that everyone she talked with lately couldn't wait to tell her that Hughes Barron had died.

"That's the one." Mr. Dauphine leaned back in his chair

and crossed his arms over his thin chest. "He make an offer on your place, too?"

"Not exactly," said Theodosia slowly. "But I did want to get in touch with his lawyer."

"Sam Sestero," said Mr. Dauphine.

"Sam Sestero," Theodosia repeated, committing the name to memory. "Do you, by any chance, have Mr. Sestero's phone number?"

"Miss Dimple keeps all that straight for me. I'm sure she can give it to you." His hand reached out and depressed the button on an old-fashioned intercom system. "Oh, Miss Dimple, see if you can find Mr. Sestero's number for Miss Browning, will you?" He turned back to Theodosia. "As I recall, Mr. Sestero's office isn't far from here."

Theodosia found that it wasn't far at all. In fact, Samuel and his brother, Edward Sestero, the two managing partners of Sestero & Sestero Professional Association, turned out to have their offices just down from the stately Romanesque buildings at the intersection of Meeting and Broad Streets, known affectionately to Charlestonians as the Four Corners of Law.

CHAPTER 22

*Y*OU *IDIOT*! *YOU* must have been out of your mind!"
Brimming with anger, the man's voice reverberated
loudly down the cavernous hallway, bouncing off marble
floors with thunderous consequences.

"What was I supposed to do?" a second voice countered. This voice was also a loud male voice but pitched
higher, with a tone more pleading than enraged.

Theodosia stopped in her tracks. She had been wandering down the hallway of the venerable old Endicott Building, looking for the office of Sestero & Sestero. From the
angry sounds coming to her from around the corner, it
would appear she might have found it.

"I expect my attorney to show a little smarts!" screamed
the first voice.

"What was I supposed to do, for crying out loud?" This
from the second voice now. "The man's a detective first
grade. Tidwell could haul my ass before a judge and
charge me with obstructing an investigation."

Tidwell? Theodosia put a hand to the corridor wall and
edged forward quietly, instantly on the alert.

"What about attorney-client privilege?" the first voice countered stridently.

"Oh, please."

"You rolled, you miserable little weasel. That's all there is to it."

"Calm down, Mr. Dante. Nothing could be further from the truth. I merely answered a few innocuous questions. You're acting as if it was a subpoena from a Federal Court judge. Take it easy, awright?"

Well, well, thought Theodosia. So the infamous Mr. Lleveret Dante was paying his lawyer a little visit. And wasn't he awfully hot under the collar. Screaming and badgering and carrying on, giving the other man, obviously Sam Sestero, an earful.

On the heels of that thought came the notion that Sam Sestero might not be the sharpest tack around if he thought for a minute that Burt Tidwell had been asking what he termed "innocuous questions."

"I'm in enough hot water as it is!" yelled Lleveret Dante. "All I need is for the AG in Kentucky to make an inquiry down here!"

The AG? Surely, thought Theodosia, Lleveret Dante had to mean the attorney general. That would wash with the information Jory Davis had given her about Lleveret Dante being under indictment in Kentucky for a mortgage flipping scheme.

"Did he ask about the partnership agreement?" screamed Lleveret Dante.

There was a mumbled answer.

"You pathetic wimp, I bet you told him about the business-preservation clause."

"Mr. Dante, I revealed nothing."

"If that idiot Tidwell knows I automatically received Barron's half of the business upon his death, he'll put me under a microscope! You ought to be disbarred, you worthless sack of shit!"

Isn't it amazing what one overhears in hallways, Theodosia mused. So Hughes Barron and Lleveret Dante *did* have a buy-sell agreement, with what Dante termed a "business-preservation clause." That meant, in this case, that should one of them die, the other automatically received the dead partner's share of the business!

But wasn't that more of a *death clause?* And couldn't it also be a motive for murder?

A door slammed shut, and Theodosia was suddenly aware of footsteps coming toward her.

My God! It had to be Lleveret Dante who was barreling down the hallway at full steam. She could hear footsteps ratcheting loudly, the man huffing and puffing like an over-worked steam engine. In a matter of seconds, he would be rounding the corner, and she would be face-to-face with him.

Frantically casting about, Theodosia spied an old-fashioned wooden telephone booth next to a pedestal water fountain. She dove into the phone booth, grabbed the receiver off the hook, and held it to her face.

"Oh, did she really?" said Theodosia loudly, pantomiming a phone call. "Is that a fact. Then what happened?"

Lleveret Dante stormed past her, and Theodosia finally grabbed her first look at Hughes Barron's infamous business partner.

Lleveret Dante was a short man, maybe five foot five at best, with a shock of white hair that went off in all directions, as if he might have a giant cowlick on top of his head. Dante's face was the color of a ripe plum against the crisp white of his three-piece suit.

Dante paced back and forth impatiently as he waited for the elevator. Every time he spun on his heel, his white suit coat flared out slightly. Made him look like a top spinning on its axis.

What a bizarre vision, Theodosia thought to herself as she rose on tiptoes and peered around the corner of the telephone booth to catch a final glimpse of the man. And yes, her hunch was correct. The man was wearing white socks and shoes as well. Well, that iced the cake. Aside from his hideous temper, Lleveret Dante was obviously a strange duck, one that would bear watching.

CHAPTER 23

━━❈━━

IN MOST CITIES and states, the position once known as the coroner has evolved into that of medical examiner. *Coroner,* at one time, meant any person in authority—a sheriff, judge, or deputy—who was empowered to make the final pronouncement that a person was deceased. But as forensic investigations became more sophisticated over the years, most jurisdictions found a pressing need for a medical examiner, one person in charge who was a doctor as well as a trained pathologist.

In Charleston, the coroner was still an elected four-year position and had been since 1868. Before that, justices of the county court selected coroners. Previous to that, they were appointed by the king of England.

Theodosia stood in the ornate marble entrance of the County Services Building. She had wandered over when she realized it was just a block down from the Endicott Building, where she'd just experienced her first sighting of Mr. Lleveret Dante.

I can't do this, she told herself. *There's no way I can waltz downstairs to the coroner's office and be convincing.*

Yes, you can, goaded a determined little voice inside her

head. It was the voice that often pushed her, told her to take chances. *You're here. What have you got to lose?*

Well, she thought, *if Burt Tidwell had been snooping around Sam Sestero's office, looking for information about Hughes Barron and Lleveret Dante, then I might not be barking up the wrong tree after all.*

Theodosia gripped the metal railing and, like Alice tumbling into the rabbit hole, descended the circular staircase that led to the basement.

"County Morgue, help ya?" a receptionist with a heroic beehive hairdo was screeching loudly into her headset. She held court behind a black laminate counter where she alternately handled incoming calls, signed for deliveries, and paged through *The National Enquirer.* A second ringing phone line was currently vying for her attention.

"I'm here to check on a body," Theodosia told the receptionist. She clung to the counter for support. Even though she felt giddy and scared, she tried to sound casual, as though she'd done this a hundred times before.

The woman smiled briefly and held up an index finger. A third line had begun to ring.

Theodosia noted that the receptionist's two-inch-long acrylic nails were painted blood red. Very Vampyra.

"Delivery," announced a man in a blue uniform who suddenly appeared at Theodosia's elbow. He thumped a large cardboard box onto the counter. The office was suddenly as busy as Grand Central Station.

"Which one, honey?" the receptionist asked Theodosia as she signed for the newly arrived packaged and consulted her clipboard. "No!" the receptionist suddenly bellowed into her headset before Theodosia could reply. "We do not issue death certificates! Cremation permits, yes. Death certificates, no. That would be Records and Registration." She raised her penciled eyebrows skyward in frustration and rolled her eyes.

"Hughes Barron," Theodosia said finally.

But the receptionist was still wrangling with the caller. "Did this person die *outside* of a hospital?" the receptionist asked. "They did? Sir, you should have given me that information in the first place. That means you need a burial transit permit." She covered the mouthpiece with a chubby hand and addressed Theodosia.

"Sorry, honey. Check down the hall. Second door on the left, ask for Jeeter Clark."

The antiseptic green hallway was a traffic jam of occupied gurneys, shiny, silver conveyances all holding body bags. Full body bags, Theodosia noted. The noxious smell of formalin and formaldehyde assaulted her as she squeamishly edged past.

"Jeeter?"

Jeeter Clark jumped to his feet, startled. He'd been drinking a can of orange soda pop and munching a ham sandwich. When he saw it wasn't his boss at the door or a disgruntled bookie come to call, he seemed to relax.

"Jeez, lady, you scared me." Jeeter put the hand that held his half-eaten ham sandwich to his chest. He was wearing green scrubs, the kind doctors wear in an operating room.

"Didn't mean to," said Theodosia. "The receptionist said I'd find you in here."

"Trudy sent you?" he asked.

"Sure did," said Theodosia, falling into his folksy pattern of speech.

"Okay, sure," Jeeter replied, satisfied that she had business there. "You must be from Edenvale."

Theodosia suddenly realized that, dressed as she was in black jacket and slacks, this man had just mistaken her for one of the many funeral directors who routinely called on the County Morgue to pick up bodies!

Oh, be honest, now. Wasn't this what you had in mind all along?

"No, Indigo," said Theodosia, almost choking on her words. *Lord love a duck,* she thought. *Now I've really done it.*

"Not familiar with that one," Jeeter muttered. "And you're here to fetch . . . ?"

"Barron. Hughes Barron," said Theodosia, again trying to sound like a disinterested funeral professional who did this routinely. Whatever that was supposed to sound like.

Jeeter snatched up a clipboard and consulted it. And, wonder of wonders, Hughes Barron's name was listed.

"Yeah, I got that name," said Jeeter. " I suppose you want to know when the body's going to be released."

The ridiculousness of the situation made her bold. "That's right."

Jeeter squinted at his clipboard. "You guys are always trying to bust my hump, aren't you? Well, I guess you gotta make a buck, too." He scanned what must have been a fairly long list. "Let's see, lab work's done. They've taken tissue samples. Lung, stomach, liver, brain . . ."

"Does it say what killed him?" asked Theodosia.

"That'd be on the pathologist's report." Jeeter slid open a drawer, ran his finger down a row of file folders, and pulled one out. He flipped it open and thumbed through a dozen or so sheets. "Bradycardia," he announced.

"Bradycardia," repeated Theodosia.

But Jeeter wasn't finished. "Heart and respiratory failure induced by a toxic substance." Jeeter looked up. "Some kind of poison. Guess they haven't got a complete report from the lab yet." He smiled at Theodosia affably. "They're always backed up. But don't worry, that's no problem. You can take him anyway. Funeral's in two days, huh?"

Was it?

"That's right," said Theodosia. "The family was planning to hold services Thursday morning."

"Then you've got plenty time to get him prepped and primped. In fact, if your meat wagon's out back, I can have one of my guys haul him out right now."

"Thanks anyway," said Theodosia, fighting hard to keep a straight face, "but I'll be sending my meat wagon by this afternoon."

CHAPTER 24

◆◆◆

*C*LEVERET *D*ANTE *SAT* scrunched down in the front seat of his Range Rover. He'd been sitting there for a good ten minutes when he saw the woman with the curly auburn hair and black slacks suit emerge from the Endicott Building.

He'd caught her out of the corner of his eye as he strode past her after leaving the office of that idiot, Sam Sestero. Something about the tone of the woman's voice or the way she had appeared so decidedly blasé had raised his radar. Suspicious by nature, he had tuned her in, like a wolf with his nose to the wind. Once again, his sixth sense hadn't disappointed him. The woman had seemed to be watching him. *Spying* on him.

He'd waited for her to emerge from Sestero's building. Then what a big surprise he'd gotten as he watched her saunter down the street and disappear into the County Services Building! That had blown his mind slightly, but it had also confirmed his suspicions. He knew damn well what was housed in the basement of that innocuous building.

Such a curious coincidence that his lawyer's office was

just down the street from where the body of his dead partner lay on a metal table.

But even more curious was that this strange woman was so interested in both of them.

He would follow this woman, to be sure. Find out who she was, where she lived. Tuck that information away for future use.

CHAPTER 25

✳︎✳︎✳︎

I CAN'T BELIEVE what I just did, I can't believe it! Theodosia repeated to herself as she drove back toward the Indigo Tea Shop.

She was truly waiting for the proverbial bolt of lightning to descend from the heavens and strike her dead. She'd told so many fibs today that her head was spinning. And she figured her karma bank had to be operating at a deficit.

No, Theodosia consoled herself as she spun down Tradd Street, *this is a murder investigation. You think Burt Tidwell worries about stretching the truth when he's questioning a suspect?*

She braked suddenly to avoid sideswiping a horse-drawn carriage packed full of tourists.

No way, she grumbled to herself. *Burt Tidwell probably pulls out a rubber hose and threatens his suspects. And that's only after he's intimidated them into tears.*

"You're finally back!" exclaimed Drayton. "You must have had an amazingly long meeting with Mr. Dauphine. Did he regale you with tales of his days in the Merchant Marines during World War II?"

Drayton was seated at Theodosia's desk, wholesalers' catalogs spread out around him. He had gathered up the papers and files Theodosia had dumped earlier and arranged them in neat little stacks on her bookcase.

"Don't even ask," said Theodosia as she plopped her handbag on the side chair. "Oh, Brown Betty Teapots." She squinted at the colorful brochures from her upside-down view.

"We're positively down to the dregs on teapot selection," said Drayton. "I know you've been preoccupied lately, so I thought I'd make the first pass on a reorder. Besides these traditional English Brown Bettys and Blue Willow pots, Marrington Imports has some stunning contemporary ceramics. A trifle edgy, but still your taste." Drayton slid the catalog toward her. "And look at these Victorian styles with matching tea towels."

"Wonderful," agreed Theodosia. She sat down and balanced on the edge of her side chair, staring straight across at Drayton's lined countenance. "But, Drayton, don't apologize for doing my job. I should be thanking *you*. As the Indigo Tea Shop's benevolent taskmaster, you keep us all moving forward."

"Thank you, Theodosia," said Drayton. A smile lit his face, and a look of satisfaction softened the lines around his eyes. "That means a lot to me."

Theodosia jumped up and peered into the little mirror that hung on the back of the door. It was slightly pitted and wavy from age, but she gamely reapplied her lipstick and fluffed her hair.

"My goodness!" She whirled about, suddenly remembering her three o'clock meeting. "Tanner Joseph. I was supposed to meet with him. About the labels for the holiday blends!"

"No need to panic," Drayton replied mildly. "He's here." Drayton consulted his watch, an ancient Piaget that seemed to perpetually run ten minutes slow. "Has been for almost fifteen, no twenty-five, minutes. Haley took the initiative. She offered to give him the nickel tour."

"She did?" Theodosia allowed herself to relax. For all Haley's indecision about choosing a major and amassing enough credits to graduate, she could sometimes exhibit an amazing take-charge attitude.

But it was Bethany, not Haley, who was seated across the table from Tanner Joseph as Theodosia parted the green velvet curtains and stepped somewhat breathlessly into the tea room.

"Mr. Joseph," said Theodosia as she approached him, her smile warm and apologetic. "Forgive me. I am *so* sorry to have kept you waiting."

"Hello, Miss Browning." Tanner Joseph rose from his chair. Dressed in a faded chambray shirt and khaki slacks, he looked more like the executive director of a nonprofit group that he really was, and less the beach bum from two days ago. "Nice to see you again, but please don't apologize. Your very capable assistant here has been kind enough to bring me up to speed."

Bethany gazed anxiously toward Theodosia, a look that said she hoped she hadn't overstepped her bounds.

"Excellent," replied Theodosia with a reassuring smile for Bethany that conveyed *Thank you, well done.*

"I have to be honest," said Tanner Joseph with a lopsided grin. "My tea drinking has been limited to English breakfast teas and flavored ice teas that come in bottles. But all of this is fascinating. I had no idea so many varieties of tea even existed. Or that water temperature or steeping time was critical. Plus, my taste buds have just been awakened and treated to this rather amazing Japanese green tea. Gyokuro, isn't that what you called it, Bethany?"

Tanner Joseph smiled down at Bethany, and something seemed to pass between them.

Interesting, mused Theodosia as she caught the exchange. *I would have guessed Haley would be the one attracted to this likable young man.* Up until this moment, Bethany hadn't displayed a whit of interest in meeting anyone new.

"I'm delighted we had a hand in helping nurture yet another tea aficionado, Mr. Joseph," Theodosia laughed as she sat down at the table and helped herself to a cup of the flavorful green tea as well.

"Call me Tanner, please." He sat back down in his chair, picked up his cup of tea, and took a sip.

"Okay then, Tanner," said Theodosia. "You've seen our shop, enjoyed a cup of tea. By chance, has Bethany mentioned our holiday blends?"

Tanner Joseph held up an oversized artist's sketch pad. One page was covered with notes and thumbnail drawings.

"We've already been through it," he said. "She told me all about Drayton's different blends, the names you came up with, even your ideas on design. See . . ." He laughed. "I'm pumped. I've already noodled a few sketches."

"You work pretty fast," said Theodosia. This *was* a surprise.

"Oh, yeah," said Tanner Joseph with great enthusiasm. "You have no idea what a fun project this is versus the tedium of waging constant war against environmental robbers and plunderers."

Theodosia sat with Bethany and Tanner Joseph for ten more minutes, expressing her thoughts on the holiday blends and what she called the "look and feel" of the label design. Tanner Joseph, in turn, shared his few quick sketches with her, and Theodosia saw that he'd grasped the concept immediately.

They went over timing and budget for a few minutes more, then Theodosia and Bethany walked Tanner Joseph to the door and bade him good-bye.

"I had no idea you knew so much about the holiday blends," said Theodosia as Bethany closed and locked the double doors. She was pleased but a little taken aback, wondering how Bethany had gleaned so much information.

"Drayton told me all about the holiday blends this morning while we were putting together boxes of tea samplers. He really loves to share his knowledge of tea."

"To anyone who will listen," Theodosia agreed with a laugh. "But I daresay, he's taken *you* under his wing."

"It's such a rare talent to know which teas combine with different spices and fruits. And Drayton really seems to come up with some wonderful blends."

"Bethany," said Theodosia, thoroughly pleased, "you're an amazingly quick study."

Bethany blushed. "But tea is such a fun subject. And something Drayton is so obviously passionate about."

"It's been his life," agreed Theodosia.

"I didn't mean that *you're* not passionate," blushed Bethany. "It's just that . . ."

"It's just that I haven't been around much lately," finished Theodosia. "Don't worry, dear. I'm passionate about a lot of subjects."

"Like finding out what killed Hughes Barron?" Bethany asked in a quiet voice.

"Well . . . yes," said Theodosia, a little surprised by the quick change of subject. "It *is* a rather compelling mystery."

"And you love mysteries," said Bethany, her eyes twinkling. "I mean, getting *involved* in them."

"I guess I do," said Theodosia. She was somewhat taken aback by Bethany's insight. Although she loved nothing better than curling up in front of the fireplace with a good mystery, a P. D. James or a Mary Higgins Clark, she'd never consciously considered the fact that she was itching to get entangled in a real-life mystery. A *murder mystery,* no less.

She sighed. Well, like it or not, she was hip deep in one now.

CHAPTER 26

✨❈✨

$\mathcal{G}$ATEWAY WALK IS a hidden pathway that begins on Church Street, near Saint Philip's graveyard, and meanders four blocks through quiet gardens. Visitors who venture in are led past the Gibbes Museum of Art, the Charleston Library Society, and various fountains and sculptures to Saint John's Church on Archdale Street. The picturesque Gateway Walk, named for the wrought-iron Governor Aiken Gates along the way, enchants visitors with its plaque that reads:

> *Through handwrought gates, alluring paths*
> *Lead on to pleasant places.*
> *Where ghosts of long forgotten things*
> *Have left elusive traces.*

Theodosia had always found the Gateway Walk a lovely, contemplative spot, conducive to deep thought and relaxation. But tonight, with darkness already fallen, she hurried along the brick path, pointedly ignoring the marble tablets and gravestones that loomed on either side of her.

She had spent the entire morning and afternoon at the

Indigo Tea Shop waiting tables, focusing on tea shop business, going over the Web site designs, trying to get back in touch. She knew she hadn't really given careful attention to her business since the night of Hughes Barron's murder; she knew her priorities were slightly out of whack. The Indigo Tea Shop was her bread and butter. Her life. And nosing about the County Morgue shouldn't have taken precedence over her meeting with Tanner Joseph on label illustrations. That had been thoughtless.

Of course, sleuthing was exciting, she told herself as she passed by a marble statue of a weeping angel, a silent, solitary inhabitant of the graveyard. And trying to solve a murder did set one's blood to racing.

Feeling her guilt slightly absolved, for the time being, Theodosia's footsteps echoed softly as she moved quickly along the dark path as it wound behind the Charleston Library Society.

She realized full well that she was headed for Timothy Neville's home not just for an evening of music. Her ulterior motive was to spy.

In a patch of crape myrtle there was a whir of cicadas, the rustle of some small, nocturnal creature, claiming the darkness as its domain.

Six blocks had seemed too short to drive, so Theodosia had walked, taking this shortcut through the cemetery and various gardens. Now, ducking through a crumbling arch with trumpet vine twining at her feet, the Gateway Walk suddenly seemed too dark, too secret, too secluded.

Stepping up her pace, she emerged two minutes later into soft, dreamy light cast by the old-fashioned wrought-iron lamps that lined Archdale Street.

Drayton had said he'd meet her at eight o'clock, just outside the gates of Timothy Neville's Georgian-style mansion. And from the looks of things, she had only moments to spare.

Cars were parked bumper to bumper up and down Archdale, and lights blazed from every window of Timothy Neville's enormous, sprawling home. As Theodosia hurried up the walk, she was suddenly reminded of the Avis Melbourne Home the night of the Lamplighter Tour. Its lamps had also been lit festively. Swarms of visitors had crowded the walks and piazzas.

She fervently hoped that an evening at this grand home would yield far better consequences.

"Right on time." Drayton emerged from the shadows and offered her his arm. He was dressed in black tie and looked more at ease in formal attire than most mere mortals could ever hope for. When an invitation specified black tie, Drayton always complied with elegance and polish.

Theodosia had worn a floor-length, pale blue sleeveless dress, shimmery as moonlight. As an afterthought, she'd tossed a silver gray pashmina shawl over her shoulders. With her hair long and flowing and a dab of mascara and lipstick to highlight her expressive eyes and full lips, she looked like an elegant lady out for a night on the town.

But I'm here to spy, Theodosia reminded herself as she and Drayton climbed the stone steps.

They nodded to familiar faces standing in groups on the piazza, passed through elegant cathedral doors and were greeted inside by Henry, Timothy Neville's butler.

Henry was dressed in full liveried regalia, and rumor held that Henry had been employed by Timothy Neville for almost forty years. There weren't many people Theodosia knew who had live-in help or had help that stayed with them for so long.

"Cocktails are being served in the solarium," Henry announced solemnly. He had the sad, unblinking eyes of an old turtle and the ramrod backbone of an English Beefeater. "Or feel free to join Mr. Neville's other guests in the salon, where Mr. Calhoun is playing a piece from Scarlatti." Henry gestured slowly toward a gilded archway through which harpsichord notes flowed freely.

Theodosia noted that the venerable Henry seemed to move in slow motion. It was like watching a Japanese Noh drama.

"Wine or song?" Drayton asked good-naturedly.

"Let's get a drink first," suggested Theodosia. She knew if they repaired to the salon, courtesy required them to pay strict attention to the music, not exactly her motive for coming here tonight. But if they grabbed a cocktail first, they'd be free to move about the house and greet other guests.

And get the lay of the land, Theodosia told herself. Try to get a better fix on the very strange Mr. Timothy Neville.

Although she had passed Timothy Neville's house many times on her walks with Earl Grey, Theodosia had never before been inside this enormous mansion. She was in awe as she gazed around. This was splendor unlike anything she'd seen before. A dramatic stairway dominated the foyer and rose three floors. Double parlors flanked the main hallway, and Theodosia saw that they contained Italian black marble fireplaces, Hepplewhite furnishings, and ornate chandeliers. Gleaming oil paintings and copperplate engravings hung on the walls.

Built during the Civil War by an infamous blockade runner, this home was reputed to have sliding panels that led to secret passageways and hidden rooms. Some folks in the historic district even whispered that the house was haunted. The fact that Timothy Neville's home had once served as residence for a former governor and was a private girl's school for a short time, only added to the intrigue.

"Theodosia!" The shrill voice of Samantha Rabathan rose above the undercurrent of conversational buzz as Theodosia and Drayton entered the solarium. Then Samantha, resplendent in fuschia silk, came determinedly toward them, like the prow of a ship cutting the waves.

"I didn't expect to see you here tonight," cooed Samantha as she adjusted the front of her dress to show off just the right amount of décolletage. "Drayton, too. Hello there, dear fellow."

Drayton inclined his head slightly and allowed Samantha to peck him on the cheek.

"Our illustrious chairwoman from the Lamplighter Tour," he said in greeting. "You're looking lovely this evening."

Samantha held a finger to her matching fuschia-colored mouth. "I think it best we downplay the Lamplighter Tour." She grasped each of them by an elbow and started to haul them toward the bar. "That is, until this nastiness blows over." She smiled broadly, seemed to really notice Theodosia for the first time, and instantly shifted her look of amusement to one of concern. "How *are* you holding up, Theodosia? So many rumors flying, it's hard to know what to believe. And how is that poor, dear child . . . What is her name again?"

"Bethany," replied Theodosia. Samantha was being incredibly overbearing tonight, and Theodosia was already searching for an excuse to escape her clutches.

Just as a waiter offered flutes of champagne from a silver tray, the perfect excuse arrived in the form of Henry, announcing that the Balfour Quartet was about to begin their evening's performance.

"Got to run," burbled Samantha. "I'm sitting with Cleo and Raymond Hovle. From Santa Barbara. You remember them, Theodosia. They also have a house on Seabrook Island."

Theodosia didn't remember Cleo and Raymond at all, but she smiled hello out of politeness when Samantha pointedly nudged a small suntanned couple as she and Drayton entered the parlor for the concert.

They found seats in the back row, not in cushioned splendor as did the guests at the front of the pack, but on somewhat uncomfortable folding chairs.

Unaccustomed as she was to wearing three-inch high-heeled sandals, Theodosia surreptitiously slipped them off her feet and waited for the music to start.

CHAPTER 27

TIMOTHY NEVILLE TUCKED his violin under his chin and gave a nod to begin. He had done a brief introduction of the other three members of the Balfour Quartet. The two men, the one who'd played the harpsichord earlier and was now on the violin, and a red-faced man on the viola, were also members of the Charleston Symphony. The fourth member, a young woman who played the cello, was from Columbia, South Carolina's capital, located just northwest of Charleston.

As Timothy Neville played the opening notes of Beethoven's *Die Mittleren Streichquartette,* he was surprised to note that the Browning woman was sitting in the back row. He gave a quick dip of his head to position himself for a slightly better view and saw immediately that she was sitting next to Drayton Conneley.

Of course. Drayton worked at the woman's little tea shop. It was logical that she might accompany him tonight. His command-performance concerts were legendary throughout the historic district, and it wasn't unusual for his invited guests to bring along guests of their own.

He frowned. The Browning woman was staring sharply

at him as though she were waiting for something to happen. Silly girl. They had just begun the allegro, and there were a good fifty minutes to go. Still, she had been bold to come see him at the Heritage Society and plead the young intern's case. Even though he may have been dismissive of Theodosia Browning, it didn't mean he didn't admire her spirit. Lots of complacency these days. Hard to find the plucky ones. All the same, he would keep a close watch on her. She had stuck her nose in matters that didn't concern her, especially her inquiry about the Peregrine Building. That just wouldn't do at all.

The Balfour Quartet was very good, far better than Theodosia had expected they'd be, and she soon found herself lost in the musical depths of Beethoven's Quartet no. 9.

It was haunting and evocative, pulling her in and holding her complete attention until it came to a crashing conclusion.

Theodosia, suddenly reminded of why she was there in the first place, applauded briefly, then dashed out the door ahead of the crowd. There would be a twenty-minute intermission, an opportunity for men to refill drinks and ladies to visit the powder room.

Theodosia headed up that grand staircase, her toes sinking deep into plush white wool, and dashed down the long, arched hallway when she hit the second floor. Peeking into several bedrooms along the way, she found that all were elegantly furnished, and yet none showed signs of being occupied. Finally, at what would be the front of the house, she found the set of double doors that led to Timothy Neville's private suite of rooms.

As she pushed one of the massive doors slowly inward on its hinges, it emitted a protesting groan. Theodosia held her breath, looking back over her shoulder to see if anyone had heard or might even be watching her. No. Nothing. She swallowed hard, stepped inside Timothy Neville's private office, and closed the door behind her.

A single desk lamp, what looked like an original Tiffany

dragonfly design, cast low light in the suite. Massive furnishings were dark, shadowy lumps. Flames danced in the ornate marble fireplace.

Theodosia's sandals whispered across the Aubusson carpet. Even in the dim light she could see portraits of Timothy Neville's ancestors, various fiery Huguenots scowling down at her from their vantage point on the burgundy-colored walls.

Then she was standing at Timothy Neville's Louis XIV desk, her hand on the brass knob, about to pull open the top drawer. She hesitated as a pang of guilt shot through her. This was snooping of the first magnitude, she told herself. Not terribly above board. Then she also remembered Timothy Neville's incredible rage and Hughes Barron clutching his teacup.

She slid the drawer open.

Inside were pens, stamps, personalized stationery, eyeglasses, a sheaf of household papers, and Timothy Neville's passport. Everything in an orderly arrangement, nothing of great interest.

What were you expecting to find? she asked herself. *A little blue glass bottle of arsenic? A crackling paper packet of strychnine?*

She padded back across the room to the door opposite the desk and sneaked it open. Timothy Neville's rather splendid bedroom met her eyes. Four-poster bed draped in heavy wine- and rust-colored brocades. Small Chippendale tables flanking each side of the bed. An elegant linen press that looked as though it might have been created by the famous Charleston cabinetmaker, Robert Walker. Two armchairs in matching brocade sat next to the small fireplace. And, on the walls, more oil paintings. Not ancestral portraits but eighteenth-century portraits of women. Women in gardens, women with children, women staring out dreamily.

The paintings hinted at a softer, more humane side of Timothy Neville than Theodosia wouldn't have guessed.

In the bathroom, next to a large walk-in closet, Theodosia hit the light switch. The bathroom was restful and elegant, replete with enormous claw-foot tub, dark green wallpaper, and brass wall sconces and towel racks. Without hesitation, Theodosia pulled open the medicine cabinet and scanned the shelves.

It was as predictable as his desk drawer had been. Shaving cream, toothpaste, aspirin, a bottle of Kiehl's After Shave Balm, a bottle of prescription medicine. Theodosia reached for the brown tinted bottle and scanned the label.

Halcion. Five milligrams. *Sleeping pills.*

She pondered this for a moment. Incriminating evidence? No, not really, she decided. Timothy Neville was an old man. Older people often had difficulty sleeping.

Theodosia placed the medicine back on the shelf, swung the mirrored door shut, and turned out the bathroom light. She crossed back through the bedroom into Timothy Neville's private office. She scanned the room again and shook her head. *Nope, nothing unusual here.*

Her hand rested on the doorknob when she noticed a tall English secretary just to the right of the door. Rather than housing fine porcelains behind its glass doors, as it had been designed to do, it now appeared to hold a collection of antique pistols.

Theodosia hesitated a split second, then decided this might be worth investigating.

Yes, they were pistols, all right. She gazed at the engraved plates that identified each weapon. Here was an 1842 Augustin-Lock Austrian cavalry pistol. And here an Early American flintlock. Fascinated, she pulled open one of the glass doors, slid her hand across the smooth walnut grip, and touched the intricate silver with her fingertips. These pieces were fascinating. Some had been used in the Civil War, the American Revolution, or quite possibly in gentlemen's duels of honor. They were retired now, on display. But their history and silent power were awe inspiring.

In the stillness of the room, a slight noise, an almost imperceptible tick, caught her attention, caused her to glance toward the door. In the dim light, she could see the brass doorknob slowly turning.

In a flash, Theodosia flattened herself against the wall, praying that whoever opened the door wouldn't peer around and see her hidden here in the shadows.

The heavy door creaked slowly inward on its hinges.

Needs a shot of WD-40, Theodosia thought wildly as she pressed closer to the wall and held her breath.

Whoever had opened the door halfway was standing there now, silently surveying the room. Only two inches of wood separated her from this mysterious person who, quite possibly, had followed her!

Theodosia willed her heart to stop beating so loudly. Surely, whoever was there must be able to hear it thumping mightily in her chest! Her mind raced, recalling Edgar Allan Poe's prophetic story, "The Tell Tale Heart."

That's me, she thought. *They'll hear the wild, troubled beating of my heart!*

But whoever stood there—Timothy Neville, the butler, Henry, another curious guest—had peeked into the room for only a few seconds, then pulled the door shut behind them.

Had they been satisfied no one was there?

Theodosia hoped so as she slumped against the wall, feeling hollow and weak-kneed. *Time to get out of here,* she decided. This little adventure had suddenly gone far enough. She moved toward the door.

Then she remembered the gun collection.

Theodosia glanced quickly toward the cabinet. In the half-light, the polished guns winked enticingly. *All right,* she told herself, *one quick peek. Then I will skedaddle out of here and join the others downstairs.*

The guns were all displayed in custom-made wooden holders. Beautiful to behold. Probably quite expensive to create. A key stuck out from the drop-leaf center panel. She turned it, lowering the leaf into the writing desk position.

Tucked in the cubbyholes were polishing cloths, various gun-cleaning kits, and a bottle of clear liquid.

Theodosia squinted at the label on the bottle. Sulfuric acid.

It was a compound often used to remove rust and corrosion from antique bronze statues, metal frames, and guns. And, unless she was mistaken, sulfuric acid was also a deadly poison.

If Timothy Neville had slipped something toxic into Hughes Barron's tea, could it have been this substance? That was the 64,000-dollar question, wasn't it? And nobody was saying yet. Not the coroner. Not Burt Tidwell. Certainly not Timothy Neville.

The Balfour Quartet had resumed playing when Theodosia slipped into the room and took her seat beside Drayton. As she adjusted her shawl around her shoulders, she felt his eyes on her.

"You look guilty," Drayton finally whispered.

"I do?" Her eyes went wide as she turned toward him.

"No, not really," he answered. "But you should. Where in heaven's name have you been?" he fussed. "I've been worried sick!"

Theodosia fidgeted through the second half of the concert, unable to concentrate and really enjoy the Balfour Quartet's rendition of Beethoven's Opus 18, no. 6. When the group finished with a flourish and the crowd rose to its collective feet, cheering and applauding, she breathed a giant sigh of relief.

Jumping up with the rest of the guests, Theodosia leaned toward Drayton. "I'll tell you all about it," she finally whispered in his ear. "But first, let's go back to the shop and have a nice calming cup of tea!"

CHAPTER 28

"YOU LOOK LIKE the cat who swallowed the canary," said Drayton.

Haley was bent over the counter, artfully arranging tea roses in a pink-and-white-flowered Victorian teapot.

"Who me?" asked Haley with wide-eyed innocence. She tied a lace bow to the teapot's arched handle and stood back to admire her handiwork.

Drayton had been asked to organize a bridal shower tea for that afternoon, and everyone was pitching in to help. Since a nasty squall had blown in overnight, causing the temperature to plummet and drenching Charleston with a frigid, pounding rain, it didn't appear that many customers would be dropping by the tea shop anyway.

"Come on, what gives?" prompted Drayton. He had carefully wrapped a dozen bone china teacups in tissue paper and was gently placing them in a large wicker basket atop a white lace tablecloth. With the weather so miserable, he would have to add a protective layer of plastic to keep everything tidy and dry.

"What time do you have to be at the Lady Goodwood Inn?" Haley asked with feigned indifference.

"Haley . . ." pleaded the exasperated Drayton. When Drayton thought someone was nursing a secret, he was like a curious child—impish, impatient, prodding.

"Well," said Haley, "it's a trifle premature to say anything."

"But . . ." prompted Drayton.

"But Bethany was out on a date last night," Haley chortled triumphantly.

"A date!" exclaimed Theodosia. Up until now she had stayed out of Drayton and Haley's little go-round. Let them have their fun, she'd thought. But this was news. Big news. While she and Drayton had been attending the concert at Timothy Neville's last night, Bethany had been out with a young man. Theodosia wondered what special person had coaxed the wistful and reclusive Bethany out of her shell. This had to be the first time Bethany had ventured out since her husband passed away.

"Dare I ask who with?" inquired Drayton. He was positively dying to know all the details.

"Why, with Theodosia's friend, of course," said Haley.

A thunderclap exploded loudly overhead at the same moment a jar of lemon curd Theodosia had been holding went crashing to the floor. As lightning strobed and windows rattled, glass shards and huge yellow globs scattered.

For some reason the name Jory Davis had popped into Theodosia's head. "Which friend do you mean?" she asked quickly.

"Oh, don't move, Theo!" cried Haley. "There's a huge sliver of glass pointing right at your foot. Move one inch, and it's liable to slice through your shoe. Hang on, and I'll get the dust pan and broom." She scurried off to fetch cleaning supplies.

"Who did she mean?" Theodosia asked Drayton.

"I'm just as much in the dark as you." Drayton shrugged.

"Okay, stand still!" Haley laid the dustpan down, hooked two large shards of glass with the broom, and slid them onto the dust pan. She surveyed the smaller pieces of glass and the pools of yellow liquid. "Gosh, what a mess."

She furrowed her brow, ready to go on the attack. A compulsive neatnik and organizer, Haley always relished a cleanup challenge.

"Haley." Drayton snapped his fingers, amused by her fierce concentration. "Which one of our fine lads had the honor of squiring Bethany last evening?"

Haley looked up at Drayton and blinked, trying to regain her train of thought. "Oh. Tanner Joseph. The fellow who's doing the illustrations for the holiday tea labels."

"Tanner Joseph," repeated Theodosia. Now it made perfect sense. Bethany had been so cordial and helpful the other day, explaining teas and holiday blends to him.

"Of course, that fellow," said Drayton. Now that he knew who Bethany's date had been, his interest level had waned. If it had been someone new, someone who'd just opened a clever new shop on Church Street or someone who'd just bought a home in the nearby historic district and was going to renovate in a historically accurate way, then Drayton would have demanded all the details. Who were his family? Where had he gone to school? What did he do for a living?

"Where is Bethany, by the way?" asked Theodosia.

Haley scooped up more of the splintery mess. "Doing deliveries."

"In this rain?" said Drayton.

"She said she wanted to clear her head," replied Haley. "Besides, she's a jogger. Joggers are used to being out in all sorts of weather." She gazed out a fogged window toward the deserted, rain-slick street. "At least I think they are."

His curiosity satisfied, Drayton turned his attention back to preparations for the bridal shower tea. "I wish it weren't pouring buckets," he fussed.

"They weren't planning on holding the bridal shower tea outdoors, were they?" asked Haley.

He grimaced. "Yes, they were. Obviously that's not a possibility now." Drayton reached up and took a tiny tea candle nestled in a white porcelain bowl from the shelf. "The whole thing will have to be rethought," he said mournfully as he gazed down at the little candle in his hand.

"Doesn't the Lady Goodwood have a solarium?" asked Theodosia. "Just off the dining room?"

Drayton considered her question. "I believe they do. Very much on the order of a greenhouse. Verdant, lots of plants, a few tables. I think there might even be a small fountain. Of course the space is abysmally hot when the sun is shining, but on a day like today, cool, rainy, it might be just right." His face began to brighten significantly as he weighed the merits of this new locale. "Maybe even a touch romantic, what with rain pattering down on the glass roof."

"What a nice image, Drayton," said Haley, smiling. "I like that."

"Theodosia," Drayton said as he frantically scanned the tall shelves where all manner of tea candles, jams, and jellies were displayed. "Don't we have some floating candles?"

He whirled about as Theodosia, a step ahead of him, plunked four boxes of the miniature round disks into his hands.

"That's it!" cried Drayton. "What else?"

"Tea cozies for all the pots!" exclaimed Haley, getting into the spirit. "And exchange the wrought-iron chairs that are probably there now for upholstered chairs from the dining room."

"Perfect," declared Drayton.

"What about food?" inquired Theodosia. "What's on the menu so far?"

"Chocolate-dipped strawberries, shortbread cakes, apricot chutney, and Stilton cheese tea sandwiches," said Drayton.

"Okay," said Theodosia. "Now just add some of Haley's hot crab dip with Irish soda bread."

"My God, Theo, you're a genius," declared Drayton. He whirled about. "Haley, do you have time to whip up crab dip?"

"Drayton. Please." Haley had already shifted into her search-and-rescue mode and was headed for the kitchen.

It was after eleven when Bethany finally returned to the Indigo Tea Shop, face shiny, hair wet and smelling faintly of fresh rain.

"You all look so busy," she cried. "Can I help?"

Theodosia took one look at her. "You're soaked clear through. Better pop across the alley and change first. You're liable to catch cold."

"Colds come from viruses," said Haley. "Not cold weather." She had finished the crab dip and was now tying raffia and gilded leaves around bunches of cinnamon sticks.

"Which is why you drink my hibiscus and orange spice tea in winter? To thwart any possible virus?" asked Drayton in a faintly critical tone.

"Well, not exactly," said Haley.

"You're right, Theodosia. I'd feel better if I changed into dry clothes," said Bethany. "Want me to take Earl Grey out for a walk first?"

"Would you?" asked Theodosia.

"Love to," said Bethany.

"She really is in a wonderful mood," Drayton remarked in an offhand manner to Haley.

Bethany stood stock-still in the middle of the tea room, and her eyes searched out the three of them. "You all have been talking about me!" she declared. "Haley, you told!" She admonished Haley's retreating back as Haley decided to quickly disappear into the safe confines of her kitchen.

"What is with that girl?" declared Bethany. Her face was pulled into a frown, and she was vexed over Haley's obvious revelation about her previous night's date.

Theodosia put a hand on Bethany's damp shoulder to reassure her. "She's happy for you, dear. That's all."

"I suppose she told you it was Tanner Joseph. We only went to a gallery opening. The Ariel Gallery over on George Street had a show of black-and-white photography. By Sidney Didion, a local photographer."

"Did you enjoy yourself?" asked Theodosia. She had read a review of the Didion exhibit, and it had sounded quite good. Titled "Ghosts," the show consisted of moody black-and-white photo essays of old plantations.

"I did." Now Bethany's eyes shone brightly. "Did you know Tanner spent an entire year in the Amazon? He has a master's degree in ecology from the University of Minnesota, and he went down to South America to study the ecosystem of the rain forest."

"Yes, he mentioned that to me."

"Isn't it fascinating?" Bethany's face had taken on a curious glow.

Why, she seems to really care for this young man, thought Theodosia. *It's heartening to see her coming out of mourning and actually take an interest in someone.*

"Tanner spent a week living in a six-by-eight-foot tree house in the rain forest canopy," said Bethany. "Apparently he had this whole system of pulleys and harnesses and long ropes that allowed him to ride from one treetop to another and collect samples. Of course, I have acrophobia and absolutely *die* if I venture more than four feet off the ground, but it does sound like an amazing adventure."

"I've seen photos of researchers doing that in *National Geographic,*" said Theodosia. "You really do need to be fearless about heights."

"There's a whole microcosm of plant and animal life up in those trees!" Bethany went on. "Insects, botanicals, birds. Most of them never touch the ground. Tanner told me all about these weird little green frogs."

Hairs suddenly prickled on the back of Theodosia's neck. "What did he tell you about frogs, Bethany?"

"Just that there's a certain type of frog the natives collect. They're very beautiful, bright green and yellow, but they're venomous. So the Indians dip the tips of their arrows into the frog's venom, then use those arrows for hunting. And Tanner told me about the most amazing orchids that grow up there, too. Bromeliads, actually. Orchid cousins. He says some of them have blooms that are ten inches across. Isn't that amazing?"

"It is," agreed Theodosia, but her mind was elsewhere.

For some reason, she had gotten a terribly uneasy feeling the moment Bethany mentioned the frogs. Uneasy, she supposed, because it meant Tanner Joseph had a working knowledge of a certain kind of poison. And, she realized that the first time she had met Tanner Joseph, he had been outspoken about having a problem . . . no, make that a fairly substantial grudge . . . against Hughes Barron.

After Bethany left on her walk with Earl Grey, Theodosia sat in her office alone, pondering this new information. Could this just be a bizarre coincidence? Was truth, indeed, stranger than fiction? Take your pick, she thought. If it was a coincidence, it certainly was an odd one. And if Tanner Joseph was somehow *not* the mild-mannered eco-crusader he portrayed himself as (and she suddenly remembered how Tanner Joseph had shown a cold satisfaction when he'd spoken of Hughes Barron's karmic death), then it meant Bethany could be in serious danger.

And she was the one who'd put her in harm's way.

Theodosia lowered her head into her hands and rubbed her eyes tiredly. Damn! In her eagerness to get her tea labels done, she seemed to have opened up yet another can of worms.

Worse yet, if Bethany was still a suspect in the eyes of Bert Tidwell, and Tanner Joseph was somehow connected . . . Well . . . the possibilities weren't good at all.

Theodosia sighed heavily and gazed about her office distractedly. A piece of paper sitting on the corner of her desk caught her attention. It was the sheet she'd begun two days ago. The sheet that looked like a family tree. But instead of family names she had written "Hughes Barron" and "Poison?" at the top and the names "Timothy Neville" and "Lleveret Dante" underneath.

Theodosia picked up a silver pen. Purposefully, but with a good deal of anguish, she added a third name to her sheet: the name of Tanner Joseph.

CHAPTER 29

❧

BY EVENING, THE rain still showed no sign of letting up. A tropical disturbance had swept in from the Atlantic and hunkered down over the grand strand and the sea islands. Its fury extended a hundred miles in either direction, north to Myrtle Beach, south to Savannah.

Above the tea shop, in her little apartment just six blocks from Charleston Harbor, Theodosia could feel the full fury of the storm. Rain pounded the roof, lashed at the windows, and gurgled noisily down drain spouts. At moments when the storm's saber rattling seemed to abate slightly, she swore she could hear a foghorn from somewhere over near Patriots Point.

Lighting a fire in the fireplace in the face of so much wind would have meant losing precious warmth. Instead Theodosia lit a dozen white candles of varying sizes and placed them inside the fireplace. Now they danced and flickered merrily. Maybe not imparting warmth in terms of temperature, but certainly lending a cozy, tucked-in kind of feeling.

Curled up on her couch, a handmade afghan snugged around her, Theodosia sipped a cup of Egyptian chamomile. The taste was slightly sweet, reminiscent of almonds and apples. A good evening calm-you-down tea.

Calming was exactly what she needed, because instead of conducting a quiet investigation and perhaps discovering a lead on Hughes Barron's murderer, she seemed to have uncovered a number of potential suspects.

Timothy Neville hated Hughes Barron with white-hot passion, despised the man because of Barron's callous disregard for historic buildings and architecture. Somehow Timothy had known that Hughes Barron was making a play for the Peregrine Building. Timothy's assumption had been that Hughes Barron would have made significant changes to it. Would that have enraged Timothy Neville enough for him to commit murder? Perhaps. He was old, inflexible, used to getting his way. And Timothy Neville had a bottle of sulfuric acid in his study.

She had told Drayton about her discovery last night, after they'd departed Timothy Neville's house. He'd reinforced the notion that sulfuric acid was, indeed, used to remove rust and corrosion from old metal. But Timothy Neville going so far as actually pouring a dollop in Hughes Barron's teacup? Well, they didn't really have the toxicologist's report, did they? And neither of them could recall Timothy Neville's exact movements the night of the Lamplighter Tour. They only remembered that, for a short time, he'd been a guest in the back garden at the Avis Melbourne Home.

Then there was Lleveret Dante. From the conversation she'd overheard outside Sam Sestero's office, Hughes Barron's portion of Goose Creek Holdings fell neatly into Lleveret Dante's hands as a result of Barron's death. Plus, the man was obviously a scoundrel, since he was under indictment in another state. Theodosia wondered if Dante had fled Kentucky just steps ahead of an arrest or, like so many unsavory business characters today, had a slick Kentucky lawyer working on his behalf, firing off a constant barrage of appeals and paperwork until the case all but faded away.

Finally, there was Tanner Joseph, executive director of the Shorebird Environmentalist Group. *She* had brought him into their lives, had invited Tanner Joseph into the safety and security of their little tea shop. Could an environmentalist be overzealous? Consumed with bitterness at losing a battle?

Theodosia knew the answer was yes. The papers were full of stories about people who routinely risked their own lives to save the whales, the dolphins, the redwoods. Did those people ever kill others who stood in the way of their conservation efforts? Unfortunately, the answer was yes on that point, too. Redwoods were often spiked with metal pieces that bounced saw blades back into loggers' faces. Some animal rights activists, bitterly opposed to hunting, actually opened fire on hunters. It wasn't inconceivable that Tanner Joseph could be such a fanatic. History had proven that passion unchecked yields freely to fanaticism.

Theodosia shucked off her afghan, stretched her long legs, and stood. She padded to the kitchen in her stocking feet. From his woven rag rug in front of the fireplace, Earl Grey lifted his fine head and gazed at her with concern.

"Be right back," she told him.

In the kitchen, Theodosia took an English shortbread cookie from one of the pretty tins that rested on her counter. From a red and yellow tin decorated with pictures of noble hunting dogs she took a dog biscuit.

Doggy biscotti, she thought to herself as she returned to the living room where the two of them munched their cookies companionably. *Could be a profitable sideline.* Just last month she'd seen a magazine article about the booming business of gourmet dog treats.

Finishing off her cookie, Theodosia swiveled around and scanned the floor-to-ceiling bookshelf directly behind her. She selected a small, leather-bound volume and settled back comfortably again to reread her Agatha Christie.

The book she'd chosen was a fascinating primer on poison. She read eagerly as Agatha Christie described in delicious detail a "tasteless, odorless white powder that is poorly soluble in cold water but excellent to dissolve in hot cocoa, milk, or tea."

This terrible poison, arsenic, Theodosia learned, was completely undetectable. But one tablespoon could administer ten to thirty times the lethal dose.

As if on cue, the lights flickered, lending a strange magic lantern feel to the living room. Ever the guard dog, Earl Grey rose up a few inches and growled in response. Then there was a low hum, as though the generators at South Carolina Light and Power were lodging a mighty protest, and the lights burned strong and steady again.

When the lights had dimmed momentarily, Theodosia's startled reaction had been to close her book. Now she sat with the slim volume in her lap, staring out the rain-spattered window, catching an occasional flash of lightning from far away.

She considered what she had just read. Arsenic was amazingly lethal and extremely fast acting. Death occurred almost instantaneously.

But from what she had been able to piece together, Hughes Barron had walked into the garden under his own power and probably sat at the far table, drinking tea, for a good half hour. So Hughes Barron must have died slowly, perhaps not even knowing he was dying. Poisoned, to be sure, but some type of poison that deliberately slowed his heart until, like a pocket watch not properly wound, it simply stopped.

CHAPTER 30

D RAYTON WAS DEEP in thought behind the counter, his gray head bent over the black leather ledger. He scratched numbers onto a yellow legal pad, then added them up using a tiny credit card–sized calculator. When he saw the total, he frowned. Painstakingly, he added the numbers again. Unfortunately, he arrived at the same total the second time through.

Sighing heavily, Drayton massaged the bridge of his nose where his glasses had pinched and looked out at the tea shop. Haley and Bethany were doing a masterful job, pouring tea, waiting on tables, coaxing customers into having a second slice of cream cake or taking home a few scones for tomorrow's breakfast. But once again, only half the tables were occupied.

Clearly, business was down, and his numbers told him they were down almost 40 percent from the same week a year ago. Granted, Thanksgiving was two weeks away, Christmas just around the corner. With the holidays would come the inevitable Christmas rush. But that rush should have showed signs of starting by now, shouldn't it?

The tourist trade brought in revenue, to be sure, as did

the special tea parties they catered, like the bridal shower tea yesterday or the various birthday celebration teas. But the real bread and butter for the Indigo Tea Shop was repeat customers from around the neighborhood. For whatever reason (although in his heart Drayton was quite confident he knew the reason) many of the locals were skittishly staying away.

"We need to talk." Drayton's quiet but carefully modulated voice carried above the light jazz that played on the radio in Theodosia's office.

When she saw Drayton standing in the doorway, trusty ledger and sheaf of papers clutched in hand, she snapped off the music. "Rats. You've got that look on your face."

Drayton crossed the faded Oriental carpet, hooked a leg of the upholstered side chair with his toe, and pulled it toward him. He deposited his ledger and papers atop Theodosia's desk and sat down heavily in the chair.

"It's not good," she said.

"It's not good," he replied.

"Are we talking tailspin or just awfully slow?" asked Theodosia.

Drayton chewed his lower lip thoughtfully.

"I see," said Theodosia. She leaned back in her high-backed leather chair and closed her eyes. According to the Tea Council of the USA, tea was a five-billion-dollar industry, poised to boom in much the same way coffee had. Tea shops and tea salons were opening at a dizzying rate. Coffee shops were hastily adding tea to their repertoire. And bottled teas, although she didn't care for them personally, were highly popular.

All of that was great, she mused. Tea was making a comeback, big time. But all she wanted to do was make a secure little living and keep everyone here on the payroll. Would that be possible? Judging by the somber look on Drayton's face, perhaps not.

Theodosia pulled herself up straight in her chair. "Okay, what do we do?" she asked. "Try to roll out the Web site fast? Open up a second front?" She knew the battlefield analogy would appeal to Drayton, since he was such a World War II buff.

"We probably should have done exactly that earlier," said Drayton. His eyes shone with regret rather than reproach.

Theodosia's manicured fingers fluttered through the cards in her Rolodex. "Let me call Jessica at Todd & Lambeau. See what can be done." She dialed the phone and, while waiting for it to be answered, reached over to her bookcase and grabbed the stack of Web designs. "Here. Pick one." She thrust the storyboards toward Drayton.

"Hello," said Theodosia. "Jessica Todd, please. Tell her it's Theodosia Browning at the Indigo Tea Shop." She covered the mouthpiece with her hand. "They're putting me through," she said.

Drayton nodded.

"Hello, Jessica? I'm sorry, who? Oh, her assistant." Theodosia listened intently. "You don't say. An online brokerage. And you're sure it won't be any sooner? No, not really. Well, have Jessica call me once she's back in the office."

Theodosia grinned crookedly as she set the phone down. "Plan B."

Drayton lifted one eyebrow, amused at the magnitude of his employer's energy and undaunted spirit. "Which is?"

"Until this entire mess is cleared up, a dark cloud is going to be hanging over all of us." Theodosia stood, as if to punctuate her sentence.

"You're probably right, but you make it sound terribly ominous," said Drayton. "What is this plan B that you spoke of?"

Theodosia flashed him a brilliant smile. "I'm going to a funeral."

CHAPTER 31

❦

IT ISN'T FOR naught that Charleston has been dubbed the Holy City. One hundred eighty-one church steeples, spires, bell towers, and crosses thrust majestically into the sky above the low-profile cityscape, a testament to Charleston's 300-year history as well as its acceptance of those fleeing religious persecution.

The First Presbyterian Church, known as Scots Kirk, was founded in 1731 by twelve Scottish families.

Saint Michael's Episcopal Church, established in 1751, was where George Washington and the Marquis de Lafayette worshiped.

The Unitarian Church, conceived as the Independent Church in 1772, was appropriated by the British militia during the Revolutionary War and used briefly to stable horses.

It was in this Unitarian Church, with its stately Gothic design, that mourners now gathered. Heads bowed, listening to a sorrowful dirge by Mozart echo off the vast, vaulted ceiling with its delicate plaster fantracery that painstakingly replicated the Henry VII Chapel at Westminster Abbey.

Theodosia stood in the arched stone doorway and shivered. The weather was still chilly, not more than fifty degrees, and this great stone church with its heavy buttresses never seemed to quite warm up inside. The stained glass windows, so beautiful and conducive to contemplation, also served to deflect the sun's warming rays.

So far, more than three dozen mourners had streamed past her and taken seats inside the church. Theodosia wondered just who these people were. Relatives? Friends? Business acquaintances? Certainly not the residents of Edgewater Estates!

Theodosia knew it was standard police technique to stake out funerals. In cases of murder and sometimes arson, perpetrators often displayed a morbid curiosity, showing up at funerals and graveside services.

Would that be the case today? she wondered. Just hanging out, hoping for someone to show up, seemed like a very Sherlock Holmesian thing to do, outdated, a trifle simplistic. Unfortunately, it was the best she'd been able to come up with for the moment.

"My goodness, Theodosia!"

Theodosia whirled about and found herself staring into the smooth, unlined face of Samantha Rabathan. She noted that Samantha looked very fetching, dressed in a purple suit and jaunty black felt hat set with a matching purple plume.

"Don't you look charming in your shopkeeper's black velvet," Samantha purred.

Theodosia had made a last-minute decision to attend Hughes Barron's funeral, hadn't had time to change, and, thus had jumped into her Jeep Cherokee dressed in a black turtleneck sweater, long black velvet skirt, and comfortable short black boots. She supposed she might look a trifle dowdy compared to Samantha's bright purple. And it certainly wasn't uncharacteristic of Samantha to insinuate so.

"I had no idea you were friends with Hughes Barron," began Theodosia.

Samantha smiled sadly. "We made our acquaintance at the Heritage Society. He was a new board member. I was . . ."

She was about to say long-term member but quickly changed her answer.

"I was Lamplighter chairperson."

Theodosia nodded. It made sense. Samantha was always doing what was proper or decorous or neighborly. Even if she sometimes added her own special twist.

The two women walked into the church and stood at the rear overlooking the many rows of pews.

Samantha nudged Theodosia with an elbow. "I understand," Samantha whispered, "that woman in the first row is Hughes Barron's cousin." She nodded toward the back of a woman wearing a mustard-colored coat. "Lucille Dunn from North Carolina."

The woman sat alone, head bowed. "That's the only relative?" Theodosia asked.

"So far as I know," Samantha whispered, then tottered up the aisle, for she had already spotted someone else she wanted to chat with.

Slipping into one of the back pews, Theodosia sat quietly as the organ continued to thunder. From her vantage point, she could now study the funeral attendees. She saw several members of the Heritage Society, the lawyer, Sam Sestero, and a man who looked like an older Xerox copy, probably the brother, Edward, of Sestero & Sestero. There was Lleveret Dante, dressed conservatively in brown instead of a flashy white suit. And Burt Tidwell. She might have known.

But no Timothy Neville. And no Tanner Joseph.

The service was simple and oddly sad. A gunmetal gray coffin draped in black crepe, a minister who talked of resurrection and salvation but allowed as to how he had never really acquainted himself with Hughes Barron.

Struck by melancholy, Theodosia wondered who would attend her funeral, should she meet an early and untimely end. Aunt Libby, Drayton, Haley, Bethany, Samantha, Delaine, Angie and Mark Congdon of the Featherbed House, probably Father Jonathan, and some of her old advertising cronies.

How about Jory Davis? Would he crowd in with the other mourners? Would he remember her fondly? Should she call and invite him to dinner?

Theodosia was still lost in thought when the congregation launched into its final musical tribute, a slightly off-key rendition of "Amazing Grace."

As was tradition at funeral services, the mourners in the front rose first and made their way down the aisle, while those folks in the back kept the singing going as best they could. That, of course, put Theodosia at the very end of the line for expressing condolences to Hughes Barron's only relative, Lucille Dunn.

She stood in the nave of the church, a small woman with watery blue eyes, pale skin and brownish blond hair worn in a tired shag style. The mustard color of her coat did not complement her skin tone and only served to make her appear more faded and worn out.

"You were a friend?" Lucille Dunn asked, her red-rimmed eyes focused on a point somewhere over Theodosia's right shoulder.

"Yes, I was." Theodosia managed an appropriately pained expression.

"A close friend?" Lucille Dunn's pale blue eyes suddenly honed in on Theodosia sharply.

Lord, thought Theodosia, *where is this conversation going?*

"We had been close." Close at the hour of his death, thought Theodosia, then was immediately struck by a pang of guilt. *Here I am,* she told herself guiltily, *lying to the relative of a dead man. And on the day of his funeral.* She glanced into the dark recess of the church, almost fearful that a band of enraged angels might be advancing upon her.

Lucille Dunn reached out her small hand to clutch Theodosia's hand. "If there's anything you'd like from the condo, a memento or keepsake, be sure to . . ." The cousin finished with a tight grimace, and her whole body seemed to sag. Then her eyes turned hard. "Angelique won't want anything. She didn't even bother flying back for the funeral."

"Angelique?" Theodosia held her breath.

"His wife. *Estranged* wife. She's off in Provence doing God knows what." Lucille Dunn daubed at her nose with a tissue. "Heartless," she whispered.

From a short distance away, Lleveret Dante made small talk with two commercial realtors while he kept his dark eyes squarely focused on the woman with the curly auburn hair. It was the same woman he'd seen acting suspiciously, trying to stake him out at Sam Sestero's office. The same one he'd followed back to that tea shop. And now, like a bad penny, she'd turned up again. Theodosia Browning.

Oh, yes, he knew exactly who she was. He enjoyed an extensive network of informants and tipsters. Highly advantageous. Especially when you needed to learn the contents of a sealed bid or there was an opportunity to undercut a competitor. His sources had informed him that the Browning woman had been in the garden the night his ex-partner, Hughes Barron, had died. Wasn't that so very interesting? The question was, what was she suspicious about? Obviously something, because she'd been snooping around. She and that overbearing fool, Tidwell. Well, the hell with them. Just let them try to put a move on him. He knew how to play hardball. Hell, in his younger days, he'd done jail time.

Gravel crunched loudly on the parking lot surface behind her, and Theodosia was aware of heavy, nasal breathing. It had to be Tidwell coming to speak with her, and she was in no mood for a verbal joust.

She spun around. "What are you doing here?" she demanded. She knew she was being rude, but she didn't care.

"Keeping an eye out," Tidwell replied mildly. He pulled a small packet of Sen-Sen out of his jacket pocket, shook out a piece and stuck the packet back in his pocket without bothering to offer any to her.

"You should keep an eye on *him.*" Theodosia nodded sharply toward Lleveret Dante. Down the line of cars, Dante had pulled himself apart from a small cluster of people and was hoisting himself up into a chocolate brown Range Rover. Theodosia noted that the SUV was tricked out ridiculously with every option known to man. Grill guard, fog lights, roof rack, the works.

Tidwell didn't even try to hide his smirk. "There's enough people keeping an eye on him. It's the quiet ones I worry about."

Quiet like Bethany, Theodosia thought angrily. "When are you going to get off Bethany's case?" she demanded. "The more you continue to harass her, the more you look like a rank amateur."

Bert Tidwell guffawed loudly.

"Oh, Theo!" a voice tinkled merrily.

Theodosia and Bert Tidwell both looked around to see Samantha bearing down upon them.

"What is it, Samantha?"

"I was going to ride with Tandy and George Bostwick, but they're going to go out to Magnolia Cemetery, and I need to get back for an appointment. Can you be a dear and give me a lift? Just a few blocks over, drop me near your shop?" she inquired breathlessly.

"Of course, Samantha. I'd be delighted." And without a fare-thee-well to Burt Tidwell, Theodosia wrenched open the passenger door for Samantha, then stalked around the rear of her Jeep and climbed in.

"What was *that* all about?" Samantha asked as she fastened her seatbelt, plopped her purse atop the center console, and ran a quick check of her lipstick in the rearview mirror.

Theodosia turned the key in the ignition and gunned the engine. "That was Bert Tidwell being a boor." She double-clutched from first into third, and the Jeep lurched ahead. "Thanks for the rescue."

"It is you who . . . Oh, Theodosia!" cried Samantha with great consternation as the Jeep careened onto the curb, swished perilously close to an enormous clump of tea olive trees, then swerved back onto the street again. "Kindly restrain yourself. I am in no way ready for one of your so-called off-road experiences!"

CHAPTER 32

❧

BY THE TIME she dropped Samantha at Church Street and Wentworth, Lucille Dunn's words, "If there's anything you'd like from the condo, a keepsake, a memento," were echoing feverishly in her brain. So Theodosia sailed right on by the Indigo Tea Shop and drove the few blocks down to The Battery.

Pulling into one of the parking lots, Theodosia noted that the wind was still driving hard. Had to be at least twenty knots. Flags were flapping and snapping, only a handful of people strolled the shoreline or walked the gardens, and then with some difficulty.

Out in the bay, there was a nasty chop on the water. Overhead, a few high, stringy gray clouds scudded along. Squinting and shielding her eyes from the hazy bright sun, Theodosia could see a few commercial boats on the bay, probably shrimpers. But only one sailboat. Had to be at least a forty-footer, and it was heeled over nicely, coming in fast, racing down the slot between Patriots Point and Fort Sumter. It would be heaven to be out sailing today, gulls wheeling overhead, mast creaking and straining, focusing your efforts only on pounding ocean.

"If there's anything you'd like from the condo, a keepsake, a memento."

Enough, already, thought Theodosia as the thought jerked her back to the here and now. Lucille Dunn had obviously mistaken her for a close female friend of Hughes Barron. Of that she had no doubt. Okay, maybe that wasn't all bad. It gave her a kind of tacit permission to go to Hughes Barron's condo.

Well, *permission* might be an awfully strong word. At the very least, Lucille Dunn's words had bolstered her resolve to investigate further.

But what condo had Lucille Dunn been referring to? Had Hughes Barron actually lived at that ghastly Edgewater Estates? Or did he have a place somewhere else? She vaguely recalled Drayton saying something once about the Isle of Palms.

Theodosia sat in the patchy sun, watching waves slap the rocky shoreline and tapping her fingers idly on the dashboard. Only one way to find out.

She dug in the Jeep's console for her cell phone, punched it on, and dialed information.

She told the operator, "I need the number for a Hughes Barron. That's B-A-R-R-O-N." She waited impatiently as the operator consulted her computer listings, praying that the number hadn't been disconnected yet and there'd be no information available. But, lo and behold, there was a listing, the only listing, for a Hughes Barron. The address was 617 Prometheus on the Isle of Palms. It definitely had to be him.

Grace Memorial Bridge is an amalgam of metal latticework that rises up steeply from the swamps and lowlands to span the Cooper River. The bridge affords a spectacular view of the surrounding environs and offers a bit of a thrill ride, so sharply does it rise and then descend.

Theodosia whipped across Grace Memorial in her Jeep, reveling in the view, grateful that the one- and sometimes two-hour backup that often occurred during rush hour was still hours away.

Twenty minutes later, she was on the Isle of Palms. This bedroom community of 5,000 often swelled to triple the population in the summer months when all hotels, motels, resorts, and beach houses were occupied by seasonal renters, eager to dip their toes in the pristine waters and enjoy the Isles of Palms' seven unbroken miles of sandy beach.

Hurricane Hugo had hit hard here back in 1989, but you'd hardly know it now. Little wooden beach homes had been replaced by larger, sturdier homes built on stilts. Shiny new resorts and luxury hotels had sprung up where old motels and tourist cabins had been washed away.

Theodosia had little trouble locating Hughes Barron's condo. It was just off the main road, a few hundred yards down from a cozy-looking Victorian hotel of gray clapboard called the Rosedawn Inn.

Located directly on the beach, Hughes Barron's condo was part of a row of approximately twenty-four contemporary-looking condos. Judging from their low-slung, beach-hugging design, they were far more townhouse than condo.

After consulting the mailboxes and finding Hughes Barron's unit number, Theodosia headed for Barron's condo via a wooden boardwalk that zigzagged through waving clusters of dune grass. Pretty, she thought, and certainly a lot more upscale than his development, Edgewater Estates.

Had Hughes Barron developed these condos, too? she wondered. Or had he purchased a unit here because he saw it as a good investment? Just maybe, Theodosia thought, Hughes Barron was smarter than anyone had given him credit for. The over-the-top garishness of Edgewater Estates and its apparent success meant he had thoroughly understood the taste of his audience.

The front door of unit eight stood open on its hinges.

Slightly unnerved, Theodosia rapped loudly on the doorjamb. "Hello," she called. "Anyone home?"

A juggernaut of a woman wearing yellow rubber gloves

appeared at the door. Had to be the cleaning lady, Theodosia immediately guessed.

"You with the police?" the woman asked.

Theodosia noted that the cleaning lady's tone was as dull as her gray hair and as nondescript as her enormous smock.

"I've been working with them," replied Theodosia, crossing her fingers behind her back at the little white lie.

"Private investigator?"

"You could say that," said Theodosia.

"Um hm." The cleaning lady bobbed her head tiredly. "I'm Mrs. Finster. I come in twice a week to clean. Course, I don't know what's going to happen now that Mr. Barron is gone." She retreated into the condo, and picked up a crystal vase filled with dead, brackish-looking flowers. "They already took some things, left me with a nice mess," she said unhappily.

By "they," Theodosia presumed Mrs. Finster meant the police.

Theodosia followed Mrs. Finster into the condo. It was a spacious, contemporary place. Low cocoa-colored leather couch, nice wood coffee table, wall filled with high-tech stereo gear, potted plants, lots of windows. She watched as Mrs. Finster halfheartedly moved things about in the kitchen.

"You just come from the funeral?" asked Mrs. Finster. She flipped the top on a bottle of Lysol and gave the counter a good squirt.

"Yes."

"Nice?"

"It was very dignified."

"Good." Mrs. Finster set the Lysol down, pulled off her rubber gloves, and brushed quickly at her eyes. "The man deserved as much. Me, I don't attend any kind of church service anymore. My first husband was an atheist."

Theodosia thought there might be more of an explanation for that somewhat strange statement, but nothing seemed to be forthcoming.

"Had you worked for Mr. Barron a long time?" she asked.

"A year, give or take," replied Mrs. Finster. "Him and the Missus."

Theodosia could barely contain her excitement. "His wife lived here, too?"

Mrs. Finster looked at her sharply.

"I only say that," said Theodosia, "because I had heard his wife was overseas."

Mrs. Finster considered her statement and shrugged. "Well, *someone* lived here with him. At least her things were always around. I never met the lady personally. People are funny that way. Most of 'em get out of the house when it comes time for someone to clean. Probably embarrassing for them. Having somebody else scrub their toilets or wipe toothpaste drips and drops out of the sink."

"Could be," agreed Theodosia.

"Anyhoo," continued Mrs. Finster, "now her stuff's gone. Moved out, I guess."

"Did you tell the police that?" asked Theodosia.

"That the lady moved out?"

"Yes," said Theodosia.

"Why?" Mrs. Finster planted her hands on her formidable hips. "They didn't ask."

The revelation of a lady friend was news to Theodosia. She pondered the ramifications of her new discovery on her drive back to Charleston.

Obviously, the woman who'd been living at the Isle of Palms condo wasn't the wife, Angelique, who was still languishing in Provence somewhere. Yet Hughes Barron had obviously been playing house with someone. Someone who might be able to shed considerable light on his death. Or maybe even know of a motive for his murder.

How involved had this mystery woman been in Barron's business dealings? Theodosia wondered. And where was she now? Had she been in attendance at the funeral today? Or was she hiding out for fear she might be the next victim?

CHAPTER 33

❈❈❈

SOFT BACKGROUND MUSIC played as Bethany and Haley leaned over the counter, giggling. At the large table in the corner, Drayton sat with three guests, presiding over a tea tasting. For some reason, the women had wanted to focus only on Indian teas, so Drayton had brewed pots of Kamal Terai, Okayti Darjeeling, and Chamraj Nilgiri.

Now, as Theodosia sat at a small table near the window, ruminating over the events of the day, she could hear the four of them using tea-taster terms such as *biscuity*, a reference to tea that's been fired, and *soft*, which meant a tea had been purposely underfermented.

Indian teas were all well and good, but today Theodosia needed a little extra fortification. She'd opted for a pot of Chinese Pai Mu Tan, a rare white tea from southern China, also known as White Peony. With its soft aroma and smooth flavor, it was also known to aid digestion. After the roller-coaster ride of the past week, and the surprising revelations of today, Theodosia figured her digestive system could use a little settling.

"Bethany," Theodosia called quietly from where she was seated.

Bethany immediately came over to Theodosia's table and favored her with a wan smile.

"Sit with me for a minute."

Bethany's smile slipped off her face. "Am I fired? I'm not fired, am I?" She twisted her head around to peer at Haley. "I know it looks like we were goofing off over there, but I've got a—"

"Bethany, you're not fired. Please, try to relax." Theodosia smiled warmly to show Bethany she really meant it.

"Sorry." Bethany cast her eyes downward. "You must think I'm some kind of paranoid goose."

Theodosia poured Bethany a cup of tea. "No, I think you were treated unfairly at the Heritage Society, and it stuck in your craw. The experience has left your confidence more than a little shaken."

"You're right," Bethany admitted shyly. "It has."

"But I want to ask you something," said Theodosia, "and I don't want you to read anything more into it than the fact that it's just a simple, straightforward question, okay?"

"Okay," said Bethany, looking nervous again.

Theodosia leaned forward. "Bethany, you got into an argument with Hughes Barron, is that correct?"

"I spoke up to him at one meeting at the Heritage Society, but I wouldn't call it arguing. Really. You can ask Drayton."

"I believe you," said Theodosia. "And later, after that same meeting where Timothy Neville took offense at Hughes Barron and verbally chastised him—"

"He certainly did," Bethany agreed.

"You talked to Hughes Barron again. *After* the meeting?"

"I . . . I did. To tell you the truth, I felt kind of sorry for him. He was a new board member who had made a generous donation and then was treated badly. I know it wasn't my place, me being the new kid, but I kind of apologized to him. I didn't want him to think we were all maniacs.

After all, *he* wasn't the one who lost his temper, it was Timothy Neville."

"Bethany, I have to ask this. Are you . . . did you have any dealings with Hughes Barron outside the Heritage Society?"

The stricken look on Bethany's face was the only answer she needed.

"I never talked to him alone except for that one time, after the meeting. That was the one and only time. On the night of the Lamplighter Tour, I didn't serve him. Haley did. I only . . ." Her voice trailed off.

Theodosia nodded and sat back. In her wildest dreams she hadn't believed that Bethany could be the mysterious girlfriend. But she had to ask. And if Bethany *had* spoken to Hughes Barron after that meeting, *apologized* to him like she said, maybe Timothy Neville had overheard her words and been enraged. That would certainly account for her being summarily fired. *Fired for an act of kindness,* thought Theodosia. *What is the world coming to?*

Bethany was smiling shyly at Theodosia. "Haley and I were working on a new idea."

"What's that, Bethany?" My God, the girl had looked so stricken. How could she have even *thought* she might have been involved with Hughes Barron?

"At the photo exhibition the other night, I ran into a friend. We got to talking, and I told her I was working here. Anyway, she called this morning and asked if we could cater a teddy bear tea. For her daughter's eighth birthday party."

Theodosia considered the request. She'd heard of teddy bear teas for children. They'd just never done one.

"I said we could do it." Bethany paused. "Can we do it?"

Theodosia smiled at Bethany's hopeful eagerness. "I suppose so. Have you talked to Drayton yet? He's major domo in charge of all catering."

"I have, and he suggested I take a shot at working up a

menu and a few party activities, then submit a proposal to my friend."

"Bethany, I think that's a fine idea."

"You do?"

"Is that what you and Haley were working on?"

"Yes, we've already got three pages of notes."

"Good for you." Theodosia smiled.

The bell over the door suddenly tinkled merrily.

"Two for tea?" asked Tanner Joseph as he stood in the doorway smiling at the two women seated at the small table.

Bethany rose awkwardly. "Hello, Mr. Jo—Tanner. Could I get you a cup of . . . Oh, excuse me." She suddenly spotted the stack of art boards under his arm. "You're here on business. The labels." She suddenly bolted, leaving Theodosia to contend with an amused Tanner Joseph.

"She's a wonderful girl," he said, sitting down.

"We think so," agreed Theodosia. She was determined to play it cool and carry on with her review of his label ideas.

Tanner set a stack of art boards on the table between them. "Tea labels, as promised," he said. "But I must confess, I took them a bit beyond the pencil stage."

"Whatever you did, it certainly didn't take you long," said Theodosia.

"You could say I threw myself into it." He favored her with a grin.

Dressed today in dark green slacks and a green military-looking sweater with cotton shoulder epaulets, Tanner Joseph looked rather dashing and every inch an eco commando. Though Theodosia had the distinct feeling he used his good looks to leverage every possible advantage, she could certainly see why Bethany had accepted a date with him. He was a handsome young man.

"Let's take a look at what you've got," said Theodosia. For the next few minutes, she banished all thoughts of poison frogs from her head as she studied the four label illustrations Tanner Joseph had created.

They were good. Better, in fact, than anything Theodosia had hoped for. Rendered in black and white, they were punchy and strong. They weren't just sketches but finished art, beautifully finished at that. Theodosia knew that once Tanner received approval from her, it was a simple matter of adding a bit of color.

"These are wonderful," declared Theodosia. She was particularly delighted by the free-flowing brush strokes and the calligraphy he had managed to incorporate.

"I tried to capture a bit of a Zen feeling," said Tanner, "but still convey the zest of your flavors."

"Drayton." Theodosia raised her voice just a touch.

Drayton looked over at her and held up a finger. His tea-tasting group was jabbering amongst themselves, and it looked like he would be able to extricate himself for a few moments.

"How long will it take to add color?" asked Theodosia.

"Not long, a few hours," said Tanner. "Oh, hello." He smiled up at Drayton. "I guess you're the gentleman who created the tea blends."

He extended his hand, and Drayton shook it even as his eyes roved over the drawings.

"I like these," Drayton declared. "I've not seen anything like this before. Most tea labels are flowery or carry coats of arms or clipper ships or drawings of tea leaves. These are like . . ." Drayton searched for the right words. "Like the wood-block prints I saw in Kyoto when I was there on a buying trip."

Tanner Joseph smiled. "I'll admit Japanese prints were in the back of my mind. Indian manuscript paintings, as well."

Drayton's eyes shone. "Well, that really makes it perfect then, doesn't it?"

"I'd say so," agreed Theodosia.

"And when will these be ready to go to the printer?" asked Drayton.

Theodosia and Tanner gazed at each other.

"Tanner thinks he can add the color in a matter of hours," said Theodosia.

Drayton half closed his eyes as he calculated the time frame. "The printer needs at least a week to do the adhesive-backed labels. Theodosia, did you order the tins yet?"

"Yes," she replied.

"Gold or silver?"

"Gold."

"Two more days to sticker the tins and fill them," said Drayton. "So perhaps seven or eight working days at the outset."

"That's right," said Theodosia.

Drayton smiled at Tanner Joseph. "I think you've done a masterful job, young man. You certainly have my blessing."

Tanner bobbed his head, looking pleased. "Great." He smiled at Theodosia. "It's been a labor of love."

The bell over the door rang again, and a half dozen people entered the tea shop. Four immediately seated themselves at a table, and two began oohing and ahing over a display of Russell Hobbs tea kettles. At that same moment, both phone lines began to ring.

"Looks like your tea shop just got busy," declared Tanner. He began to collect his art boards. "I'd better get out of here and let you folks tend to business."

"Theodosia," called Haley from the counter, "telephone. A Mrs. Finster. Said she talked to you this morning. Something about Hughes Barron?"

Tanner Joseph's lip curled at the mention of Hughes Barron's name, and his eyes fastened on Theodosia. "The infamous developer," he spat out. "I wasn't aware Hughes Barron had been a friend of yours."

"He wasn't," replied Theodosia evenly, "but *you* certainly seem to have a strong aversion to the man. Or at least to his memory, since he's now deceased."

"Hughes Barron was a charlatan and an environmental pirate," Tanner declared vehemently. "I'm delighted he came to a well-deserved end."

"I see," said Theodosia, and a cold chill touched her heart. Their polite, enthusiastic meeting of a moment ago seemed to have rapidly deteriorated into a nasty go-round concerning Hughes Barron.

"Excuse me," said Theodosia. She rose from her chair and stalked off to take Mrs. Finster's call.

What an extraordinary woman, Tanner Joseph thought to himself as he quietly departed the Indigo Tea Shop. Confident, worldly, so full of energy. Since the moment she'd first walked into his office at the Shorebird Environmentalist Group, he had longed to learn everything there was to know about Theodosia Browning. Where had she grown up? What had she studied in college? What kind of man did she find attractive?

He had always found the simplest way to obtain a reliable dossier on someone was through their friends and acquaintances. So he had invited Bethany, her employee, to the gallery opening the other night. Of the two young women he had met in the tea shop, she had seemed the most needful, the most eager to talk. So he had flattered the girl, plied her with a few questions, appeared interested in her problems and her work. It had been simple enough.

Tanner Joseph glanced back at the brick-and-shingle facade of the Indigo Tea Shop and smiled to himself. What a fine joke that Hughes Barron had succumbed at the Lamplighter Tour's garden tea with a cup of Darjeeling clutched in his money-grubbing hand. Now he, Tanner Joseph, was designing a set of tea labels. It was those little touches of irony that made life so delightful.

Yes, he would keep an eye on this extraordinary creature, Theodosia. She was like some wonderful, rare tropical bird. But you couldn't just walk up and grab something like that. You had to charm it, woo it, make it feel safe. Only then could you hope to possess it.

CHAPTER 34

✖

"*HELLO, MRS. FINSTER.*" Inwardly, Theodosia was shaking with anger from her conversation with Tanner Joseph.

"Miss Browning," said Mrs. Finster in her flat voice, "you asked me to call if I remembered anything that might pertain to the woman who lived with Mr. Barron."

"Yes," replied Theodosia, her voice almost a whisper, so upset was she.

"Well, I haven't," said Mrs. Finster.

"Then why—" began Theodosia.

"Because another detective came by after you."

"Tidwell," said Theodosia.

"That's right," said Mrs. Finster rather crossly, "and he showed me a badge. He had *credentials.*"

Theodosia didn't say a word, but apparently Mrs. Finster wasn't that upset by her ruse because she continued after a moment.

"This Tidwell character acted like a bull in a china shop," she said. "At least you were polite. You showed concern for Mr. Barron."

"Did he ask many questions?" asked Theodosia.

"A few. Wanted to know if the woman living with Hughes Barron was a much *younger* woman."

"Thank you, Mrs. Finster," said Theodosia. "I really appreciate your calling."

Theodosia replaced the receiver in the cradle and glanced at the door. Drayton was shepherding his tea-tasting ladies outside, bidding them farewell. Theodosia tried to stifle the rising tide of anxiety inside her. She knew Drayton's good-byes were always prolonged.

When he finally approached the counter a good five minutes later, she beckoned him to follow her into her office.

"Drayton." She closed the door softly. "I fear I've made a terrible mistake."

"What is it?" he said, instantly concerned.

"With Tanner Joseph."

His face had started to mirror her anxiety, but now it relaxed. "Oh, no, the labels are going to be perfect," he reassured her. "True, they are a trifle beyond the realm of traditional, but that's what makes them so charming. They're—" Drayton stopped midsentence and peered at Theodosia. Amazingly, he had detected a quiver to her lower lip, and her eyes seemed to sparkle a little too brightly. Could those be tears threatening to spill down her cheeks? He couldn't remember ever having seen Theodosia quite this upset. She was always so strong, so spunky.

"You weren't referring to the labels, were you?" Drayton asked.

Theodosia pursed her lips and shook her head. "No," she said hoarsely, finally getting her emotions under control.

He pulled out her desk chair. "Sit, please."

She did, and Drayton sat on the edge of her desk, facing her.

"Now tell me," he said quietly.

She looked up at him, worry clouding her blue eyes. "Drayton, Tanner Joseph is hiding something. Every time

Hughes Barron's name is mentioned, he gets this hard, calculating look."

Drayton stared at her for a moment and stroked a hand across his chin. "I thought you were casting your suspicions toward Timothy Neville. Or Hughes Barron's awful partner. What was his name again?"

"Lleveret Dante. Yes, I have been," Theodosia said. "But that was before Tanner Joseph reacted so oddly."

"Oddly like a murderer?"

"I'm not sure," answered Theodosia. "But my main concern right now is with Bethany."

"She went out with him," Drayton said, suddenly catching on to why Theodosia seemed so upset.

"Yes, she did," said Theodosia.

"Then let's talk to her," Drayton urged. "See if we really do have something to fret over." He rose from the desk, moved swiftly to the door, and opened it. "Bethany," he called.

Haley appeared in the doorway. "We just sold two of those Hobbs teakettles, isn't that a scream? Two of them!" she announced delightedly. "One stainless steel, one millennium style." She paused, staring at the grim faces on Drayton and Theodosia. "What's wrong?"

"Everything," snapped Drayton.

"For gosh sakes, Drayton, lighten up a little," said Haley. She smiled brightly at Theodosia. "Hey, don't quote me on this, but I think business is turning around."

"We're not pulling our hair out over business," said Theodosia. "It's about Bethany. And Tanner Joseph."

"Oh," said Haley. She frowned quizzically and stared at the two of them.

"Theodosia thinks there's something a trifle off about Tanner Joseph," said Drayton.

"More than a trifle, Drayton," interjected Theodosia.

"In particular," said Drayton, "his attitude toward the late Mr. Hughes Barron."

Haley sobered immediately. "I think Bethany really likes that guy Tanner."

"What time is it?" asked Theodosia.

Drayton consulted his wristwatch. "Four-twen . . . four-thirty."

"Let's close early," suggested Theodosia. "Haley, would you latch the front door? And send Bethany back."

Haley glanced from one to the other, knowing something was up. "Sure."

Bethany had gathered her notes from her earlier brainstorming session on the teddy bear tea, fully prepared to present what she thought were some fun, innovative ideas. But the moment she set foot inside Theodosia's office, she knew the conversation was going to be a serious one.

"We want to ask you a few questions, Bethany," Theodosia began.

"Okay," said Bethany. She awkwardly shifted from one foot to the other.

"Do you want to sit down?" offered Theodosia.

"I'm fine." Bethany tilted her chin up, preparing for whatever was about to come her way.

Theodosia fumbled about, trying to figure out just where to start. Finally she plunged right in. "When you were with Tanner Joseph the other night, did he ask questions about Hughes Barron's death?"

"Not exactly," said Bethany slowly. "I mean, Tanner was already aware Hughes Barron had died. And we did sort of chat about it, but I think he could see it made me uncomfortable."

Bethany's eyes sought out Theodosia's and silently appealed to her. *See,* her eyes pleaded, *this makes me uncomfortable, too. This makes me relive that terrible night.*

"Did Tanner Joseph ask probing questions?" asked Drayton.

Bethany frowned. "No. At least they didn't feel probing. We talked, that's pretty much it." She stared unhappily at the two of them. "What is this really about?"

"We think Tanner Joseph had a slightly unhealthy interest in Hughes Barron's death," said Theodosia.

"Theodosia," returned Bethany, "I think *you* have more than a passing interest in Hughes Barron's death."

"Tell Drayton about the frogs, Bethany."

Now•Bethany just looked confused. "The frogs?"

"You know, the rain forest frogs," prompted Theodosia.

"Oh, God," said Drayton.

"Tanner Joseph just told me about his work in the Amazon rain forest. Studying the ecosystem up in the canopy."

"And he told you about poison frogs, Bethany. Frogs that exude toxins. Tanner Joseph knows all about toxins," said Theodosia determinedly.

Haley had suddenly appeared back in the doorway, anxious to know what was being said. Each time Theodosia's voice hit hard on the word *toxins,* she grimaced.

"There have to be dozens of plants and animals in the Amazon that are toxic," countered Bethany. "So what! To even *think* that Tanner Joseph had something to do with Hughes Barron's death is so unfair!"

"No, Bethany," said Theodosia. "Unfair is Bert Tidwell thinking *you* killed Hughes Barron."

Tears streamed down Bethany's face, and Haley quickly went to her side and put an arm around her.

"There, there," Haley tried to reassure Bethany. "Don't cry," she cooed softly. She gazed up at Theodosia. "You don't need to do this!" Her voice was strident, defensive.

Drayton's face blanched white. "Please!" he cried out. "I cannot stand to have us all squabble and argue. This terrible thing is wrenching us apart!" His hands were outstretched, as if imploring them all to calm down.

"Drayton's right," said Theodosia finally. "I'm so sorry, Bethany. I truly didn't mean to upset you." She slipped out of her chair and squeezed around her desk. Putting her hands on Bethany's glistening cheeks, she stared raptly into the girl's troubled eyes. "Know this, Bethany. I did not mean to push this so far."

Tears continued to stream down Bethany's face, and she hiccuped softly. Haley continued to pat her back and mur-

mur, "There, there." Drayton twisted his hands in anguish at this display of feminine angst.

Finally, Bethany was able to stem her flow of tears and blow her nose. She took a deep breath, held her head up high. "I'm not upset that you think Tanner Joseph might be a murderer," she declared.

The three stared at her in stunned surprise.

"You're not?" said Theodosia.

Bethany stared at Theodosia. "I'm upset because he asked so many questions about you!"

CHAPTER 35

※※

WHILE SPAGHETTI NOODLES bobbed and swirled in a pot of boiling water, Theodosia heated butter and olive oil in a large skillet.

"How are you coming with the pancetta, Drayton?" she asked.

He was bent over the cutting board, knife in hand, chopping the pancetta into thin strips.

"Done," he said, stepping away. "Want me to add it to the skillet?"

Theodosia checked the wall clock. Everything seemed to be timing out just right. "Yes."

Through the arched doorway they could hear Haley and Bethany talking quietly, setting the table. Ever since Theodosia had made the suggestion that everyone come upstairs for dinner and all had enthusiastically agreed, the mood had been considerably calmer and more copacetic.

Theodosia popped the cork on a bottle of Vouvray and measured out a third of a cup.

Drayton peered at the label. "You use this for *cooking?* This is awfully good wine."

Theodosia interrupted her stirring to reach overhead for

two wineglasses. She poured each of them a half glass. "That's the whole idea," she said.

"Salut." Drayton tipped the glass toward her, took an appraising sip. "Excellent. Love that dry finish."

Theodosia poured her one-third cup of white wine into the skillet and watched it hiss and bubble.

"Now reduce it to half?" asked Drayton.

Theodosia nodded as she stirred the mixture that was beginning to exude an enticing aroma.

"And you really use eggs instead of cream?"

She nodded again. "Egg yolks."

"I think I'm going to *adore* this spaghetti carbonara," said Drayton. "Of course, it's not exactly the cholesterol-buster's version."

"That's where the wine comes in," said Theodosia. "Supposed to have a neutralizing effect. Well, at least we hope it does."

"You mean like the French paradox," said Drayton. He was making reference to the staple diet in France that consists of bread, rich cheeses, eggs, cream, and lots of chocolate desserts. Yet, because of their almost daily consumption of wine, the French have an extremely low incidence of heart disease.

"My God," declared Haley as she tasted her first bite of the creamy spaghetti carbonara. "This is incredible!"

"It's amazing how far a little cheese, butter, olive oil, pancetta, and egg yolks will go toward making mere noodles palatable," said Drayton as he passed a loaf of crusty French bread across the table to Haley.

"That's what's in this?" asked Bethany. "Yikes! I'm going to be on lettuce and water for a week."

"Two weeks," said Theodosia.

"Isn't it worth it?" grinned Drayton.

The four of them, their squabbles put aside and forgotten, sat around Theodosia's dining table. They were dining on Theodosia's good china, the Picard, with tall pink tapers glowing in the center of the table. Looking through the French doors, the diners could observe a fire crackling in the fireplace and hear light jazz as it poured from the CD player. Earl Grey lay under the table, snoring softly. It was hard to believe that just an hour ago they had been upset, angry, suspicious.

"This was worth blowing off night school for," declared Haley as she wound the creamy pasta around her fork and took a final bite.

"Which class was it?" asked Bethany. Candlelight danced on her cheeks, and she certainly didn't look as though she'd been sobbing her heart out earlier.

"Abnormal psychology," said Haley.

There was silence around the table, then Theodosia spoke up. "I didn't realize you were taking a psych course, Haley."

Haley nodded brightly. "It's my second one."

"I thought you were majoring in communications," said Drayton.

"I changed my mind," said Haley.

"I'd like to propose a toast," said Bethany. She held up her glass of wine, and the other three followed suit.

"To friendship," she said.

"To friendship," they repeated.

"And solving mysteries," added Haley.

They all gazed at her quietly, not sure she was even being serious.

"Hey, come on," urged Haley. "We opened Pandora's box. Or at least Theodosia lifted the lid and peeked in. Now we've got to see it through."

"Haley's right," agreed Drayton. "Let's lay it all out on the table right now."

"You mean everything we know about the suspects?" said Theodosia.

"Yes. If you shared the information you've been able to gather," he said, "maybe working together, we could all add our perspective and come up with something."

"That's a great idea," said Haley. "Kind of like a mystery dinner."

"Or a mystery tea," spoke up Bethany. "Wouldn't that

be a unique thing to offer! If you can do bridal shower teas and teddy bear teas and Valentine teas, why not mystery teas?"

Theodosia had to chuckle. Right in the middle of a serious conversation, Bethany had come up with a terrific marketing idea. Themed teas. And why not? Why not mystery teas or book lovers' teas or chamber music teas? Such catered affairs—downstairs at the tea shop, in local inns, in people's homes—would open up whole new directions for profitability.

"I positively adore the idea, Bethany," said Theodosia. "And I cheerfully pass the torch of marketing director along to you!"

"Oh, no! When all this is cleared up, I'm going back to the museum world. It's a lot quieter than a tea shop."

"A lot safer, too, I'll warrant," said Haley. "Now, Theodosia, fill us in on what you've found out about Hughes Barron. Share your suspicions concerning Timothy Neville and Tanner Joseph, too. And who's that weird partner again?"

"Lleveret Dante," said Drayton, carefully enunciating every syllable. "Anyone for a cup of Chinese Hao Ya?"

Everyone nodded, and Drayton scooted into the kitchen. Measuring four teaspoons of the smoky black Chinese tea into a teapot, he splashed in hot water and returned to the table.

Theodosia leaned forward and, in her quiet voice, shared her suspicions as well as the subsequent discoveries she'd made during the past few days. She spoke uninterrupted for at least thirty minutes. When she finished, the group was wide-eyed with wonderment, literally sitting on the edge of their chairs.

"Wow," whispered Haley. "You actually went to the morgue?"

Theodosia nodded.

"And you snooped in Timothy Neville's medicine cabinet?" asked Bethany.

"I can't say I'm proud of that," said Theodosia.

"How brave you were," Bethany replied. "I would have been scared to death."

"Lleveret Dante is really the wild card in all this, isn't he?" said Haley.

"What do you mean?" asked Theodosia.

"He's the one we don't know all that much about."

"I suppose you're right," said Theodosia.

"How do we go about changing that?" asked Drayton.

"Spy on him," piped up Haley matter-of-factly. "Run a background check, ask around, follow him if need be. Try to put together a profile."

"You go, girl," urged Bethany.

"Haley," said Theodosia, "are you sure you're not taking classes in criminology?"

"What about Tanner Joseph?" said Drayton. He gazed evenly at Theodosia. "He's still working on our tea labels."

"Leave him to me," said Theodosia.

It was eight o'clock when they all trooped down the stairs, a yawning Earl Grey padding after them. Everyone still felt sated from the rich dinner, talked out, yet heartened by a renewed sense of camaraderie.

"Someone's pinned a note to the door," remarked Drayton.

"I bet it's for me," said Haley as she slipped her sweater on. "One of the delivery services probably arrived late and found us closed."

Drayton pulled the paper from the door, where one corner had been stuck into the wood trim that framed the small window. "Let me put on my spectacles." He pulled wire-rim glasses from his jacket pocket, hooked the bows behind his ears, and studied the note. "Oh, no," he said, his face crumpling in dismay.

"What is it?" asked Theodosia, instantly on the alert. She snatched the note from Drayton's hand and scanned it quickly. When she looked up, she was white as a sheet.

"Someone's threatened Earl Grey," she said softly.

"What!" exclaimed Haley. "Threatened . . . How do you mean?"

"The note," said Theodosia in a strangled voice, "threatened him with . . ." But her throat had closed up, and she wasn't able to finish.

"With poison," whispered Drayton.

"Oh, God!" Haley put a hand to her mouth, shocked.

Theodosia dropped to her knees and pulled Earl Grey close to her, placing her head against his own soft head. "I can't believe it," she murmured softly. "I don't know what I'd do if something happened to Earl Grey."

"Theodosia." Above her, Drayton's lined countenance was grave. "This threat has hit too close to home. I know what we talked about . . . agreed to . . . earlier, but now . . . Well, perhaps the prudent move is to bow out of the investigation entirely."

"Drayton, we haven't really been *in* the investigation," Theodosia shot back. "Up till now, we've only been on the periphery."

"You know what I mean." Drayton dropped his large hand to gently touch Earl Grey's sleek head reassuringly. "We would all be heartbroken should something happen to this fine fellow."

"Something's already happened," said Theodosia tightly. Her fingers kneaded at the dog's soft fur.

"But, Theodosia—" Haley began.

"When someone threatens anyone close to me, people or pet, they're threatening *me,*" continued Theodosia, her voice shaking. "I take it personally. However, I do not take it well. So this *will* end. And *I* shall be the one who brings it to a crashing conclusion."

"My God, Theodosia, you can't be serious," implored Drayton. "After this terrible note—"

"I've never been more serious, Drayton," she said in a hoarse whisper. She stared up at him, fire smoldering in her eyes, her breath coming in short, choked gasps, her cheeks flushed with color.

Drayton gazed back at his beloved employer, knowing the depth of her emotions and the firmness of her resolve.

"All right, then," he said finally. "Good for you. Damn good for you. You know we're all in this with you."

All hands reached down to touch Earl Grey, a silent acknowledgment of solidarity.

Upstairs in her apartment, alone with Earl Grey, Theodosia shook with rage. She had promised everyone she would lock the door and set the alarm. And, yes, she had done exactly that. But she had another idea cooking in her head. A good idea that would insure Earl Grey's safety and allow her to focus all her energy, once and for all.

Take Earl Grey to Aunt Libby's. Tonight. Right now.

Then, tomorrow morning, when she could think with a clear head and a lighter heart, she'd figure something out. Maybe even get in touch with Burt Tidwell. Who knows.

But she knew she had to do something. She couldn't just sit idly by, feeling scared and impotent. If some sick individual had threatened an innocent dog with poison, what would they do to a person?

Of course, she already knew that answer. They'd already done it once before. To Hughes Barron.

CHAPTER 36

❧❦❧

$\mathcal{B}$UNDLED IN A wool sweater, sipping a cup of tea, Theodosia sat on the wide wooden porch, enjoying the warmth of the early-morning sun. Secure in the knowledge that Earl Grey was safe, feeling comforted by the familiar old surroundings of Libby's house, she had slept well last night, had enjoyed deep, restful sleep for the first time in two weeks.

Now, her body refreshed and spirits slightly buoyed by the sun peeping over the trees, Theodosia gazed contentedly at the golden woods and fields spread out around her. Birds chirped dozens of melodies and darted about. Some even fluttered hopefully just above Aunt Libby's head as she poured thistle and cracked corn into large ceramic dishes set on the lawn.

Earl Grey, deliriously glad to be running off his leash where there were such interesting places to explore and things to sniff, circled around Libby exuberantly.

Now that the weather had turned cooler, Libby had switched to high-oil-content sunflower seeds. She claimed that migratory birds would soon be arriving exhausted from their long flight from the north and needed extra oil to restore their energy.

Theodosia wondered what it would take to restore *her* energy. The preparations to bring Earl Grey to Aunt Libby's last night had been nerve-racking. She'd had to make three trips just to get the dog bed, canister of food, aluminum food and water bowls, and Earl Grey, himself, down to her Jeep.

Then, just on the off chance that she was being watched or even followed, she'd circled through the historic district a few times, scanning her rearview mirror for any suspicious cars. She spent another fifty minutes driving and, upon arrival, giving a careful explanation to Aunt Libby so she wouldn't be thrown into hysterics.

But Libby hadn't gone into hysterics. She had listened with a sort of dead calm to Theodosia's disclosure of her sleuthing efforts following the death of Hughes Barron, as well as her explanation as to exactly why she'd brought her companion animal out to the plantation.

Libby had stretched a hand out to Earl Grey and patted him on the head. "It will do him good to spend time on the plantation," she'd said. "Let him stretch his legs and chase critters in the woods. He can be a country dog for a while."

Now Theodosia had to figure out her next move, and it had to be a careful one. Judging from the note last night, someone had been angered by her snooping around. Somehow, some way, she had rattled the cage of Hughes Barron's murderer.

It was a terrifying thought, one that chilled her to the marrow. At the same time, it also gave her an odd feeling of pride at the success of her own amateur sleuthing efforts.

"Breakfast's served." Margaret Rose Reese, Libby's live-in housekeeper, set a yawning platter of food down on the small pine table that sat outside on the porch.

"My goodness, Margaret Rose, breakfast's ready so soon?" said Libby as she climbed the stairs to the porch. Dressed in a tobacco-colored suede jacket, khaki slacks, and old felt hat, she looked like a seasoned plantation owner, even though she no longer grew her own crops.

Margaret Rose was a white-haired, rail-thin woman who seemed to have the metabolism of a gerbil. Between Libby and Margaret Rose, Theodosia didn't know which one exuded more nervous energy. In fact, if that energy were to be harnessed, it could probably generate enough power to keep the lights burning in the entire state of South Carolina.

"I swear," said Libby, pulling off her leather gloves and sitting down to the table laden with orange juice, tea, fresh fruit, croissants, and a platter of bacon and scrambled eggs. "The older you get, Margaret Rose, the earlier you get up. Pretty soon you'll have us eating breakfast at four A.M."

Margaret Rose grinned. She had been with Libby for almost fifteen years. In fact, Libby had hired her right after Theodosia went off to college and Margaret Rose's former employer, the Reverend Earl Dilworth, passed away.

Theodosia had always suspected Libby's reasons for hiring Margaret Rose were twofold. First, Margaret Rose didn't really have a place to go after old Reverend Dilworth died, and Libby was too kindhearted to see her left at odds and ends. Second, Libby finally realized how lonely she was, rattling around in that huge old house by herself.

True, Libby had two neighbors, good friends, who leased much of her land for growing crops and spent time around the house and old barn (now the equipment shed) on an almost daily basis. But that wasn't the same. The house would still have been empty.

"You're driving back to Charleston this morning?" asked Libby as she helped herself to juice, coffee, and a small serving of scrambled eggs.

Theodosia nodded.

"You know that Leyland Hartwell at your father's old law firm would be delighted to assist you in any way," said Libby.

She was trying not to show her deep-seated worry, but concern shone in her eyes.

"I've already spoken with Leyland," said Theodosia. "He helped me obtain some information I needed. He and another lawyer, Jory Davis."

Theodosia wondered if she shouldn't perhaps call Jory Davis and see if he could give her a referral on a good private security company. It might not be a bad idea to have someone keep an eye on the tea shop as well as Haley and Bethany's apartment across the alley. She decided she'd better include Drayton's house, too. His place was so old, over 160 years, that a clever person could easily pick one of the ancient locks or pry open one of the rattly windows. And, because any restoration Drayton had done had been to make it as historically accurate as possible, she knew there was no way he'd ever install a security system.

Their breakfasts eaten, Theodosia and Libby watched as an unsuspecting woodchuck lumbered out of the woods to go facedown in a platter of seeds. Then, abruptly startled by a playful, pouncing Earl Grey, the woodchuck was forced to beat a hasty retreat and hole up in a hollow log. Nonplused, Earl Grey circled the woodchuck's temporary hideout with a mournful but proprietary air.

"Walk with me for a while, dear," invited Libby, and the two descended the wooden steps and slowly crossed the broad carpet of lawn.

"So peaceful," murmured Theodosia as they wandered past the small family cemetery surrounded by a low, slightly tumbledown rock wall. In one corner of the family plot was a grape arbor with decorative urns underneath. The grapes from the thick twining vines had long since been carried away by grackles, and dry, papery leaves rustled in the gentle wind. An enormous live oak, that sentinel of the South, rose from another corner and spread its canopy over the small area.

"It's comforting to know our family is still nearby," said Libby. "Oh, look." She stuck her gloved hand into a large, dark green clump of foliage and pulled out a cluster of white blossoms that resembled delicate butterfly wings. Smiling, she held out the branch to Theodosia.

"Ginger lily," murmured Theodosia. It was a tropical plant that had long ago been brought over from Asia to grace Southern gardens. It was also one of the few plants that flowered in the autumn. Theodosia accepted the blossoms, inhaling the delicate fragrance so reminiscent of gardenias.

"Just a moment," she whispered, and slipped through the archway into the small cemetery to lay the blossoms on the simple marble tablet that marked her mother's grave.

Libby smiled her approval.

Circling around the pond with its shoreline of cattails and waving golden grasses, past the old barn that decades ago had held prize cattle and fine Thoroughbred horses, they came to a cluster of small, dilapidated wood-frame buildings. The elements had long since erased any evidence of paint, and now the wood had weathered silver. Red-brick chimneys had begun to crumble.

These were the outbuildings that long ago had been slave quarters.

When one of Libby's neighbors had once suggested to her that the buildings were an eyesore and should be torn down, Libby had steadfastly demurred and explained her strong feelings about preserving them just as they were.

"No," she'd said, "let people see how it really was, no tearing it down, no disguising the issue. Slavery was a disgrace and the worst kind of black mark against the South."

And so Aunt Libby's dilapidated slave quarters remained. Every so often, a group of schoolchildren or a history professor, filmmaker, or TV station would call and ask permission for a visit or to shoot film footage. Libby always said yes. She knew it was an abomination, but she also knew it was an irrefutable part of Southern history.

"Theodosia." Libby Revelle stopped in her tracks and turned to face her niece. Her wise, sharp eyes stared intently into the younger woman's face. "You will be very careful, won't you?"

CHAPTER 37

"YOU'LL NEVER GUESS what happened!" exclaimed Haley. Theodosia held her breath. She had just driven back from Aunt Libby's and quietly let herself in through the back door of the Indigo Tea Shop. Now, judging by the curious, startled look on Haley's face, it would appear that an event of major proportion had just taken place.

"Mr. Dauphine died!" Haley announced in hushed tones.

"Oh, no, how awful!" cried Theodosia, sinking into a chair. "The poor man." She let the news wash over her. Of course, she had just been to see Mr. Dauphine three days ago, checking with him about offers he might have received on the Peregrine Building. They'd had a pleasant enough discussion and Mr. Dauphine had seemed in good spirits. He may have been a little tired, and his coughing hadn't been good, but he certainly hadn't looked like a man who was about to die.

"They just took his body away," said Haley. "Did you see the ambulance?"

"No, I parked in back," said Theodosia.

"That's where the ambulance was," said Haley. "Miss

Dimple had them pull around to the back. She didn't want to upset the tourists. Wasn't that sweet?"

"How did he . . . ?" began Theodosia.

Haley shook her head sadly. "Miss Dimple found him on the second-floor landing. She went looking for him when he didn't show up for work. Apparently, he was always punctual, always arrived by nine A.M. Anyway, by the time she got to him, he wasn't breathing. She phoned for an ambulance, but it was too late. The paramedics thought Mr. Dauphine might have had a heart attack."

Perhaps the four flights of stairs *had* finally done him in, thought Theodosia. How awful. And poor Miss Dimple; how awful to find her beloved employer of almost forty years crumpled in a sad heap, no longer able to breathe. Now there would be yet another funeral in the historic district.

The sudden memory of Hughes Barron's recent funeral service caused Theodosia to chase after Haley, who, shaking her head at the sad incident, had wandered out front to exchange additional bits of information with Drayton. Right after the ambulance had arrived, Drayton had gone up and down Church Street, chatting with the other shopkeepers, clucking over the sad news.

"Haley," said Theodosia, catching up to her, "they're sure it was a heart attack?"

There was an immediate flicker of understanding in Haley's eyes. "Well, everyone's saying it was a heart attack. But . . ."

"But what if it was something else that *caused* a heart attack?" asked Theodosia.

"My God," whispered Haley as she put a hand to her mouth, "you don't think someone bumped off Mr. Dauphine, do you?"

Theodosia reached for the phone. "Right now I don't know what to think."

"Who are you calling? The hospital?"

"No," replied Theodosia. "Burt Tidwell."

CHAPTER 38

*B*URT *TIDWELL DIDN'T* show up at the Indigo Tea Shop until midafternoon. Even then, he didn't make his presence known immediately.

He sauntered in, sampled a cup of Ceylon white tea, and scarfed a cranberry scone, all the while keeping Bethany in a state of near panic as she waited on him. Finally, Burt Tidwell told Bethany that she could kindly inform Theodosia of his arrival. Told her to tell Miss Browning that, per her invitation to drop by the tea shop, he was, voilà, now at her disposal.

"Mr. Tidwell, lovely to see you again," said Theodosia. She arrived at his small table by the window bearing a plate of freshly baked lemon and sour cream muffins drizzled with powdered sugar frosting. Haley had just pulled them from the oven, and the aroma was enough to tempt the devil. The way to a man's heart may be through his stomach, Theodosia had reasoned, but you could just as often tap his inner thoughts via his stomach, too. And Burt Tidwell had a very ample stomach.

"And pray tell what are these?" Tidwell asked as Theodosia set the plate of muffins on the table between them.

His nose quivered like a bunny rabbit, and his lips puckered in delight. "I declare, you folks certainly offer the most delightful repertoire of baked goods."

"Just our lemon and sour cream muffins," said Theodosia, waving her hand as if the pastries were nothing at all. In fact, she had instructed Haley to knock herself out.

"May I?" asked Burt Tidwell. He was just this side of salivating.

"Of course," said Theodosia in her warmest, coziest tone as she inched the plate and accompanying butter dish closer to him. Aunt Libby would have laughingly told her it was like dangling a minnow for spottail bass. "I'm glad you could drop by," she said. "I wanted to find out how the investigation was going and ask you a couple of peripheral questions."

"Peripheral questions," Tidwell repeated. "You have a gift for phrasing, don't you, Miss Browning? You're able to make unimportant data seem important and critical issues appear insignificant. A fine tactic often used by the police."

"Yes," she continued, trying to ignore his jab but being reminded, once again, of just how maddening the man could be.

"Such goings-on you've had in your neighborhood," chided Tidwell. His pink tongue flicked out to catch a bit of frosting that clung to his upper lip.

"Enjoying that, are you?" Theodosia asked archly.

"Delicious," replied Tidwell. "As I was saying, your poor neighborhood has endured more than its share of tragedy. First, Mr. Hughes Barron so inelegantly drops dead at your little tea party. Now Mr. Dauphine, your next-door neighbor in the Peregrine Building, has succumbed. Could you, perchance, be the common denominator?"

There's my opener, thought Theodosia. *As infuriating and off base as Tidwell's implication is, there is my opener.*

"But no one from the Indigo Tea Shop was *near* Mr. Dauphine when he died," said Theodosia. "And I was under the impression the poor man suffered a heart attack."

"But *you* were with Mr. Dauphine three days ago," said Tidwell. "His very capable associate, Miss Dimple, keeps a detailed log of all visitors and all incoming phone calls. And"—Tidwell paused—"she has shared that with me."

Good, thought Theodosia, *now if you'll just share a little bit more of that information with me.*

"Yes, I did go to Mr. Dauphine's office," said Theodosia, struggling to control her temper. "We *are* neighbors, and I was talking to him about the offer Hughes Barron put forth on his building." Theodosia took a deep breath. "Have *you* learned anything more about someone trying to buy the Peregrine Building?" She knew it was a stab in the dark.

Tidwell's huge hands handled the tiny butter knife with the sureness of a surgeon. Deftly he sliced a wedge of unsalted butter and applied it to a second muffin. "I understand the surviving business partner, Mr. Lleveret Dante, made an offer on the building only yesterday," he said.

"That's very interesting," said Theodosia. *Now we're getting somewhere,* she thought.

"Not that interesting," replied Tidwell mildly. "Hughes Barron had already made an overture to purchase the Peregrine Building. That was fairly common knowledge. It's only logical to assume that the remaining partner would follow up on any proposition that had already been put into motion."

"And you think Dante made a legitimate offer?"

Tidwell pursed his lips. "Highly doubtful. A leopard doesn't change his spots, Miss Browning. Mr. Lleveret Dante had many nefarious dealings in his home state of Kentucky."

The door to the shop opened, and Delaine Dish walked in. She took one look at Theodosia, deep in conversation with Burt Tidwell, and sat down at the table farthest from them.

Oh, dear, thought Theodosia, *just what I don't need right now—Delaine Dish making the rounds, whispering in hushed tones about the death of Mr. Dauphine.*

"Of course," continued Tidwell, "it makes no difference if Lleveret Dante offered three times market value on the Peregrine Building. He shall never own it now."

"Why do you say that?" asked Theodosia. She snapped her attention from Delaine back to Tidwell. *He knows something,* she thought with a jolt. Why else would his sharp eyes be focused on her like a cat doing sentry duty outside a mouse hole?

Tidwell rocked back in his chair. "Because Mr. Dauphine left a very specific last will and testament." He paused for a moment, then continued. "Mr. Dauphine's will clearly stated that, should he die before disposing of the Peregrine Building, ownership of it passes to the Heritage Society."

CHAPTER 39

❧

$\mathcal{T}$HEODOSIA, PLEASE," BEGAN Delaine, "someone's got to tell you, and it may as well be me."

"Tell me what, Delaine?" Theodosia slipped into the chair across from Delaine Dish. She was still rankled by Tidwell's attitude and shocked at his revelation that the Heritage Society was suddenly on the receiving end of poor Mr. Dauphine's generosity. This certainly was a surprising turn of events.

Delaine cocked her head in mock surprise. "Surely you're aware of Timothy Neville's mud-slinging campaign. It has reached epidemic proportions."

So Delaine hadn't come here to talk about Mr. Dauphine. She still had a bee in her bonnet over Timothy Neville. Theodosia settled back in her chair and gazed at Delaine. She was dressed head to toe in cashmere, pale pink cowl-neck sweater that draped elegantly, and matching hip-skimming skirt. Even her handbag was cashmere, a multicolored soft baguette bag in coordinating pinks, purples, and reds. Theodosia slid her chair back a notch and peeked at Delaine's shoes. Ostrich. Holy smokes. The clothing business must be good these days, very good. Certainly far better than the tea shop business.

"Delaine," said Theodosia tiredly, "I have so much going on right now. I appreciate your concern, but—"

"Theodosia, I cannot stand idly by and tolerate this much longer. The man is spreading lies. Lies!"

Theodosia smiled and nodded as Angie Congdon from the Featherbed House entered the shop. "Hello, Angie," she called, then turned back to Delaine. "What kind of lies?" Theodosia asked, the smile tight on her face.

Delaine Dish leaned forward eagerly. "Innuendoes, really. About the night of the Lamplighter Tour."

"Oh, that," said Theodosia.

"About your snooping around inside his house during one of his concerts." Delaine's cupid lips were curled in a smile, but her look clearly questioned the truthfulness of this allegation.

"He said that?" Theodosia tried her best to appear injured and innocent.

"That's what Timothy told George Harper when he stopped by the Antiquarian Map Store."

"Really," said Theodosia. *So maybe Timothy Neville had been the one who'd opened the door that night,* she thought. Come to check if she was snooping about. And she cowering in the dark. Truly, another proud moment in what had been an insane last couple weeks. "What else, Delaine?" Theodosia asked.

Delaine looked pained. "Something about the young woman who served as an intern at the Heritage Society. Now works for you."

"Bethany."

"That's the one."

"Let me guess, Delaine. Timothy Neville is convinced Bethany had some kind of *relationship* with Hughes Barron."

"Yes, he is!" said Delaine, enormously pleased that Theodosia seemed to be finally getting into the spirit of this juicy discussion.

"Forget it," said Theodosia. "It's not true. None of it's true." Well, she reluctantly admitted to herself, the snooping part was true, but she wasn't about to confess her sins to Delaine Dish. If she did, they'd be headline news all over Charleston.

"I know that, Theodosia," assured Delaine. "But Timothy Neville carries a lot of clout around here. You do, too, of course. Your family is almost as old as his. But *he* is being verbal. *You* remain silent."

"I do not need to dignify his lies with a rebuttal."

"Oh, *hello,* Angie," said Delaine excitedly. She turned in her chair, the better to greet Angie Congdon. "Wasn't it a *shame* about Mr. Dauphine? Such a pity. Dear, do you have just a *moment?*" Delaine stood in a swirl of perfect pink and reached out to catch Angie's arm. "I just received the most *tantalizing* shipment of silks in the most *amazing* jewel tones and, of course, I *immediately* thought of your olive complexion and dark hair." Delaine was off and running.

Theodosia rose and began clearing the table, all the while pondering what Delaine had just related to her. As much as she wanted to, perhaps she couldn't ignore these issues any longer. Maybe she had to do something about Timothy Neville. The question was, what?

If he had been the one who left the note last night, it meant he was truly dangerous, a threat to everyone at the tea shop. But she still didn't have any hard evidence to use against him.

It was obvious now that Timothy Neville had been secretly fearful that Hughes Barron's offer on the Peregrine Building would be accepted. If the Peregrine Building had been sold before the event of Mr. Dauphine's death, the Heritage Society would have lost out completely.

Was that motive enough to do away with Hughes Barron? Perhaps.

And now, with Mr. Dauphine's very convenient death, the deed to the property slid over to the Heritage Society, no questions asked. Timothy Neville would, once again, look like a shining star in the eyes of his board of directors and roster of high-profile donors.

So did that make Timothy Neville a double murderer? It was a chilling thought.

There was yet another dark possibility. Only yesterday, Mr. Lleveret Dante had put forth an offer on the Peregrine Building. But what if Mr. Dauphine had turned him down flat? Could being rebuffed have sent Lleveret Dante into a vicious rage? A rage that prompted him to kill Mr. Dauphine?

Not knowing about Mr. Dauphine's will, Lleveret Dante might have assumed that, with the aging owner's death, the property would have been sold off hastily. He was already the likely suitor, already in a position to pounce on the Peregrine Building!

Her theories reminded Theodosia of the logic course she'd taken in college. If A equals D, then B equals C. Logic hadn't made any sense to her then, and her suppositions on Hughes Barron's murder or Mr. Dauphine's death weren't yielding anything constructive, either. They were just puzzles within puzzles that made her head spin.

The phone shrilled on the counter next to her, and Theodosia automatically reached for it. "Indigo Tea Shop, how may I help you?" she said.

"Theodosia, Tanner Joseph here. Good news. I've just finished your labels."

"Wonderful," she said in a flat voice.

"Hey, don't sound so excited."

Tanner Joseph's tone was upbeat and breezy. A far cry, Theodosia thought, from the anger and hostility he'd radiated when she'd made mention of Hughes Barron the day before. She suddenly wondered if *he* knew something about the Peregrine Building. Everyone else certainly did.

"Will you be home this evening?" Tanner asked her. "I'm driving into the city, and I could easily drop them—"

"No," interrupted Theodosia. "Don't bother. I prefer to come pick them up." She thought quickly. "You'll be at your office tomorrow morning?"

"Yes," Tanner said, "but there's really no need to—"

"It's no trouble," said Theodosia and hung up the phone.

The labels. Damn. She'd forgotten about them for the moment. They were one more futzy detail to follow up on, one more reminder that she wasn't really tending to business here. Theodosia stared out into the tea shop where Delaine was still deep in conversation with Angie Congdon.

"Do we need to talk?" Drayton, reaching for a fresh jar of honey, saw consternation mingled with weariness on Theodosia's face.

Theodosia nodded. "My office, though."

When the two were alone, Theodosia related her conversation with Delaine.

"Pay no attention," counseled Drayton. "Everyone knows Delaine is a confirmed gossip." He peered at her, knowing something else was gnawing at her. "Did Burt Tidwell say something to you as well?"

"Drayton," said Theodosia, "you're on the board of directors of the Heritage Society. Were you aware that Mr. Dauphine had willed the Peregrine Building to the Heritage Society?"

"He did?" Drayton frowned. "Seriously? No, I knew nothing. It's news to me."

"So board members aren't privy to such information?"

"That kind of thing comes under the category of directed donation. So usually just the board president, in this case Timothy Neville, and the Heritage Society's legal counsel are privy to details."

"I see."

Drayton gazed at her. "You're getting frown lines."

"Not now, Drayton," she snapped.

"Oh, we're going to be that way, are we?" he said. "Once again, you have assumed the entire weight of the world on your small but capable shoulders." He continued even as she glowered at him. "As you wish, Theodosia. I shall play along, then." He crossed his arms and tried to appear thoughtful. "Let me guess. Suddenly you are envisioning a scenario where Timothy Neville also decides to hasten the death of Mr. Dauphine?"

"It's a possibility," admitted Theodosia.

"Perhaps. Or a second scenario might place our mystery man, Lleveret Dante, at the scene of that crime as well. Mr. Mustard in the library, so to speak."

"It's no joking matter, Drayton."

"No, it's not, Theodosia. I'm as concerned as you about everything that's gone on. And I certainly don't take the threat against Earl Grey lightly, either. I hope you informed Detective Tidwell about that incident."

He took her silence as a no.

"That's what I was afraid of," he said wearily.

"Last night, you said you were in this with me," she cried.

"That was before Mr. Dauphine turned up dead!" He rolled his eyes skyward as if to implore, *Heaven help me.*

"I'm not afraid," murmured Theodosia. "I'm not afraid of anything."

"Really," said Drayton. He planted both hands on her desk and leaned toward her. "Then, pray tell, why did you spirit Earl Grey off to your Aunt Libby's in the middle of the night?"

CHAPTER 40

TANNER JOSEPH HEARD the muffled slam of the car door outside his office. She was here, he told himself excitedly. Theodosia Browning had arrived to fetch the tea labels. Evening before last, he had worked long into the night, adding subtle touches of color to the black-and-white drawings, so intense had been his desire to please Theodosia and see her again.

After his call to her yesterday, when she told him she wanted to wait till morning, preferred to drive out to Johns Island and pick up the labels herself, he had been terribly dismayed. But when the day had dawned and a gloriously sunny day revealed itself, his spirits had greatly improved, and he saw now that he might turn her visit to his advantage. He simply had to convince Theodosia to stay. To spend the rest of the day with him. And, he hoped, the evening. That would finally give the two of them the time and space they needed to really get to know each other.

The door flew open, and Tanner Joseph greeted Theodosia with a smile. It was the boyish grin he had practiced many times in his bathroom mirror. It was also a grin that, more often than not, worked rather well on girls.

Only Theodosia was not a girl, he reminded himself. She was a woman. A beautiful, enchanting woman.

"Hello, Tanner." Theodosia stood in front of his desk, gazing down at him. She wore a plum-colored pant suit and carried a slim leather attaché case. Her face was impassive, her voice brisk and businesslike.

Theodosia had to remind herself that this young man who sat before her, looking rather innocuous and innocent, had quite possibly used Bethany to obtain information about her. She wasn't certain why Tanner Joseph wanted to collect this information but, since she still viewed him as a wild-card suspect in Hughes Barron's murder, his attempt at familiarity was extremely unsettling. As she met Tanner Joseph's piercing blue eyes, she assured herself this would be a quick, by-the-book business transaction.

Tanner Joseph took in her business garb and snappy attitude, and his hopes slipped a bit. Perhaps Theodosia hadn't taken time to fully appreciate the thousand-watt glow of his boyish grin. No, he could see she obviously hadn't. She was all but tapping her toe to get going.

"Here are the finished pieces, Theo." He held the art boards out to Theodosia and watched as she took them from his hands. Their fingers touched for a moment. Could she feel the spark? The electricity? He certainly could.

Theodosia quickly shuffled through the four boards, studying the finished art. "These are very good," she declared.

Tanner Joseph frowned. The gush of compliments he'd hoped for didn't seem to be forthcoming. Instead, her comment was more a calculated, measured appraisal. A pro forma "job well done."

"You finished them in tempera paint?" Theodosia asked. She tapped at one of the drawings with a fingernail.

"Colored markers," replied Tanner Joseph. He eased himself back in his chair. She was pleased, he knew she was. He could read it in her face.

Theodosia laid her attaché case on Tanner Joseph's desk and opened it.

"Drayton is going to love these," she said. "You did a first-class job." She placed the art boards carefully in her case, closed it, snapped the latch.

"That's it?" he inquired lazily.

"That's it," replied Theodosia. "Send me your invoice, and I'll make sure you receive samples as soon as everything's printed." She spun on her heel, heading for the door.

Tanner Joseph stood up so quickly his chair snapped back loudly. "Don't rush off," he implored. "I was hoping we could—"

But Theodosia was already out the door, striding across the hardpan toward her Jeep.

"Hey!" Tanner Joseph slumped unhappily in the doorway of the Shorebird Environmentalist Group headquarters and waved helplessly at her.

"Bye!" called Theodosia as the Jeep roared to life. The last thing she saw as she pulled into traffic was a forlorn-looking Tanner Joseph, wondering how things had gone so wrong.

CHAPTER 41

"WHAT ARE YOU drinking?" asked Bethany.

Drayton answered her without looking up from his writing. "Cinnamon plum."

He sat at the table nearest the counter, working on his article. It was 2:00 P.M., and Bethany and Haley were bored. The lunchtime customers had left, and afternoon tea customers hadn't yet arrived. Baked goods cooled on racks, shelves were fully stocked, and tables were set.

"Cinnamon plum sounds awfully sweet. I thought you said you never drink sweet teas," responded Bethany.

"I consider it more flavorful than sweet," said Drayton as he continued writing.

"What are you working on?" asked Haley.

"I *was* working on an article for *Beverage & Hospitality* magazine," said Drayton as he sighed heavily and put down his pen.

"About tea?" said Haley.

"Yes, about tea. I can't seem to put my finger on the precise reason, but I seem to have completely lost my train of thought."

"No need to get snippy, Drayton." Haley peered over

Drayton's shoulder. "You always write your articles in longhand?"

"Naturally. I'm a Luddite. I abhor modern contraptions such as computers. No soul."

"Is that why you live in that quaint, rundown house?" asked Bethany.

"The dwelling you are referring to is neither quaint nor rundown. It is a historic home that has been lovingly and authentically restored. A time capsule of history, if you will."

"Oh," said Haley, and the two girls burst out giggling.

Drayton turned to face them. "Instead of plaguing me, ladies, why don't you just come right out and admit it? You're nervous about Theodosia's errand."

When he saw their faces suddenly crumple and real worry appear, Drayton immediately changed his tune. "Well, don't be," he replied airily. "She's highly capable, I assure you."

"It's just that everything's been so topsy-turvy around here," said Haley. "And now with that awful note . . ." Her voice trailed off. "I wish it hadn't been typed. If it was someone's handwriting, we'd have something to go on."

"Listen to yourself," scolded Drayton. "You're *still* talking about investigating. Don't you know we may be in real danger? Dear girl, there's a reason Theodosia hired a private security guard."

"She did?" Bethany's eyes were as round as saucers. This was news to her!

The doorknob rattled, then turned, and they all held their breath, watching.

But it was Miss Dimple.

Drayton rose from his seat and rushed over to greet her. He extended an arm to lead her to a table. "Get Miss Dimple a cup of tea, girls."

He sat down next to her, patted her arm. "How are you doing, dear?"

Miss Dimple's sadness was apparent. Her shoulders were slumped, her usual pink complexion doughy. "Terrible. I was just up in the office and I kept waiting for Mr. Dauphine to come clumping up the stairs." A tear trickled down her cheek. "I can't believe he's really gone."

Drayton pulled a white linen handkerchief from his pocket and passed it to her. She accepted it gratefully.

Bethany and Haley arrived with a steaming teapot and teacups. "Tea, Miss Dimple?" asked Haley.

"Don't mind if I do," she said, blotting her tears.

Drayton poured a cup of tea for Miss Dimple and, without asking, added a lump of sugar and a splash of cream.

"Thank you," she whispered and took a sip. "Good." She smiled weakly, glancing around at the three of them.

"We were all very sorry to hear about Mr. Dauphine," volunteered Haley. "He was such a nice man. He parked his car in the alley outside our apartment. He was always worried that he'd disturb us or something. Of course, he never did."

"I came to tell you all," said Miss Dimple, "that there will be a memorial service for Mr. Dauphine. Day after tomorrow."

"At Saint Philip's?" asked Drayton.

"Yes," Mrs. Dimple squeaked, and a few more tears slid down her cheeks. "He loved Saint Philip's," she said tremulously.

"As do we all," murmured Drayton.

Thirty minutes later, when Theodosia walked in, Drayton was back at his table working on his article, while Haley and Bethany were waiting on customers. Even though almost all the tables were filled, the mood in the tea shop seemed somber and quiet.

"Who died?" asked Theodosia, sitting down across from Drayton. Then she remembered. Mr. Dauphine had. "Oh, dear," she said contritely, "how could I have even said that! How thoughtless of me. Forgive me, Drayton." She went to pour a cup of tea and spilled it, so flustered was she by her inappropriate remark.

Drayton waved a hand. "Not to worry. I think the stress is getting to all of us. And of course it didn't help that poor

Miss Dimple stopped in here a while ago. She's going around to all the shops. Well, the ones up and down Church Street anyway. Telling folks that Mr. Dauphine's funeral will be held day after tomorrow."

Theodosia nodded.

"You picked up the artwork?" Drayton pointed his pen toward her attaché case.

"Already dropped it by the printer. They're probably making color plates even as we speak."

"No problems out there?" he asked, a pointed reference to Tanner Joseph.

"None at all."

"Excellent. FedEx delivered the tea tins while you were out. There are ten cartons in back stacked floor to ceiling. Your office now resembles a warehouse. All you need is a hard hat and forklift."

"Let me get you a fresh cup, Theodosia." Bethany reached over and carefully retrieved Theodosia's cup and saucer with its overflow of tea.

"Thank you, Bethany," murmured Theodosia.

Bethany transferred the cup and saucer to her silver serving tray. She hesitated. "Everything was fine with the artwork?"

Theodosia nodded. "Bethany, you wouldn't go out on a date with Tanner Joseph again, would you?" Theodosia asked the question as gently as possible.

"No chance of that," declared Bethany.

"I'm glad," said Theodosia, "because there is something decidedly unsettling about his—"

"I think so, too," whispered Bethany as she hurriedly slipped away to the kitchen.

"Theodosia. Telephone!" Haley called from the counter.

Theodosia hurried to the counter and picked up the phone. "This is Theodosia."

"Hi, it's Jory Davis," said the voice on the other end.

"Oh, *hello.*"

"I just wanted to tell you that your private security

guard has reported no unusual incidents over the last two days."

"He's been watching us for two days? Are you sure? Because I haven't seen hide nor hair of anyone."

Jory Davis chuckled. "You're not supposed to. That's the whole point."

Theodosia considered his remark. "You're probably right. I certainly appreciate your arranging for this. I'm not entirely convinced it's necessary, but still it feels comforting."

"Again," said Jory, "that is the point." He hesitated. "Theodosia, I have two tickets for the opera tomorrow evening. *Madame Bovary,* to be exact."

She smiled, her first genuine, heartfelt smile in days.

"Realizing this is a rather late invitation, I offer, by way of explanation, that they are my mother's season tickets, actually quite excellent seats, and she is just now unable to attend. But I would love it if you'd accompany me."

"As it so happens, Mr. Davis, I am free."

"Wonderful. Black tie, of course. There's a cocktail party preceding the performance and afterwards a number of small parties to choose from. I shall call for you at precisely six-thirty P.M."

"I look forward to it."

Theodosia hung up the phone and whirled about to face the tea shop. So genuine was the smile that graced her face that two elderly ladies seated near the door smiled back at her.

What a delight! she told herself. *A date with Jory Davis. And to the opera, which was always fabulous. With parties before and after!*

"You look energized, Theodosia," commented Haley. "Your face is absolutely glowing."

"Drayton." Theodosia fairly skipped over to where he was sitting. "Why don't we start filling the tea tins with the holiday blends? Get a jump on the whole process?"

"Today? Now?" he asked, surprised by her shift in mood.

"As soon as the customers leave. I've been dragging everybody down with my snooping and sleuthing, and all it's done is put us farther and farther behind. Jeopardize business."

He was still staring at her.

"Where's the tea?" she asked. "Over at Gallagher's?"

"Of course."

Drayton always used the extensive food-prep facilities at nearby Gallagher's Food Service to blend his teas. Now they were stored there as well, all four of the holiday blends, in their twenty-gallon airtight canisters.

"Can they deliver today?"

"With their fleet of delivery trucks, they can probably have the tea here in thirty minutes."

"Perfect," said Theodosia.

CHAPTER 42

❦

TABLES PUSHED TOGETHER, empty gold tins laid out upon them, glinting under overhead lights, the group was ready to begin.

"Okay," began Drayton, "this is going to be assembly-line style. Haley and I will begin at opposite ends. She'll measure out the black currant blend, and I'll do the Indian spice. You two—" he nodded at Theodosia and Bethany— "have to keep tabs and let each of us know when we've filled two hundred fifty tins. Then we'll put covers on and restack the filled tins back in their original cartons to await the labels."

Bethany looked at the daunting task that loomed ahead. "Machines can't do this?" she asked.

Drayton snorted disdainfully. "Can machines create the perfect blend? Can machines add just the right touch of bergamot oil? Can machines impart care and love into each tin? I hardly think so." Drayton dipped a glass scoop into the twenty-gallon canister, filled it to equal approximately six ounces of tea, and began pouring tea into tins at his end of the table.

"Trust me, dear," said Theodosia. "It won't feel like love an hour from now. It will just feel like a sore back."

"You got that right," agreed Haley, who'd done this chore for the last two years.

"And remember," warned Drayton, "when you close up the filled tins and put them back into the cartons, mark each carton carefully as to the blend. We don't want to mix them up!"

"Yes, Drayton," said Theodosia obediently, and the two girls chuckled.

They worked quickly and efficiently. Soon the aroma of the spicy teas filled the air, and bits of loose tea clung to their clothing.

"This is like working in an aromatherapy factory," joked Haley. "There are so many different essences and aromas swirling around, I don't know whether to feel relaxed or invigorated."

"Just feel diligent," said Drayton. His personality was so task-oriented that, once he started a project, he doggedly kept at it until he finished.

"My back is killing me," complained Haley. She had just added a fourth layer of filled tins to one of the cartons and was bending over it, about to close it up.

"We're almost done," said Drayton. "It can't be more than . . ." He carefully surveyed the table of empty tins. "Perhaps forty more tins to fill with cranberry orange blend."

"Tell you what," said Theodosia. "Why don't you let me finish up?"

"Okay," agreed Haley. She was tired and ready to throw in the towel.

"But we're almost done," protested Drayton.

"Exactly," said Theodosia. "It's late. It's been a long day. I don't mind finishing myself. It'll be fun."

"Well . . ." said Drayton. "Be sure to mark each . . ."

"I'll mark each carton, Drayton," she assured him. "Now, you folks scoot!"

Theodosia breathed a sigh of relief as she turned the latch on the door.

It was nice to be alone in the tea shop, she decided. Nice to be able to finish this chore at her own pace instead of whipping along, trying to keep up with Drayton's production line.

She turned on the radio and found a station that was playing a whole set of songs by Harry Connick. She sang and hummed along, thoroughly enjoying herself. It took her almost an hour to finish filling the tins, replace the lids securely, pack them up, and stack the boxes in her office. When she was done, she enjoyed a real sense of accomplishment. All that was needed now were the printed labels.

Drayton was right, Theodosia decided as she surveyed the wall of floor-to-ceiling cartons. She did need a hard hat and forklift. What a huge amount of tea to sell. She definitely had to buckle down to business!

Once upstairs in her apartment for the evening, Theodosia's thoughts turned to her date tomorrow night. She was determined to find just the right moment to tell Jory Davis all about her private sleuthing and what she'd uncovered. He was a smart man, a lawyer. It would be valuable to get his input and hard-nosed advice. She certainly didn't seem to be making much headway. Maybe Jory Davis would see an angle that had eluded her.

Now, she asked herself, what would she wear? Jory Davis had specified black tie, so that narrowed it down. And the weather was still cool, so that was a factor, too. Were we talking black cocktail dress and beaded jacket or long gown with velvet opera cape? she wondered. Even though a long gown was technically not black tie, women in Charleston did tend to favor them. Especially for opening night at the opera. Oh, and there was that wonderful hand-painted velvet jacket hanging in her closet, too. Could she wear it with black velvet slacks and get away with it? Hmm . . . probably not. Might be just a tad casual. Better to go with the black dress and beaded jacket. That outfit would be classy and slimming.

Now, what about jewelry? Small, tasteful diamond stud earrings or glitzy drop earrings?

Just as she was beginning to think she should get Delaine on the line and do a quick consultation with the fashion police, Theodosia straightened up, cocked an ear. She'd heard a noise downstairs. A slight rattle. Subtle. Surreptitious.

Rattle? Like someone trying to open the back door? Maybe the same someone who left a threatening note two nights ago?

Panic gripped her heart. Her hand flailed for the light switch and hit it, dousing the lights. Now she pressed her face up close against the window and peered down into the alley.

There was a car down there, all right. Its lights were off, but she could hear the low throb of an engine. It sounded almost as loud as the pounding in her chest.

She contorted her head, trying to see more. A shadowy figure moved from her doorway to the car and climbed inside.

What to do? Where was the security guard? She had a phone number to call—should she dial it? Yes!

She scurried into the living room, fumbled through her purse, and found the number. Grabbing the phone, she punched in digits.

Someone picked up on the first ring. "Gold Shield Security."

"This is Theodosia Browning at the Indigo Tea Shop." Her words tumbled out, one on top of the other. "Someone's downstairs in the alley. Right behind my shop. Someone who shouldn't be."

"Calm down," replied the voice. "Let me check my screen." There was a pause. "Miss Browning, the security guard patrolling your area is about three blocks away. I've flashed him a message. Is the prowler still in the alley?"

"Just a minute." Clutching the cordless phone, she scurried back into the bedroom and pressed her face against the window. "Yes," she whispered into the phone.

"Stay on the line, please. I'll get back to you as soon as I get a response. Can you do that?"

"Yes. Of course."

Then Theodosia was standing there in the shadows,

watching the dark car in the alley below, hoping the prowler hadn't ducked back in his car for a lock pick or sledgehammer, praying he wasn't going to step across the alley to Haley's and Bethany's apartment and knock on the door. Because, trusting souls that they were, they'd probably let him in!

"Miss Browning, our guard should be there any moment. Do you see anything?" asked the voice on the phone.

"No . . . yes!" She suddenly saw a car turn in to her alley, glide swiftly toward her shop. But now the prowler's car below suddenly flashed its lights on and gunned the motor. The driver hit the accelerator, and the tires screeched horribly for a few seconds, then found purchase on rough cobblestones. Roaring ahead, the prowler's car fishtailed, gaining speed. But the response car was right behind, searchlight on, accelerating full bore.

The words *in hot pursuit* formed in Theodosia's brain, then she sat down heavily on the bed.

"Miss Browning, everything okay there?" came the voice again in the phone.

"Yes, your security guard is in pursuit."

"We have him on our screen. A second security guard is en route and should be there within two minutes. He will remain parked outside your home through the night. If we get any information on your prowler, we'll call you."

"Thank you," said Theodosia gratefully.

She went to the window again and waited for what seemed like an eternity, although it probably was just two minutes, until the second security guard pulled up.

She flipped the bedroom lights back on and looked at the black dress hanging on her closet door. Well, at least she'd have an interesting story to tell over cocktails tomorrow night!

CHAPTER 43

✦✦✦✦

THESE MUGS ARE neat," said Haley. Federal Express had just delivered a large carton, and Haley was unearthing bubble-wrapped mugs from their nest of plastic peanuts.

"Did Drayton order these?" asked Bethany.

Haley nodded. "Gearing up for the holidays. We usually sell a lot of gifty items." She held a ceramic mug in each hand, one a pink peony pattern, the other a Chinese dragon design. "Look," she exclaimed, "matching tops to keep your tea warm. Pretty slick." She pushed the carton across the counter to Bethany. "Why don't you do one of your pretty arrangements while I pull my pumpkin scones out of the oven. See there, you can slide those trivets and candles over on that middle shelf."

"Sounds good," agreed Bethany as she admired the peony tea mug. "Has Theodosia seen these yet?"

"No, she's still on the phone."

Theodosia was bent over her desk, head cocked to the left, phone cradled in the crook of her neck. Her right hand clutched a black felt-tip pen. "Give me that plate number again," she said. Nodding to the disembodied voice on the other end of the phone, she wrote AUY372 on a sheet of paper. She tapped the tip of the pen against the paper sharply, making a series of zigzag doodles around the number. Nervous doodles.

"And you *did* get a response from the Motor Vehicles Department? Oh, they're faxing it now? Yes, of course I'll hold."

Theodosia continued tapping her pen nervously, and her gaze roved the room. It fell upon bookshelves filled with paperwork that demanded her attention. A chair heaped with storyboards that weren't going anywhere for a while. Cartons filled with tins of holiday teas. She groaned inwardly. That tea alone represented almost 20,000 dollars in potential gross profit. Could she sell it and jump-start business? That remained to be seen.

"Yes?" She fairly bounced out of her chair when the voice came back on the line. "I didn't realize a leased auto made a difference. Yes, it is interesting, isn't it?" she said, although she was clearly disinterested. "You have the name?" She sat up straight, eyes riveted on the plate number she'd written on her paper. "Yes? Tanner Joseph," she repeated in an odd, flat tone. "Thank you."

She slammed the phone down so hard the receiver bounced back out of its cradle.

"Damn!" she cried.

Drayton was in Theodosia's office in a heartbeat, easing the door closed behind him.

"Shhh." He held a cautionary finger to his lips. "We've got customers!"

She whirled to face Drayton, chest heaving, complexion mottled with anger, auburn hair in a mad swirl. "It was Tanner Joseph!" She spat the name out with anger and disgust.

"What was Tanner Joseph?" Drayton asked quietly. He figured the surest way to calm someone was to remain calm yourself, although he could certainly be proved wrong in this case. Theodosia seemed absolutely infuriated.

"Last night!" she raged and began pacing the confines of her small, cluttered office. "Out in the alley!"

"Someone was in the alley last night?" asked Drayton. Now his voice rose a few octaves as well. "Theodosia, did something happen after we left?" he demanded.

"That idiot, Tanner Joseph, was out there. Gold Shield Security just called. One of their security guards got a read on his plate number." She stomped her foot. "Of all the nerve!"

"But why would he . . . ?" Drayton let his sentence hang there, searching for a logical explanation. He tried again. "But you already picked up the labels, so . . ."

His eyes met hers and realization dawned. "Tanner Joseph was stalking you," whispered Drayton.

"No kidding," she said glumly.

CHAPTER 44

$\mathcal{F}$OR THE FIRST time in years, Theodosia did not find herself calmed by the simple act of sipping a cup of tea. As she gazed across her desk at Drayton, she realized he wasn't exactly the poster child for serenity either.

"What are you going to tell Haley and Bethany?" asked Drayton. He had experienced his own minimeltdown upon hearing that Tanner Joseph had been Theodosia's unwelcome caller the night before, and now his hair was ruffled from running his hands nervously through it, his tie askew. And Drayton was gulping his tea rather than sipping it.

"I suppose I'll have to tell them the truth," said Theodosia. "Even though we still have the security guard, they need to be on the alert. We don't know what this character Tanner Joseph is capable of."

"We also don't know if he was the one who left the note the other night," said Drayton.

"He could have," said Theodosia. "But I'm more inclined to believe this was the first time Tanner Joseph has shown up. My guess is he was colossally ticked that I picked up the labels and didn't hang around to schmooze with him. Although I'm afraid he might have had more on his mind than just schmoozing."

Drayton gazed at her glumly. "If that's the case, it means there are *two* nut cases walking around."

Theodosia put both hands to her temples and massaged them. "Chilling thought, isn't it?"

A gentle rap on the door interrupted them.

"What?" called Drayton.

The door cracked open no more than an inch.

"Tidwell just came in," said Haley. "He wants to speak with Theodosia."

"Get out in front right now," ordered Drayton. "You know Bethany is scared to death of that man!"

"Okay, okay," grumped Haley. "Take a chill pill. I can't be in two places at once!"

Theodosia gazed wearily at Drayton. "Everything is falling apart," she murmured. "Ever since the murder of Hughes Barron, nothing's been the same."

Drayton grabbed her hand in his, held it firmly, and met her sad-eyed gaze with genteel fervor. "Hear me, Theodosia. We *will* get to the bottom of all this. We *will* unravel this mystery. And when we do, we shall both look back on this and laugh. That's right; we will find this all terribly droll and amusing, mark my words. Now, Miss Browning, I suggest you smooth your hair and blot your eyes. That's it," he said with encouragement. "Can't have terrible Tidwell thinking anything's amiss, can we?" He fell in step behind Theodosia. "Bear up, dear girl," he whispered.

Theodosia unleashed a warm smile on Burt Tidwell that she somehow managed to dredge from the depths of her soul. "Good morning, Detective Tidwell." Her voice, still husky from anger, passed for throaty.

"Miss Browning." Tidwell favored her with a quick grimace, his rendition of a smile, and Theodosia wondered if there was a Mrs. Tidwell attached to this quaint, quirky man. Pity the poor woman.

Tidwell half stood as Theodosia seated herself, then crashed down heavily into his chair. They both kept tight smiles on their faces as Haley set cups and saucers, spoons, milk, and a pot of Dimbulla tea in front of them. But no goodies. Theodosia intended to keep this visit brief.

Tidwell's bullet-shaped head swiveled on his beefy shoulders, appraising customers at surrounding tables. "Business good?" he asked.

Theodosia raised her shoulders a notch. "Fine."

"As you know, our investigation into Hughes Barron's death has been ongoing." Tidwell paused, pursed his lips, and took a tiny sip of tea. "Where is this from?" he asked.

"Ceylon."

"It would go well with a sweet."

"It would." Theodosia sat patiently with her hands in her lap. By now she was familiar with Tidwell's oblique tactics.

Tidwell blotted his mouth and favored her with a mousy grin.

Unless . . . she thought as she watched him carefully. *Unless the man has something up his sleeve.*

"To assure ourselves of a *thorough* investigation," Tidwell continued, "we focused much of our attention on Hughes Barron's business office here in town as well as his place of residence." He peered at Theodosia over his teacup. "You may be familiar with his beach condominium. Located on the Isle of Palms?"

Theodosia gave him nothing.

"Moving along," Tidwell continued, "I should tell you that we discovered an object at said condominium. An object that carries the fingerprints of one of your employees."

"Is that a fact."

"Yes, indeed. And I'm sure you won't be at all surprised when I tell you the fingerprints—and we obtained a rather excellent four-point match—belong to Bethany Sheperd."

Theodosia fairly spat out her next words. "Why don't you rock my world, Detective Tidwell, and tell me what *object* Bethany's fingerprints were found on."

"Miss Browning." His eyes drilled at her. "*That* information remains confidential."

CHAPTER 45

❈❈❈

BURT TIDWELL SAT in his Crown Victoria and stared at the brick-and-shingle facade of the Indigo Tea Shop. He had purposely not informed the Browning woman that her dear departed neighbor, Harold Dauphine, had, indeed, died of a heart attack. A myocardial infarction, to be exact.

He knew Theodosia was probably lumping the deaths of Mr. Hughes Barron and Mr. Dauphine together. Putting two and two together, he mused. A trifle off base in this instance. But overall, she hadn't performed badly for an amateur.

Burt Tidwell sighed, reached down to his midsection, fumbled for his belt buckle, and released it one notch. There. Better. Now he could draw breath. Now he could even begin to contemplate stopping by Poogan's Porch for an early lunch. Perhaps some shrimp Creole or a bowl of their famous okra gumbo.

Tidwell turned the key in the ignition. The engine in the big car caught, then rumbled deeply.

Theodosia Browning had proved to be highly resourceful. True, she was snoopy and contentious toward him, but she had made some interesting connections and suppositions.

Best of all, she'd rattled more than a few cages here in Charleston's historic district. That had certainly served his purpose well. After all, Theodosia was an insider. He was not.

CHAPTER 46

❧❧❧

"*DID YOU LET* the police fingerprint you?" Theodosia paced back and forth in her small office while Bethany sat perched on a chair. Bethany's knees were pulled up to her chin, and her hands worked constantly, nervously twisting her long skirt.

"Yes," she said in a small voice. "Leyland Hartwell said it was okay. Anyway, the police explained that it was to rule me *out.*"

"Bethany, you don't have to be so defensive. I'm not cross-examining you."

"No, that will come later," replied a glum Bethany.

"We don't know that at all," said Theodosia. *Honestly,* she thought to herself, *the girl could be positively maddening.*

The phone on Theodosia's desk buzzed, and she snatched up the receiver, almost welcoming a diversion.

"I understand you had some excitement last night," said Jory Davis.

"The security company called you?" said Theodosia, surprised.

"Of course. I hired them." There was a long pause, then

Jory Davis asked quietly, "Theodosia, are you in over your head on this?"

She waited so long to reply that Jory Davis finally answered his own question. "Sometimes no answer *is* an answer," he said.

"I promise," Theodosia said, "to share absolutely everything with you tonight. And to listen carefully to any lawyerly advice you choose to impart." She paused. "Truly."

"Fair enough," said Jory Davis, seemingly appeased by this. "I await our evening with bated breath." His voice was tinged with faint amusement.

"Can I please go back to work?" Bethany asked. She noted that Theodosia had long since hung up the phone but was standing there in the strangest way, staring down at her desk, seemingly lost in thought.

Theodosia looked up. "What? Oh, of course, Bethany."

Bethany jumped up to make her escape.

"You don't have any idea what Tidwell was talking about, do you?" Theodosia called to her back.

Bethany spun on her heel. "About my fingerprints? No. Of course I don't." She gazed at Theodosia, the expression on her face a mixture of hurt and humiliation. "I think . . . I think this should probably be my last day here," sniffled Bethany.

"Bethany, please." This was the last thing she wanted, to upset Bethany in any way, to foster more bad feelings.

"No. My being here has become entirely too problematic."

"As you wish, Bethany," said Theodosia. She waited until Bethany pulled the door closed behind her, then sat down in her chair and sighed. What in her wildest dreams had told her she could possibly solve Hughes Barron's murder? She had followed her leads and hunches and ended up . . . nowhere. If anything, there were more unanswered questions, more strange twists and turns. Now some mysterious object had been found at Hughes Barron's condominium, something the police had run tests on and found smatters of Bethany's fingerprints!

Theodosia pulled her desk drawer open and hoisted out the Charleston phone directory. As the book thudded on top of her desk, she quickly flipped through the front pages. Just past the directory assistance and long-distance calling pages, she found the number she wanted. The Charleston Police Department.

She dialed the number nervously, knowing this was a long shot.

"Cletus Aubrey, please," she told the central operator when she came on the line.

"Which department?" asked the disinterested voice.

"Computer records," said Theodosia.

"You don't have that extension?" The operator seemed vexed.

"Sorry, I don't," said Theodosia, feeling silly for apologizing to an operator whose job it was to look up numbers.

Cletus Aubrey was a childhood friend. He had grown up in the low-country on a farm down the road from the Browning plantation. As children, she and Cletus had spent many summer days together, romping through the woods, wading in streams, and tying pieces of string around chicken necks and trolling creek bottoms to catch crabs. Interested in law enforcement early on, Cletus had received encouragement from her father, Macalester Browning. And when Cletus graduated from high school, he went on to a two-year law enforcement program, then joined the Charleston Police Department.

"Mornin', Cletus Aubrey."

"Cletus? It's Theodosia. Theodosia Browning."

She heard a sharp intake of breath and then rich, warm laughter.

"As I live and die, I don't believe it. How *are* you, Miss Browning?"

"Cletus, exactly when did I become Miss Browning?"

"When you stopped running through the swamp barefoot and started running a tea shop. Listen, girl, it *pleases* me to call you *Miss* Browning. Reminds me of how you followed in the graceful footsteps of your Aunt Libby. And, by the way, how *is* Aunt Libby?"

"Very well."

"Still treating her feathered friends with all manner of seed and millet?"

"She's extended her generosity to woodchucks, raccoons, and opossum, too."

Cletus Aubrey chuckled again. "The good things in life never change. Theo, *Miss* Browning, to what do I owe this blast from the past, this walk down memory lane?"

"Cletus, I have a favor to ask."

"Ask away."

"You used to work in the property room, am I correct?"

"For three years. Before I went to night school and turned into a computer nut."

"How big a deal would it be to snoop around in there?"

"No big deal at all if I had a general idea what I was on the lookout for."

"Let's just call it a mysterious object found in the home of a Mr. Hughes Barron."

"Uh-oh, the old mysterious object search. Yeah, I can probably pull that off. What was the name again? Barron?"

"Yes. B-A-R-R-O-N."

"The first name is Hughes?"

"That's it," said Theodosia

"One of the guys who works in property owes me twenty bucks from a bet he lost on last week's Citadel game. I'll harass him and have a look around. Kill two birds with one stone."

"Cletus, you're a gem."

"That's what I keep telling my wife, only she's not buyin' it."

Theodosia was deep in conversation with one of the sales reps at Frank & Fuller, a tea wholesaler in Montclair, New Jersey, when the other phone line lit up. It was Cletus calling back.

"You ain't gonna like this, Miss Browning," he began.

"What was it, Cletus?"

"Some tea thingamajig."

"Describe it to me," said Theodosia.

"Silver, lots of little holes."

"A tea infuser."

"You sell those?" asked Cletus.

"By the bushel," Theodosia said with a sigh.

CHAPTER 47

❧

THE LAST SIX months of sales receipts were laid out on Theodosia's desk. Haley had tried to stack them, month by month, in some semblance of order, but there were so many of the flimsy paper receipts they kept sliding around and sorting into their own piles.

"This is everything?" asked Theodosia. In an effort to gain some control and a slight appearance of tidiness, she had pinned her hair up in a bun, much to Haley's delight.

"You look like a character out of a William Faulkner novel," Haley quipped. "All you need are Drayton's reading glasses perched on the end of your nose."

Theodosia ignored her. "These are all the sales receipts, correct?"

"Should be, unless you want me to pull computer records, too." Haley sobered up. "We don't need to do that, do we? I think it would just duplicate efforts."

"If the two of us go through these, we should be able to sort out sales receipts on everyone who purchased a tea infuser."

Because the Indigo Tea Shop maintained a customer database for the purpose of sending out newsletters and direct mail, customer names and addresses were almost always entered on sales receipts.

Haley looked skeptical. "Which kind? Spoon infusers, mesh ones with handles, tea ball infusers?"

"All of them," declared Theodosia. "You take these three stacks, I'll take the others."

"What about infuser socks?" asked Haley.

"Anything having to do with tea infusers means infuser socks, too."

"Okay, okay. I'm just double-checking. I'm worried about Bethany, too." Haley bent diligently over her stacks of papers.

"You're sure Bethany didn't fill in here before six months ago?" asked Theodosia. She was concerned about the window of time they were checking.

Haley squinted thoughtfully. "Before last May? No, I don't think so."

Two hours later, they had sifted through all the receipts and found, amazingly, that the Indigo Tea Shop had sold almost fifty tea infusers in the last six months.

"Now we've got to try to rule some people out," said Theodosia, overwhelmed at the sheer number of receipts just for tea infusers.

"Such as?" said Haley.

"Tourists, for one thing. People who stopped by for a cup of tea and made a few extra purchases."

"Okay, I get it," said Haley. "Let me go through these fifty then. See what I can do."

Fifteen minutes of work produced a modicum of progress.

"I think we can safely rule out about thirty of these," reasoned Haley. She indicated a stack of receipts. "These customers are all from out of state and fairly far-flung. California, Texas, Nevada, New York . . ."

"Agreed," said Theodosia. "So now we're down to local purchases. Who have we got?"

Haley passed the remaining handful of receipts to Theodosia. "Those two sisters, Elmira and Elise, who live over the Cabbage Patch Needlepoint Shop. Reverend Jonathan at Saint Philip's. A couple of the B and Bs."

Theodosia studied the culled receipts. "Mostly friends and neighbors," she said. "Not exactly hardcore suspects."

"Lydia at the Chowder Hound Restaurant down the street bought *three* of them," said Haley. "Do you think she had it in for Hughes Barron?"

"I doubt she even knew him," murmured Theodosia. "Okay, Haley, thanks. Good job."

"Sorry we couldn't come up with something more definitive." Haley hesitated in the doorway, feeling somehow that she'd let Theodosia down.

"That's all right," said Theodosia. "Thanks again."

Theodosia reached for the clip that contained her thick hair and yanked it out. As her hair tumbled about her shoulders, she thought of all the things she had left undone at the shop, how she'd even missed this week's therapy dog session with Earl Grey.

Her heart caught in her chest. Earl Grey. The dog she'd found cowering in the alley out back, the dog that was her dear companion. Someone, quite possibly the person who had murdered Hughes Barron, had threatened to poison Earl Grey if she didn't back off.

Okay, Theodosia thought to herself. Following up on these sales receipts was going to be her last effort. And if it didn't pan out, she *would* back off.

Sitting in her chair, trying to focus, Theodosia leafed through the stack of twenty or so receipts Haley had culled out.

Lydia at the Chowder Hound. Could she have had any sort of connection to Hughes Barron? Or, for that matter, any of the possible suspects? Her gut feeling told her probably not.

And Samantha Rabathan had bought a tea infuser a few months ago. Theodosia pondered this, thought about probable connections. What if, just what if Samantha purchased the tea infuser for the Heritage Society?

Samantha was kind of a goody-goody that way. When

she wasn't out winning a blue ribbon for her spectacular La Reine Victoria roses or flitting about being a social butterfly, she spent a good portion of her time as a volunteer with the Heritage Society. She worked in the small library and helped the development director entice new donors.

So it *was* possible that Timothy Neville might be behind this after all.

Timothy Neville could have done away with Hughes Barron and somehow planted the tea infuser with Bethany's fingerprints as false evidence. He knew her prints would have thrown the police off the track. That is, if the police ever got onto that track in the first place.

Well, there was only one way to find out. She would go and ask Samantha if she'd bought a tea infuser for the Heritage Society. Samantha might think it a strange question, but she'd probably be too polite to say so.

CHAPTER 48

❧

PAVED IN ANTIQUE brick and bluestone, accented by a vine-covered arbor, Samantha Rabathan's garden was a peaceful, perfect sanctuary. Flower beds arranged in concentric circles around a small pool had lost much of their bloom for the season but, because of the great variety of carefully selected greenery, still conveyed a verdant, pleasing palette.

"Yoohoo, over here, dear," called Samantha.

She had seen Theodosia approach out of the corner of her eye, had heard her footfalls. Still on her hands and knees, Samantha looked up, a smile on her face and pruning shears in her hand.

"Artful pruning in autumn makes for healthy flowers in spring," said Samantha as though she were lecturing a garden club. She was wearing a broad-brimmed straw hat, even though the afternoon sun kept disappearing, without a moment's notice, behind large, puffy clouds.

Theodosia gazed about. The garden was beautiful, of that there was no doubt. At the same time, Samantha's garden always seemed a trifle contained. So many of Charleston's backyard gardens felt enchanting and mysterious because of their slightly wild, untamed look. Vines tumbling down crumbled brick walls, tree branches twining overhead, layers of lush foliage with statuary, rockery, and wrought iron peeking through. These were the places Theodosia thought of as secret gardens. And there were many in the old city.

"How is everyone at the tea shop?" Samantha inquired brightly.

"Good," said Theodosia. "Busy. We're right in the middle of inventory, so everything's a muddle." She thought this little story might help deflect any flak concerning her tea infuser inquiry.

"Sounds very tedious," said Samantha as she picked up a trowel, sank it deep into the rich turf, and ousted an errant weed.

"Only way we can get a handle on reorders," said Theodosia as Samantha tossed the weed into a carefully composed pile of wilted blooms and stems.

"Samantha," continued Theodosia, "did you purchase a tea infuser for the Heritage Society?"

Samantha finished tamping the divot she'd created, stood up, and gave a finishing stomp with her heel.

"Why, I think perhaps I might have. Is there a problem, Theodosia? A product recall?" Now her voice was tinged with amusement. "Tell you what. Come inside, and we'll have ourselves a nice cup of tea and a good, friendly chat."

Without waiting for an answer, Samantha stuck her steel pruning shears and trowel into the webbed pockets of the canvas tool belt she wore cinched around her waist, linked her arm through Theodosia's, and pulled her along toward the back door of her house.

"Look, over there," Samantha said, pointing, "where I planted my new La Belle Sultane roses last year. What do you bet that in five months I'll have blooms the size of your fist!"

Samantha fussed about in her kitchen, clattering dishes, while Theodosia seated herself in the small dining room. Samantha had an enviable collection of Waterford crystal, and today it was catching the light that streamed through the octagonal windows above the built-in cabinets in a most remarkable way.

"Here we are." Samantha bustled in with a silver tea service. "Perhaps not as perfect as you serve at the Indigo Tea Shop, but hopefully just as elegant."

Theodosia knew Samantha was making reference to her silver tea set. Not just silver-plated, the teapot and accompanying pieces were pure English sterling, antiques that had been in Samantha's family for over a century.

"Everything is lovely," murmured Theodosia as Samantha stood at the table, held a bone china cup under the silver spout, and poured deftly.

Theodosia accepted the steaming cup of tea, inhaling the delicate aroma. Ceylon silver tips? Kenilworth Garden? She couldn't quite place it.

As Theodosia lifted her cup to take a sip, her eyes fell upon the livid purple flowers banked so artfully on the cabinet opposite her. Funny how she hadn't noticed them before. But then the sun had been streaming in and highlighting the crystal so vividly.

The purple blooms were like curled velvet and bore a strange resemblance to the cowled hood of a monk's robe, she noted. Pretty. But also somewhat unusual.

Images suddenly drifted into Theodosia's head. Of flowers she'd seen elsewhere. Purple flowers that had graced the wrought-iron tables the evening of the Lamplighter Tour. Mrs. Finster at Hughes Barron's condominium holding a vase of dead flowers. Deep purple, almost black. Papery and shriveled.

Theodosia put her teacup down without taking a sip. The fine bone china emitted a tiny *clink* as cup met saucer. Suddenly she understood what kind of poison had been used to kill Hughes Barron and how easily the deed had been accomplished.

As understanding dawned, the chastising voice of Samantha Rabathan echoed dreamlike in Theodosia's ears.

"You're not drinking your tea," Samantha accused in a

peevish, singsong voice as she slipped quickly to Theodosia's side.

Theodosia, stunned, gazed down at the teacup filled with deadly liquor, blinked, lifted her head again, and stared at the steel-jawed pruning shears with their curved Bowie knife blade and sharp tip poised just inches from her. In a single, staggering heartbeat she saw anger and triumph etched on Samantha's face.

"Hughes Barron," whispered Theodosia. "Why?"

Samantha's mouth twisted cruelly as she spat out her answer. "I loved him. But he wouldn't divorce her. Wouldn't divorce *Angelique*. He promised he would, but then he wouldn't do it."

"So you poisoned him." It was a statement, not a question.

"Oh, please. At first I only tried to make him sick. So he would need me. Then I . . ." Samantha's eyes rolled crazily in her head as she jabbed with the pruning shears, the sharp tip pressing in, dimpling the skin of Theodosia's neck again and again.

She's having some sort of breakdown, thought Theodosia. *The nerves that connect her thoughts with her actions have somehow short-circuited. She's divorced herself from reality.* At the same time, Theodosia knew she had to try to keep Samantha talking. Keep Samantha communicating and engaged, seeing her still as a person. Theodosia shuddered, trying to keep at bay the thought of those nasty carbon steel pruning shears slicing into her neck.

"What are they?" Theodosia's voice was hoarse. "The purple flowers."

"Monkshood," snapped Samantha.

"Monkshood," repeated Theodosia. She'd learned something about this plant in the botany class she'd taken back when she first became serious about the tea business. Monkshood contained the deadly poison aconite. It had been used for centuries. The Chinese dipped arrows and spears in aconite. In England the plant was called auld wife's huid. And, indeed, the potent petals had turned many an old wife into a widow.

"Don't be impolite," taunted Samantha. "Drink your tea." The sharp point traced a circle on Theodosia's neck, slightly below and behind her left ear.

Theodosia flinched at the needlelike pain. *That's where the carotid artery is,* she thought wildly.

"The tea," spat Samantha. "You are fast becoming a rude, unwelcome guest who has severely stretched my patience!" The last half of her sentence came out in a loud, shrill tone.

Anger flickered deep within Theodosia, replacing fear. This woman, with cold, cunning calculation, had poisoned Hughes Barron. Had gone on to threaten Earl Grey. And now, this same deranged creature was within an inch of inflicting bodily harm on her! Smoldering outrage began to ignite every part of her body.

Theodosia raised her right hand slowly, extending it tentatively toward a tiny silver saucer where a half dozen cubes of sugar rested.

"May I?" asked Theodosia.

Samantha's laugh was a harsh bark. Her head jerked up and down. "What's that silly song? A spoonful of sugar helps the medicine go down? Go on, help yourself, you prim and proper little simp."

Theodosia reached for two cubes, clutched them gently between her thumb and forefinger. Feeling the fine granulation of the sugar cubes between her fingers, she was also keenly aware of cold steel pressed insistently against her neck.

As she drew her hand back, Theodosia suddenly dropped the sugar cubes as if they were a pair of hot dice. Her right hand wrapped around the handle of Samantha's handsome silver teapot, clutching it for dear life. With every bit of strength she could muster, Theodosia swung the heavy teapot, filled to the brim with hot, scalding tea, toward Samantha. The silver lid flew forward, cutting

Samantha in the cheek. Then hot tea surged out and met its intended target, splashing directly into Samantha's face.

Samantha threw back her head and howled like a scalded cat. "My face! My face!" she shrieked. The garden shears flew from her hand and clattered to the floor as her hands flailed helplessly. "You nasty witch!" She gnashed her teeth in pain and outrage. "What have you done to my face!" Samantha tottered back unsteadily, eyes blinded by the viciously hot liquid, her hair drenched.

Theodosia bent down and snatched up the pruning shears. Then she reached over and plucked the steel trowel from Samantha's webbed belt as well. Like disarming a gunslinger, Theodosia told herself recklessly.

Samantha had one hand on the wall now, hobbling along, trying to cautiously feel her way toward the kitchen. "Help me!" she yowled. She was stooped over and bedraggled. "Cold water . . . a towel!"

Theodosia pulled her cell phone from her handbag and dialed Burt Tidwell's number. Tidwell's office immediately patched her through to his mobile phone.

Theodosia barked Samantha's address at Tidwell, admonishing him to get here *now,* even as she stepped outside and stood on the front porch to finish their terse conversation. Then she collapsed tiredly on the steps and dropped her head in her hands. She tried not to listen to Samantha's pitiful cries.

CHAPTER 49

❧

"*YOU ALL RIGHT?*" Tidwell peered inquisitively into Theodosia's face. He had arrived ten minutes earlier, breathless and bug-eyed, gun drawn. Two patrol cars, lights flashing, sirens screaming, had been just seconds behind him.

Theodosia took a deep breath, then blew it out. "I'm okay." Tidwell had led her gently from her perch on the front steps to more comfortable seating on the porch's hanging swing.

"You're sure?" One of Tidwell's furry eyebrows quivered expectantly. "Because you look awfully pale. Ashen."

"It's just my post-traumatic stress look," Theodosia said slowly. "Comes from confronting murderous maniacs." There was a slight catch in her voice, but there was a touch of humor, too.

Tidwell cocked his head, studying her. "You're right. You do project a certain been-to-the-edge look." He grinned crookedly, but his manner was respectful.

Theodosia sat silently for a few moments, staring at Tidwell's big hands fidgeting at his side. "Did you talk to her?" she finally asked.

Tidwell nodded gravely. "She wasn't making a lot of sense, but, to answer your question, yes, I did."

"I was so off base," fretted Theodosia. "I was so sure Timothy Neville was the murderer. And that was only after I'd cast suspicions toward Lleveret Dante and Tanner Joseph as well."

Burt Tidwell pulled himself up to his full height, sucked in his stomach, and gave her a look dripping with reproach. "I beg your pardon, madam. Kindly do not denigrate or underestimate your efforts. Justice will be served precisely because of your actions."

As if on cue, the front door snicked open, and two uniformed officers led a handcuffed Samantha out onto the porch. The officers had allowed her to pull a pink wool blazer over her gardening clothes and tie a matching paisley scarf, turban style, around her head. Even though the scarf was pulled down across her ears, angry red blotches, the beginnings of blisters, were visible on one side of her face.

Samantha, hesitating at the top of the steps, looked around dazedly. As she suddenly spotted Theodosia, something akin to recognition dawned.

"Theodosia." Her mouth twitched in a slightly vacant smile. "Be a dear and water that basket of plumbago, will you? And do take care with the sun."

CHAPTER 50

❋❋❋

*S*HE HELD *A* knife to your throat?" squealed Haley.

"Haven't you been listening?" Drayton returned snappishly. "Theodosia just told us it was *pruning shears.*" Still shaken to the core by Theodosia's recent brush with danger, Drayton stretched an arm across the table and clasped his own hand warmly atop Theodosia's. "Anyone knows a tool like that is a deadly, dangerous weapon!"

Drayton, Haley, and Bethany had sat incredulous and openmouthed as Theodosia related the bizarre string of events that had unfolded at Samantha Rabathan's house. In fact, when Burt Tidwell led Theodosia into the tea shop some ten minutes earlier, pale and still slightly shaken, Tidwell had pulled Drayton aside for a hastily whispered conversation. Drayton listened to the amazing story and thanked Tidwell profusely. Then the usually unflappable Drayton had fairly kicked the few remaining customers out of the shop. As Haley declared later, this was the one time Indigo Tea Shop customers got the bum's rush!

"And I was beginning to believe Timothy Neville was the guilty party," spoke up Haley. "He's such an arrogant old curmudgeon."

"Timothy topped my list, too," admitted Theodosia. "I was even worried that he might have been involved in Mr. Dauphine's death. But Detective Tidwell assured me the poor man did suffer a heart attack."

"I thought it must be Tanner Joseph," said Bethany quietly. "Drayton confided to us earlier that he was snooping around outside your apartment last night."

"He really has a thing for you, Theodosia," Haley said, rolling her eyes.

"Well, he's terribly misguided," Drayton replied with indignation. "Crass fellow, sneaking around like that, peering in windows and such. I daresay he was probably planning to leave some kind of mash note until the security guard rousted him."

Bethany put a hand on Theodosia's shoulder. "So good to have you back safely," she said, her eyes glistening with tears.

"It's good to have *you* back," said Theodosia.

"Nobody cast their vote for Lleveret Dante?" asked Drayton.

"As the murderer?" said Haley. "Not hardly. But I think that's because we never knew enough about him to get really suspicious," she added.

"Burt Tidwell does," replied Theodosia. "He told me that Dante is in as much trouble here as he was in his home state of Kentucky."

"Well, I hope he gets indicted and shipped back there," said Drayton. "Good riddance to bad rubbish. We don't need unsavory chaps like that in Charleston."

"Right," declared Haley. "We've got enough of our own."

"Drayton," said Theodosia, "what time is it?"

He wrinkled his nose and peered at his ancient Piaget. "Twenty to four."

"Which means it's really ten to four," said Haley.

"Would you drive me out to Aunt Libby's?" asked Theodosia. "I want to pick up Earl Grey."

"Hear, hear," said Haley, pounding on the table. "Let's

all drive out to the low-country and pick up Earl Grey. We can stop at Catfish Jack's on the way and celebrate with beer and blackened catfish."

"I love the idea," said Theodosia. "But can we save it for another time? Tonight I've got to get right back."

"Of course you do," said Drayton graciously. "You've just been through a terrible ordeal. Best thing for you is to spend a nice cozy evening at home."

Drayton's right, Theodosia mused to herself. I should take it easy, give myself a little quiet time. And I will. Tomorrow night for sure. As for tonight, however . . . tonight I'm going to the opera!

A RECIPE FROM
THE INDIGO TEA SHOP

❧

Theodosia's Tea-Marbled Eggs
A nice summer hors d'oeuvre

3 cups water
8 small eggs
2 Tbs. loose-leaf black tea
or 4 tea bags black tea
1 Tbs. kosher salt

Place eggs in pot with cold water, cover, and bring to a boil. Reduce heat and simmer 10–12 minutes. Carefully remove eggs and reserve water. Place eggs in cold water, and when they're cool enough to handle, gently tap eggs all around with the back of a spoon to make cracks. Add tea leaves to the reserved water and place eggs back in. Add the salt and simmer, covered, for one hour. Remove pot from stove and allow eggs to soak in tea water an additional 30 minutes. Then remove eggs and cool. Eggs will now have a brown marbleized design. To serve, slice eggs in half and sprinkle with paprika and minced parsley.

DON'T MISS THE NEXT
INDIGO TEA SHOP MYSTERY

Gunpowder Green

Charleston's annual Isle of Palms Yacht Race is the perfect occasion for boiled crab, iced tea, and social tête-à-têtes. From their vantage point in White Point Gardens at the tip of the historic peninsula, Theodosia Browning and her fellow picnickers watch sleek J-24s hurtle toward the finish line, masts straining, spinnakers billowing. But the dramatic battle between Charleston's two rival yacht clubs turns tragic. The ancient Civil War pistol used for the traditional finishing line gunshot suddenly explodes, killing the patriarch of one of Charleston's oldest families. As her neighbors go into mourning, Theodosia begins to unravel a family secret that stretches back over a hundred years, making her wonder: Was this truly an accident . . . or murder?

Indigo Tea Shop owner Theodosia Browning finds herself in hot water when a body surfaces at the grand opening of Charleston's Neptune Aquarium—her ex-boyfriend Parker Scully . . .

FROM *NEW YORK TIMES* BESTSELLING AUTHOR
LAURA CHILDS

AGONY OF THE LEAVES
• *A Tea Shop Mystery* •

When Theodosia notices what look like defense wounds on Parker's hands, she realizes that someone wanted him dead, but the local police aren't keen on hearing her theory. She knows that if she wants Parker's killer brought to justice, she'll have to jump into the deep end and start her own investigation . . .

Includes delicious recipes and tea time tips!

laurachilds.com
penguin.com

The Tea Shop Mysteries by
New York Times Bestselling Author
Laura Childs

"A delightful series."
—*The Mystery Reader*

"Murder suits Laura Childs to a Tea."
—*St. Paul Pioneer Press*

laurachilds.com
penguin.com

M314AS0911

FROM THE *NEW YORK TIMES* BESTSELLING AUTHOR
· LAURA CHILDS ·

THE CACKLEBERRY CLUB MYSTERIES

Eggs to go. Murder on the side…
EGGS IN PURGATORY

Don't put all your eggs in one casket…
EGGS BENEDICT ARNOLD

Sleuthing is never over easy…
BEDEVILED EGGS

A killer has the town walking on eggshells…
STAKE & EGGS

facebook.com/TheCrimeSceneBooks
penguin.com

M1149AS0712